The Forgotten Duke

Viennese Waltz
Book 1

Sofi Laporte

Copyright © 2024 by Alice Lapuerta.

All rights reserved.
No part of this book may be reproduced in any form or by any electronic or mechanical means, including information storage and retrieval systems, without written permission from the author, except for the use of brief quotations in a book review.

This book is a work of fiction. Names, characters, businesses, organisations, places, events and incidents either are the product of the author's imagination or are used fictitiously. Any resemblance to actual persons, living or dead, events, or locales is entirely coincidental.

http://www.sofilaporte.com
sofi@sofilaporte.com

c/o Block Services
Stuttgarter Str. 106
70736 Fellbach, Germany

Editors: Julia Allen, Rebecca Paulinyi
Cover Art: Covers & Cupcakes

ISBN: 978-3-903489-04-2

All those Names!

Fictional Characters:
Julius Stafford-Hill, Duke of Aldingbourne
Catherine Stafford-Hill, Duchess of Aldingbourne, also known as Lena
Evangeline Stafford-Hill, sister

Lindenstein—Aldingbourne's friend
Georg von Hartenberg—Aldingbourne's friend

Arenheim Family:
Helena (Lena)
Simon—father, deceased
Theseus (Theo)—son
Harmonia (Mona)—daughter
Hector (Hecki)—son
Achilles (Les)—son

Minor Characters
Karl and Emma Bauer—neighbours

Agent August—an agent in the employ of the Secret Police
Adam Klein- a family friend and co-performer
Emil Mortimer—Aldingbourne's secretary

Historical Characters:

Prince Metternich—Austrian Minister of Foreign Affairs and host of the Congress
Monsieur de Talleyrand—French diplomat
Tsar Alexander—Tsar of Russia
Viscount Castlereagh—British Foreign Secretary
Lady Emily Castlereagh—his wife
Duchess Wilhelmine von Sagan—mistress of Metternich
Princess Katharina Bagration—mistress of Metternich (and Tsar Alexander)
Baron von Hager—Head of the Austrian Police and Secret Service
Emperor Francis of Austria

Chapter One

Music filled the redolent evening air.

Lena Arenheim stepped out of the shop and onto the busy street, clutching a violin case and several sheets of music to her chest. She paused, threw her head back and closed her eyes, immersing herself in the intoxicating cacophony of sounds around her.

Church bells. A tenor singing an aria. The enthusiastic plucking of a violin. Lena smiled at the scratchy, crooked melody of the waltz, which had a certain charm.

There were other sounds, too—the clatter of horse hooves, the squeaking of carriage wheels, the hurried slap of leather boots on cobblestones, and the melodic calls of street vendors hawking lavender, chestnuts, onions, and other wares.

"*Servus* Sepp!" a man greeted his friend.

An anxious woman's voice called out repeatedly, "Catherine!"

Jugglers and magicians, dancers, and travelling musi-

keeper treat her as if she were an inferior person just because she was not wearing an expensive ermine coat? What if she had actually *wanted* to spend fifty *Gulden* on a pair of stockings? What if—

"Look out, woman!" a voice roared. Horses neighed, brakes squeaked. Jerking her head up in time, Lena realised she'd nearly collided with a carriage. She jumped back, stumbled, slipped, and fell into a pile of manure. Her heart thudded violently in her chest. *Goodness, that had been dangerously close.*

"Gather your wits, Lena," she scolded herself. She pulled herself up, her fingers trembling as she wiped the manure from her skirts. Thank goodness she had clung tightly to Theo's violin; the instrument was undamaged. It was priceless, nearly a century old, passed down through generations of the Arenheim family. The thought of anything happening to it was unthinkable. The notes were scattered all over the street. Her precious music, trampled in the manure by the horses.

The coachman had stopped the carriage and was shouting curses at her. Lena ignored him and picked up the muddy sheets.

"Catherine!"

The wind scattered the papers further, and Lena scrambled after a sheet before it flew under the carriage. She bent down to pick up another when suddenly someone grabbed her arm and pulled her around.

"Catherine!"

She found herself staring into the dark eyes of a young woman who'd climbed down from the carriage that had almost run her over.

"Heavens above," the woman gasped. "How is this possible?"

And before Lena could blink, she found herself enveloped in a cloud of perfume, cashmere, and silk as the lady burst into tears.

Lena tried to pull away, but the lady sobbed into her neck and clung to her like ivy. She babbled rapidly in English.

It was clear that this woman had mistaken her for someone else. That kind of thing could happen; it was simple human error, a misunderstanding. In fact, something like that had happened to her just the other day, when a child in the crowded market square had mistaken Lena for his mother and had hugged her legs before realising his mistake. He too had burst into tears, but she had gently wiped his cheeks and waited with him until his mother came running. No doubt this must be a similar situation.

She blew away a feather from her lips that must have fallen from the woman's opulent headdress.

"Catherine, it really is you! Is this a miracle? How—how is it that you are here? After all this time? How is it that you are...alive?" The lady's mouth wobbled dangerously, as if she was about to burst into a fresh flood of tears.

Lena pulled away, alarmed. "I'm sorry. I don't know you. You've made a mistake." Her English was a little stilted. She usually had little contact with English speakers and therefore hadn't spoken English for a long time.

The woman's mouth fell open and a look of doubt crept into her eyes. "Catherine? It is you, isn't it?"

"I'm afraid not. My name is Helena Arenheim. Please, excuse me—"

"But...you are definitely Catherine!" She reached out and tilted Lena's face to the side. "You must be. You even have that heart-shaped birthmark on your cheek. There! Only Catherine had that. Of course you are Catherine!"

Lena stared at her with her mouth agape. The lady was dainty and very pretty with wild brown curls falling over a heart-shaped face, a wide mouth, and big dark eyes swimming in tears. The hands that still gripped her arm were gloved, her feet were in satin slippers, and she was wearing a fashionable pastel pink redingote and an extravagant feathered headdress that Lena couldn't afford even in her dreams. She felt awkward and self-conscious in her threadbare, simple blue cotton dress and mud-spattered coat, reeking of manure.

"I am sorry." She tried again to pull her arm away.

The lady frowned. "You have not changed at all, Catherine."

Lena huffed, partly annoyed, partly amused. Was the lady mad? She must be, for she simply refused to accept that she wasn't this Catherine. With a firm tug, Lena removed her hand from her arm. "My name is Helena, not Catherine. Now, I must go. My children are waiting. I wish you a good evening."

The woman dropped her hands. "Children? You have children?"

Lena's face lit up with pride, as it always did when discussing her children. "Yes. I have four children."

The Forgotten Duke

coloratura soprano, having memorised the score of entire Mozart operas.

Together, they performed as well as anyone—no, better. But talent wasn't everything. The world of music was competitive. If one did not know the right people, if one did not have a wealthy patron, if one was not a member of the correct guild, if one did not have the right connections, or, heaven forbid, if one was a woman, the doors would not open.

Lena was convinced that they needed only one chance, one single performance in one of those glittering aristocratic soirees. Where music was appreciated, where the intellectual elite gathered, or even better, where the diplomats and statesmen convened at Prince Metternich's palais. The most glittering, glamorous fêtes were held there. Once one performed there, one's name was made. That would be grabbing for the stars, indeed. It was an impossibility. It would never happen. Yet one could dream, could one not?

The court carriage in front of them inched forwards slowly.

"At this rate, we'll be home tomorrow morning," Karl groaned, leaning back and lighting his pipe.

"I wonder which of the guests is in that vehicle? It could be anyone, really. Do you think it could be a royal?" She sat up with a gasp. "Could it be Tsar Alexander?" He was already very popular amongst the Viennese.

Lena stared at the golden double-headed eagle engraved on the door. The carriage that had almost struck her had been a green court carriage, a four-wheeled berline with a closed roof. It had been that mad Englishwoman's carriage. A liveried footman stood at the back, and the driver sat on a black and silver embroidered cloth that draped his seat. Did that mean that the Englishwoman was one of the aristocratic visitors attending the Congress? A steep frown formed on Lena's forehead. She was troubled with the single-minded way in which the woman had insisted on calling her Catherine. Surely there was nothing to it. Lena wasn't really worried about that, was she? Then why couldn't she let go of the incident?

"Unlikely. I don't think it's the Tsar's carriage. Haven't you read the papers?"

Lena shook her head. "No time."

"The Tsar is to arrive with Frederick William, the king of Prussia, tomorrow. Our emperor will receive them. There will be a parade of pomp and glory as the three monarchs enter the city." Karl pulled out a dirty handkerchief and wiped his nose loudly. "Emma says she wouldn't miss it for the world. It can't be helped. I suppose I shall have to accompany her to gawk at them."

Lena suppressed a grin. Despite his protests, Karl was as starstruck by the foreign aristocratic visitors as much as any of them were.

"My children will want to see it too, I suppose."

She had to admit, it was a sight to behold, seeing the elite strolling along the Bastei, riding under the chestnut trees in the wide lanes of the Prater, dressed in the latest expensive fashions, conducting themselves with an air of arrogant distinction. People stopped and gaped in awe at

Before he could say anything, she rushed on. "When I was in the carriage on the way home, I saw her walking along the Kohlmarkt. I followed her in the carriage. I swear it was her. Catherine." She drew in a trembling breath. "She's alive."

Aldingbourne was not amused. "Stop making such jokes. Catherine died eight years ago." An all too familiar black streak of grief shot through him as he said the words. After all this time, it still shook him. He closed his eyes briefly as he pushed his emotions down. He'd become good at that, too. Clamping down emotions. Bottling them up deep inside, with a lid on top.

Evie shook her head with a vehemence that sent her curls flying.

"But I swear on my life, Julius. It's not a joke. It was Catherine. She's happy and healthy and very much alive."

"Impossible." He picked up the documents again, but the paper between his fingers trembled.

"It was the same figure, the same hair. Even the birthmark on her cheek. Do you remember? Only Catherine had that." She pointed to the right side of her cheek. "That slightly heart-shaped one."

That detail was unexpected, as was that agonising wrench in his gut, like someone twisting a knife. How could he have forgotten that adorable heart-shaped mole on her cheek? How could he have forgotten... her face?

"I'd recognise it anywhere, even after all this time," Evie mused. "Except when I went to talk to her, she did not recognise me at all. It was excessively odd."

Something else shot through him, but this time it

wasn't grief, but anger. He struggled with it until he managed to suppress it like he did all his emotions. His sister was merely being thoughtless, that was all.

"It is not uncommon for two people to look alike," he bit out in a measured, cold tone. "I grant you that the woman must have looked like Catherine. Maybe she even had the same mole on her cheek. A coincidence. These things happen. I dare say that if we search long enough, each of us will find another person who looks exactly like us, down to the last detail. Somewhere in this world, Evie, there is a woman who looks just like you. Why shouldn't there be? With all the millions of people living on this earth, chances are good that you have a twin somewhere, too."

Evie shook her head with a stubbornness he was all too familiar with. "Must you always be so rational and cold?"

"One must be rational in situations like this. What other choice do we have?"

"I know it was her, and not another person who merely looked like her. It *was* Catherine. I don't know how to explain it. The woman not only looked like her, but she also *felt* like her." Her voice trembled.

Something snapped inside him. He slammed the document down on the table with a vehemence that made her jump. "Enough! You will cease this talk. Catherine is dead. She is buried in our family crypt. I placed her body in the casket myself." He would never, ever forget the feeling of her cold, broken body in his arms when he placed her in that coffin. It haunted his dreams to this day. With an iron will, he pushed the memory aside. "It is a fact, it is what is true, and anything else is beside the point and a fantasy. I do not want to hear another word about you having seen Catherine."

"But—"

"Evie!"

She folded her arms over her chest and pouted.

He stood up, towering over his sister. "Evangeline," he began sternly. Then, as he saw her eyes fill with tears, his voice softened. "I know it's been difficult. You've been lonely, and like any young woman, you desire romance. Your betrothed, Hartenberg, blast the man, isn't helping by being perpetually absent. I am certain after what happened to our friend Atherton who found his lost love Mirabel after all these years, it must have filled you with ideas of finding lost love and epic romance and whatnot" —he waved a pale hand about tiredly—"and while we are all exceedingly happy that Kit and Mirabel have finally found each other, you must understand that this was an exception and that these things don't normally happen in this world. Pray, cease to attempt to recreate the same fate for me. That Catherine has been alive all this time, wandering about in the streets of Vienna is a fairy tale, a fantasy. Would that it were true. But it is not. So please, Evie. Please! Desist from this, as it leads to nowhere." His voice turned rough and gruff. "Such talk like that is— exceedingly difficult to bear." He swallowed painfully. "It merely stirs up old grief and anguish."

His sister's head snapped up and she looked at him with troubled eyes. "Oh, Julius." Now she was about to cry in earnest. "I am so thoughtless. I apologise. I do! It is not my intention to cause you distress and pain. Far from it." She threw herself impulsively around his neck. "I did not think. Pray, forgive me. I shall not insist on speaking about this any longer. Surely you are right, and there must be some sort of logical explanation for the physical resemblance between this woman and Catherine. I shall not dwell on it. There. I've already forgotten it."

He patted her back awkwardly and tried to smile, but only managed a grimace.

Evie sat in the armchair next to him. "But you are quite vexatious, Julius. You've become so hard and cold most of the time, and anyone who doesn't really know you would never know it's merely a shell surrounding you. I know you were never as romantic as me, but you didn't used to be so cynical, either. It troubles me that sometimes even I begin to believe that this is what you have become, cold and proud, without any emotion. It isn't true. I know it isn't. You've merely repressed all emotions and ceased to acknowledge you have any feelings at all. But what kind of life is that? It's not a good way to live at all."

Aldingbourne wearily pressed both his thumbs between his brows.

She lifted a hand. "I see you find this subject distasteful as well, so I shall no longer expound upon it."

"Thank you."

Evie jumped to her feet again and walked to the tall windows, pushing aside the curtains and looking down at the bustling street as if she hadn't done so at least a hundred times the past half hour. "I'll have to distract myself with something else, then," she said more to herself than him. "There is much to see in Vienna. It is such a charming place. But going shopping with Lady Castlereagh is such a bore. She drags me into every shop, inconveniences the shopkeepers by making them show her every item they have and then leaves without buying anything. I take pity on them, usually, so I inevitably end up buying something I don't need." She grimaced.

"Hm. It seems you need a female companion of your own age to distract you. I shall look into the matter. A pity that Hartenberg is not in town, otherwise it would have been his duty to escort you about town. You are to marry him, after all."

"I doubt we'll ever see that day." She dropped the curtain. "You know I don't even know what he looks like? What if he is hideously ugly and old?"

"Hmm?" Aldingbourne had immersed himself in his documents again.

Evie sighed. "Never mind."

There was silence again in the drawing room.

"I think I'll go out and buy a new bonnet," she announced, even though she'd just returned from a long shopping trip and had just bought three bonnets that she didn't need.

"Yes, yes, do that. Also, we are to have supper at the British Embassy tonight. Be back in time. Tomorrow, there is a gala dinner at Hofburg Palace with the emperors. In two days' time there is a soiree hosted by Metternich. Prepare yourself accordingly."

"Very well, Julius."

"Another thing, before I forget." He looked up, frowning. "While you are in Vienna, don't talk to any strangers and make sure you burn any kind of correspondence, as I am about to do now. Watch me." He walked to the fireplace, tore up the dispatch he'd just read, and threw the pieces into the fire. "Make sure it burns properly to ashes. Conduct yourself with the utmost discretion. Do you understand? Trust no one, not even our own servants."

"Why?"

"The city is crawling with Metternich's spies. I caught a maid going through the wastepaper bins, trying to piece together one of the letters you'd thrown in there. I had to dismiss her, of course, but it is more than likely that the new maid who's taken her place will do the same. They're all in the employ of the Austrian secret police."

Evie stared at him with round eyes. "But why? I thought the Austrians were our allies. Why would they be spying on us?"

Aldingbourne shrugged. "There has never been a Congress like this before in history. Much is at stake. Even though we are actively working for peace, there is a certain amount of suspicion towards the others. We also have our own agents collecting intelligence for us, so it goes both ways."

Evie knit her brows together. "How hypocritical. Here you have a Congress for peace, and each party distrusts each other enough to send out spies long before the Congress has even begun. Not that there was anything remotely interesting in the scribbles I produced. It was a letter to Mirabel, in which I was detailing my shopping trip with Lady Castlereagh, describing the bonnets I bought, and the scent of the famous Cologne water, which is said to cure migraines, which I recommended to her. She has been complaining of migraines, for she feels out of sorts and very uncomfortable in her confinement. I doubt there's any political relevance to this tidbit, is there?"

The ghost of a smile played across his lips. "To Metternich, everything is relevant. Be on guard, is all I'm saying. Now go and buy yourself those gloves or shoes or whatever it is you wanted to buy."

"A bonnet," Evie muttered as she turned to go.

But of course, that was just an excuse. She had another reason for leaving Julius. The truth was, she intended to find that woman again, the one who had looked so deceptively like Catherine. She would search the streets of Vienna for her. What had her name been?

Helena Arenheim.

She whispered the name aloud, which seemed strange and foreign on her lips.

She was as certain as the stars fixed in the sky that this woman was her brother's wife, Catherine, the Duchess of Aldingbourne.

Chapter Three

"Mama, Theo almost burned the house down today!"

"Mama, why is there horse manure on my violin case?"

"Mama, can we please go to the parade of emperors tomorrow, pleeeeease?"

"Mama, you won't believe what Hecki did today."

"Mama, Hecki smeared jam into my ear while I napped."

"I did not! It was Les. He was conducting an experiment!"

And then, all of them together: "I'm sooo hungry!"

"Goodness gracious!" Lena cupped her hands over her ears and laughed. "Let's see." She pointed to the tallest and oldest, a lanky twenty-one-year-old with dishevelled red hair. "Theo. Where is Marie?"

Theo wiped the violin case with his sleeve. "She had to leave suddenly to be with her father, which is why the brood is hungry. I tried to make potato soup, but I got distracted and it cooked a bit too long..."

"And it burned and now Marie's pot is ruined and the entire place almost burnt down! The potatoes turned into little black things, harder than rocks," said Achilles, a precocious, dark-haired boy of about ten, with thick spectacles that kept sliding down his small nose. "Hecki threw them up on the roof and they're stuck in the rain pipe but he also hit the neighbour's attic window, which is now broken, as is the pot. May I have it for my experiments?"

"Tattler!" Hector, the youngest, hissed at Les and elbowed him. "It was his idea to throw them on the roof! He dared me." Hector was two years younger than Les, and when together, the two were often up to no good. Theo called them the "wicked twins". Hector was a pretty boy with thick, dark brown curls and his mother's big grey eyes, which made for a striking contrast, but his angelic appearance hid a mischievous, lively personality. Les was usually the one who came up with the hare-brained ideas, while Hecki would carry them out without thinking twice.

Lena frowned. "Wait. You broke Herr Bauer's window?"

"It's just a tiny little window, it hardly matters." Les jumped to his defence.

"That's right." Hecki nodded emphatically. "He won't even notice. No one uses the attic anyway, and if you think about it, now the pigeons can use it to get in and out like a dovecote—"

"Hector Arenheim!" Lena placed her hands on her hips.

"I'll fix it, Mama, I promise, I will," the boy said.

"For sure. With newspaper and cardboard and glue." Les grinned. "I'll help him create a new kind of window altogether. It will be indestructible."

"No. You're going to Karl Bauer immediately to apologise. Tell him you'll pay for a new window by helping him sell vegetables at the market."

"Noooo! Anything but that, Mama!"

"And you, Achilles, will help him." She crossed her arms.

Both boys grumbled. Turning to Theo, she asked, "What exactly is the matter with Marie's father?"

Theo shrugged. "She received a missive saying that her father was on his deathbed. Dropped everything to catch the next mail coach to Innsbruck. Left this letter." He handed her a crumpled, soiled letter, in which Marie had scribbled an apology for her hasty departure.

Lena perused it.

"Oh dear, oh dear," she muttered. "This is sad news, indeed." Marie was their maid, cook, nanny, friend, and part of the Arenheim family. Without her, things would fall apart, as they obviously already had.

Lena inspected the ruined pot. Another household item to dispose of. Mona sidled up to her and hugged her from behind. "I don't think the boys mean to be bad," she said. "Except when they decide to put jam in my ear." She glared at them. "It's not nice. Now my ear is all sticky and it won't come out."

"I was trying an experiment to see if the jam would prevent her ear from tearing when Hecki blows his trumpet in the same room. It's for a new invention, you see," Les said to defend himself.

"It's not the ear that would tear, but the tympanic membrane," Theo said, setting his violin aside. "I listened to a lecture on the anatomy of the internal ear 'De Auribus' the other day."

Les shrugged. "Whatever, not-yet-Doctor Arenheim. My point being, it didn't work." His shoulders slumped. "When Hecki blared his trumpet in Mona's ear, she jumped up immediately and gave each of us a cuff. I daresay my tum-panic membrane is now damaged. I'll have to come up with another idea for earplugs that keep the sound out." His eyes brightened. "Do you think tar would work better?"

"Achilles Arenheim, don't you dare smear tar into my ears while I'm sleeping!" Mona picked up a broom and went after Les, who ran out of the room squealing, followed by Hecki, who egged her on.

"Children, children!" Lena didn't know whether to laugh or cry.

Mona returned, sometime later, breathless. "I told them to go to Karl Bauer and apologise for the broken attic window, or else there would be no supper."

Lena set aside the pot she'd been inspecting. "Poor Mona. Did you have a hard time with the boys today?"

"As the only woman in the house? Yes." Mona was the second eldest at almost seventeen. She was a sweet, gentle girl with straight brown hair and dreamy eyes. She was a passionate musician and played the viola better than anyone Lena knew. Because she was a young woman, people had begun to frown upon her public performances. When she was younger, she had been considered a prodigy. Now that she was a young woman, it was considered unseemly for her to play a stringed instrument in public. "She should be married, not exhibiting herself on the public stage. It is indecent," people said. Lena's heart ached because Mona wanted nothing more than to become a professional musician.

Female professional musicians? In private, by all means. But on the public stage? That was unheard of. Yet they existed, these women. They were rare and overshadowed by men, but they existed.

"I can think of three female musicians easily," Mona liked to declare. "Maria Anna Wilhelmina von Neipperg was one of them. She was an Austrian composer and music theorist. Or Mozart's sister, Nannerl. And then there was Maria Theresia von Paradis, also a pianist."

"The problem is that they all played the piano, not the viola. The viola is considered a male instrument," Theo argued. "Not that I have a problem with it, mind you. It is the way society thinks."

Mona had angrily retorted that she did not give a fig for what society thought.

Now, Lena showed her the sheet music that had been trampled in the mud.

"It's a string quartet by Schubert in E-flat. It's quite new."

Mona took it eagerly and studied it. "I can copy it easily, Mama."

"Have you found us a patron?" Theo sat down at the table and peeled the skin off one of the burnt potatoes.

Lena shook her head. "No. There were too many

people waiting outside the palais. The queue was so long, it went around the building. It was impossible to get inside. Then the rumour spread that Metternich's parties have been planned months in advance and that everything has already been decided down to the last detail. All the musicians have already been hired, and pieces they are to play have been already chosen. I'm afraid this is it, Theo." She shrugged. "I've reached the end of my wisdom."

"I went to the inn in the Seilergasse," Theo said. "You know, where all the musicians meet. To talk to Herr Beethoven and ask him for a letter of recommendation." He rubbed his neck.

Lena looked up. "Was he there?"

"Yes, but he was in a terrible temper. He was spooning his soup when I went up to introduce myself, saying I studied under one of his former pupils, Adam Klein. He claimed he didn't remember him, but judging by the way he was cursing, I suspect he remembered him all too well. I thought he was about to throw the soup bowl at me. When I asked if we could perform for him in order to receive a letter of recommendation, he said it would be pointless because he could no longer hear well enough to judge the quality of our performance." Theo frowned. "Yet he has a big performance of his newest symphony coming up soon. I wonder how he will fare then."

"You mean Beethoven can no longer hear his own music? Poor man. What a terrible fate." Mona's eyes softened in pity.

"He could barely hear what I was telling him. He was

lip-reading most of the time and lifting a ridiculous ear trumpet to his ear." Theo tugged at his right ear. "I wonder whether it is an *impedita canalis auditiva*—a blockage in the ear—or some sort of nerve damage. I don't think it's an imbalance of humours, as some doctors claim. I wonder what Papa would have diagnosed." A shadow of sadness flitted over his narrow face.

Lena reached out and rubbed his hand.

Mona tapped on the table. "Back to the issue at hand, Doctor Arenheim. We were discussing our performance opportunities, which are non-existent."

Theo shook his head as if to clear out his thoughts. "You are right. You know what I think, Mama? We are probably going about this the wrong way. If only we had someone of influence to guide us and make the right introductions..."

Lena rubbed her forehead. "Yes. Adam Klein is doing his best, you know."

"Bah. He knows nothing." Theo banged his fist on the table in frustration. "They play music everywhere, but nobody wants us. It's not fair. Klein thinks he's helping, but the truth is, his only claim to fame is that he was once Beethoven's student—hardly his best, either."

Lena sighed. She knew there was some truth in what Theo was saying—Klein did not hold much influence in the Viennese music scene. Nevertheless, she was grateful for his support. Their relationship was friendly, but she knew it could develop into something more if she encouraged him. Yet, she did not, always ensuring to keep a friendly distance between them. As a schoolteacher, he was well read and enjoyed reading as much as Lena did.

However, he seemed to live in a world much smaller, narrower than the one the Arenheims inhabited. Simon Arenheim had been a visionary, a giant, a towering intellect. He had been a talented doctor, fluent in six languages, hungry for travel and adventure, and one of the most interesting men Lena had ever known. By comparison, Adam Klein seemed bland and somewhat dull.

"If he ever develops a romantic tendre for you, he will have to deal with me first." Theo pulled himself up and puffed out his chest. "As the head of the Arenheim family, it is my duty to protect you." Lena was only eight years older than Theo, but he had always been precocious and liked to pretend like it was the other way round.

A smile tugged at the corners of Lena's mouth. "What nonsense, Theo. We are merely good friends, Adam and I, and there is nothing more to our relationship." She ruffled his hair. "And what about your flame? Any progress?"

He had been smitten with the blacksmith's daughter for two years. It was only recently that she seemed to be responding to his advances. Theo was in high spirits. His face brightened. "I have decided to ask Rosalie to go for a walk with me next Sunday after church."

Lena nodded and watched with a smile as Theo left the room with a cheerful whistle on his lips. Now, as for cooking. She pulled up the sleeves of her dress and stared at the empty shelf in the kitchen.

A cabbage, an onion, flour, raspberry jam, and dried bread.

Cabbage soup it would be. And for dessert, some plain sugar biscuits with the homemade raspberry jam.

'Twould do.

THE NEXT MORNING, Lena had planned to stay at home and make jam preserves. There was much work about the house with Marie absent. It bothered her that they had not been able to secure a single performance. She slapped her hand on the wooden table. "*Ach!* This can't be such an impossibility, can it?"

She put on her bonnet and draped her shawl across her shoulders. She would try one more time to secure an introduction to one of the noble families. Count Razumovsky, a Russian nobleman and music lover, was a patron of Beethoven. Perhaps, if she could manage to get an introduction to him...

But, as on previous days, she was turned away at the gates of the vast palatial complex.

"The count is not at home," was the lackadaisical answer.

Discouraged, she turned away.

As she turned to leave, a man in a nondescript brown suit approached her.

"Frau Helena Arenheim?" His eyes were shaded by the hat he wore low over his face.

"Yes?"

"I understand that you are seeking to be hired as a musician."

"How did you know that?" She looked at him suspiciously.

The man's eyes gleamed. "There is very little that we do not know. It is almost impossible for someone without a patron or a member of the music guild to get a commission. Especially not from them." He jerked his chin up to nod at the splendid palais in front of them. "Yet you have tried knocking on the doors of all the great ones, at all the noble families, not only Metternich, but also Arnstein, Esterhazy and Kaunitz—alas, all in vain."

Her fingers gripped her reticule tightly. "Who are you?"

"You may call me August."

Lena moistened her lips. "August. Are you a secret agent?"

She couldn't see his eyes, but his thin lips curled to an unamused smile. "I see you are quick. That is admirable."

"Are you?"

His teeth gleamed. "My employer is Baron von Hager."

Everyone knew that name. The head of the Viennese secret police. She exhaled. "Von Hager reports directly to Metternich," she muttered. Even she knew that.

August inclined his head.

Metternich had set up the most sophisticated and elaborate spy network in all of Europe. The city was swarming with spies and agents, now more than ever before all on account of the Congress, of course.

Lena tightened her grip on her reticule. "Agent August. What do you want? I don't have much time."

"Because your children are waiting for you." He smiled again and she couldn't help but feel a shiver run down her spine.

The Forgotten Duke

"I'll get straight to the point. We can help you get the commission you want. We can help you get *any* commission you want. Anywhere. Do you want to play in the Hofburg? It shall be done. No more futile knocking on closed doors, begging to be heard. All that will be a thing of the past. Because Baron von Hager—or should we say Metternich?—himself will be your patron."

Lena's heart beat heavily against her ribs. "In return for my spying for him."

He flashed his teeth at her. "That's a given."

Oh dear, oh dear, oh dear.

Her breathing increased.

It was impossible, of course. Immoral. Unethical. She could never do it. She could think of a hundred, no, a thousand reasons why she should immediately turn and run away from Agent August as fast as possible and forget she ever talked to him.

"You and your family shall begin with a performance at Metternich's soiree next Wednesday," August continued talking. "If you so wish. We can arrange it in the blink of an eye. It won't matter that there are two women in the orchestra. You'll be protected. We can ensure that in the future, you will not lack any musical commissions, either. In return, all you have to do is be our eyes and ears."

"It is espionage. It is despicable."

"But when it comes to putting food in the mouths of the hungry hordes, a parent will do anything, even spy on high and mighty aristocrats who don't care a fig about us. We must help ourselves. The welfare of my children comes before safeguarding the political secrets of the arrogant nobility. Trust me, I have four little ones myself." He leaned forwards and whispered. "As one parent to another, I would seize the opportunity."

Spying on people was abhorrent to her. "I cannot reconcile it with my conscience." She shook her head. "The very idea disgusts me."

August smiled. "You have a strong conscience, a strong sense of what is right and what is wrong. That is good. Think of it this way: what are these foreigners to us? They will be gone in a few weeks. You'll never see them again, and there won't be any harm done."

Lena picked at the little flakes of dry skin on her lower lip. He had a point. What were those foreigners to her, anyway?

Nothing at all.

"In the meantime, you'll have done our nation a great service, and you'll be regarded a true patriot. The financial rewards are not to be scoffed at. You want the opportunity to perform regularly in the salons of the toffs? It shall be done. All you have to do is find out who says what to whom and where. Metternich, the Emperor, and the entire Austrian empire will be in your debt."

"I don't care a whit about the Emperor and whether he's in my debt or not," Lena said truthfully. "It's just not right."

"Very well. I see you won't be swayed." August tipped his hat up and she looked into a pair of shrewd, pale green eyes. He was younger than she'd expected. He straightened his cuffs and made a gesture as if to leave. At the last moment, he changed his mind. "It's just that I know what happens to young widows and their children when they can't afford to keep their livelihood. Have seen it with my very own eyes. Although—forgive me—you're not exactly a widow, are you?" His jade green eyes bored into hers.

She licked her dry lips. "What...what happens to them?" She ignored his reference to her not being a widow.

"They end up in the poorhouse. You have no idea what they are like, do you? A while back I saw a whole family of six—a mother and her five children—dragged out of their house because they could no longer pay the rent. They were carted to the poorhouse. Heard there was a cholera outbreak there only yesterday. Half the people are dead. Are you certain you won't be facing the same fate when your landlord finds out you can't pay the rent and that you're not really a widow? He won't be in a charitable frame of mind once he discovers the truth of your particular circumstances."

"I have no idea what you mean," Lena stammered.

He looked at her almost pitifully. "We know that you never married Simon Arenheim."

She clenched her hands so tightly that her knuckles whitened. "What are you saying now? Are you blackmailing me?"

He shook his head and raised his hands as if to reassure her. "You misunderstand. I would never do anything so dastardly. I only sought you out because I was aware of your particular circumstances. I thought you of all people, would appreciate the opportunity rather than continuing to march down a road that ends in the poorhouse. I merely wanted to offer you a way out of this predicament."

The picture August had just painted was terrifying. She imagined her children, her beautiful children, Theo, Les, Hecki and Mona, cooped up in the squalid quarters of the poorhouse with disease ravaging the place. The poor, when they died, ended up in mass graves outside the city walls of Vienna. She'd seen it. It was horrifying beyond words.

August continued talking. "But since you're not interested and there are many other people who are—"

"Suppose I agreed. What would I have to do?" She wrung her hands.

He did not appear surprised by her change of heart. "Not much. Do what you do best. Perform. Enjoy it, without the worry of having to secure another performance afterwards. Observe who is there. If you can, keep an eye on who is talking to whom. It's not that difficult. I'd be your contact, and you'd pass your messages to me." He paused. "What do you say? Will you do it?"

Lena massaged her temples. Her mind was spinning.

Here was a golden opportunity impossible to refuse.

All her dreams would come true.

Their financial woes would be solved at a stroke.

Their rent would be paid.

If she worked for Baron von Hager, she would no longer have to fear exposure. She would receive commissions in the upper echelons of society.

They would not end in the poorhouse. Their future would be made.

"I—I—I, oh heavens." She paced up and down,

wringing her hands. Then she stopped in front of the man and pulled herself up. "I am probably selling my soul right now. You are right. I will do anything, anything at all for my children and their safety."

The man gave her a piercing look. "You'll do it?"

Lena let out a big breath that sounded like a sigh. "Very well. I'll do it."

Chapter Four

Prince Metternich's villa was one of the most magnificent estates in and around Vienna. Situated just outside the city walls opposite the Belvedere Palace, it had been built as a summer residence, a newly constructed, stately, neoclassical two-storey mansion with a vast park stretching into the distance.

"*Famos!*" Hecki and Les exclaimed in unison, their eyes wide as they gazed up at the imposing colonnades of the portico. '*Famos*,' a Viennese term for something absolutely fantastic, was currently their favourite expression. Everything was *famos*, such as *Knödel* with *Sauerkraut* that their neighbour Emma, the good soul, had cooked for them earlier; the splendid fireworks that had lit up the sky the night before; the parade of emperors; the bag of roasted chestnuts they'd bought; the performing monkey they'd seen at the fair. Now, Metternich's palace seemed to have been added to the list.

"Hector, Achilles, don't forget the music stands!" Lena called, her nerves on edge. After careful consideration, she had decided to bring the younger boys along as musical assistants. They were to assist with setting up, turning pages, and carrying instrument cases and stands.

All were dressed as eighteenth century musicians, thanks to Emma, who had unearthed a trunk full of clothes once worn by her grandparents. It was this or nothing, as Lena couldn't possibly afford new outfits for them.

"It looks like carnival started early," her husband Karl had commented with a pipe between his teeth.

Dressed in matching brocade waistcoats and jackets, complete with breeches, stockings, wigs, and buckled shoes, the boys resembled charming little page boys from a bygone century. Lena herself was dressed in an unfashionably heavy, burgundy brocade gown with a low neckline, a fitted narrow bodice, and sleeves with laced cuffs.

"Not only do I look like I've stepped out of Empress Maria Theresia's drawing room, but these lace cuffs are completely impractical for playing the piano," she remarked, lifting the lace covering her hands and shaking her head in mild frustration.

"I think it's lovely," Mona chimed in, pleased with her emerald-green robe cut in the same historic fashion.

Theo, dressed in a distinguished grey velvet suit with breeches, buckled shoes, and a grey wig looked particularly dapper.

"The fashion suits you, Theo," Lena said with a smile, appreciating his appearance. "You look like a gentleman."

Adam Klein, who had joined them as a violinist,

looked around nervously. His wig was crooked on his head and the dark blue suit seemed too tight for him.

Her dream was on the brink of realisation—they were to make their debut that night at Metternich's soiree. Yet, paradoxically, she found herself wishing they didn't have to perform. It was their first time playing in such distinguished company. What if they failed? What if they forgot their music, their fingers became unresponsive, or, worse, the boys burst out into one of their laughing fits during their performance? What if the elite discovered they were really impostors and expelled them in disgrace? Such a failure could end their budding careers.

Sweat gathered under her arms at the mere thought.

"Never fear, Mama," Theo drawled as he alighted from the carriage and picked up his cello. "We're all heading for a shipwreck for sure. Relax in the knowledge that it will all end in disaster, chaos, and infamy, and we can enjoy every minute of it."

"Thank you, Theo," Lena replied stiffly, "you're no help at all."

As she turned away, Theo tugged at her sleeve. "We know the pieces by heart. You could wake us in the middle of the night, and we'd play them perfectly half asleep. There's no one in Vienna who can match us. Deep down, you know that's true. Step Aside, Paganini, for the Arenheims are coming." With a swagger, he headed for the servants' entrance at the side of the building.

"There's nothing wrong with some self-confidence, but yours borders on arrogance, Theseus Arenheim," Lena scolded. Yet she couldn't help smiling. Theo had managed to calm her nerves. Squaring her shoulders, she followed her children through the side entrance into the grand mansion.

"This place is full of naked people, Mama," the incorrigible Hector reported. He pointed to the statue of a man that stood at the top of the marble staircase. Indeed, the entire corridor resembled a gallery of Greek gods and goddesses and heroes, all naked.

"I wonder why they always have to plant a tiny leaf over *that* particular body part..." Les muttered as he inspected the statue of his namesake, Achilles.

Mona hushed him and ushered him along. "The guests will be arriving soon, and we need to set up and tune our instruments. Help us, boys."

The rooms where they were to perform were bright and airy, with high stuccoed ceilings, buttery yellow wallpaper, freshly waxed parquet flooring and a massive marble fireplace. Gilded mirrors hung on the walls, reflecting the light from the crystal chandeliers and making the entire room sparkle.

"How wonderful," Mona gasped.

A pianoforte stood in the corner of the room. This was where they would set up their instruments.

The event turned out to be less daunting than Lena had feared. Their task was simply to provide background music in the grand salon while the guests mingled. This meant that instead of the audience sitting and staring directly at them, there was a constant buzz of conversation and movement as people came and went. This informal setting meant that their performance wasn't the sole focus, which was a relief. If they weren't the centre of attention, then minor mistakes or mishaps were less likely to be noticed.

On the other hand, this could also be a source of irritation. Could the children concentrate and perform when the room was restless?

It turned out that they could. Both Hecki and Les comported themselves well, turning the pages with unwavering concentration. Lena was proud of them.

They started with a Trio by Haydn with just the strings. Then Lena joined them on the pianoforte for a piece by Mozart. They played very well. In fact, they'd never played it so well before.

Lena was pleased.

The room began to fill with people. They were all dressed in the latest expensive fashion, and it was clear that these were people from the top echelons of society, the statesmen of the nations of Europe. A small crowd had gathered around them, clapping politely.

"The music is first-rate. They play exceptionally well," said one gentleman to another, lifting his lorgnette to study them. He tapped his fingers lightly on his palm.

Elated, Lena stood up and bowed. Pride filled her.

"Let's play Mozart's second quartet," Adam Klein said, wiping his forehead with a handkerchief.

Lena nodded and sat down at the pianoforte.

It happened in the middle of the Allegretto. Her fingers flew across the keyboard. It was as if the music absorbed her and she and the music became one. Everything around her ceased to exist, and she felt and saw nothing else.

The sharp sound of glass smashing on the marble floor nearby jolted her out of her reverie. She flinched, and there was an infinitesimal pause as the music stopped.

"Continue," Adam growled.

Lena gave a shake of her head and struggled to regain her concentration. Then her fingers continued to fly over the keys.

There was a long applause when they finished. They stood and bowed.

"Intermission," Theo mouthed.

"Well done, children, well done," she told them, wiping her moist fingers on a handkerchief. "Let's take a short rest. Afterwards Hecki and Les can perform one of their pieces." The boys had rehearsed simple folk pieces suitable for the recorder flute.

She had half an hour to mingle with the guests and do what she had been sent here to do: spy. While she had been performing, she'd been far too immersed in the music to do so.

The problem was: how did one spy when one had no idea how to go about doing it?

Her eyes swept across the room of well-dressed people. Here she encountered another problem. How was she to report who said what to whom when she had not an inkling of who these people were? Most of them spoke French. It was the common language of diplomacy.

Lena understood enough French to follow a conversation, but she was rather rusty in it.

Near the fireplace were two gentlemen. One lean gentleman in plain, dark evening clothes and a pale, angular face leaned against the mantelpiece with his arms folded across his chest as he listened coldly to the tall, moustached man in a blue uniform.

"This is unacceptable," the uniformed man said tersely. "I insist that Prussia has a historical claim to the territory in Poland, especially if we are to restore the status quo as it was before the war. As for Saxony, our aim is to create a buffer zone to protect Prussia from further French aggression. Surely, Saxony's allegiance to Napoleon during the war cannot be overlooked."

"Your Majesty," the lean gentleman replied, unmoved, "the annexation of Saxony stands in stark contradiction to the principle of legitimacy and the restoration of the political order. Britain will not budge an inch from this position."

"Damnation, Castlereagh, Britain will have to budge eventually."

So this was Castlereagh, the one Karl had mentioned the other day, the representative of the British delegation. Her eyes wandered to the tall gentleman in the blue uniform who was scowling. Could he possibly be Frederick William, the King of Prussia? Her hand wandered to her mouth to cover her gasp. If so, she was standing in the presence of a king.

"Do we?" Castlereagh raised an eyebrow, a flicker of steel in his gaze. "Prussia has much to gain from a stable Europe. Perhaps a compromise can be reached on the Polish borders. As for Saxony, surely his majesty will agree that a strong, independent, but contented Saxony would serve as a better buffer against French aggression than a resentful one under Prussian rule?"

Lena leaned forwards to listen further, but several people moved in front of the couple by the fireside, so she could no longer hear what they were saying.

That would have to do, she decided. Her heart pounded and her mouth was dry. Espionage made one thirsty. She grabbed a glass of champagne from the tray of the nearest footman, not caring that it might be inappropriate as she was not a guest.

She wandered into the next room, drinking thirstily. There, too, were groups of people standing about, deep in conversation.

Her eyes fell on a handsome man who seemed to be watching her. He was well-dressed, medium height, with receding dark blond hair slicked back from his high forehead. When their eyes met, he curled his lips into a half-smile and—goodness! Had he just *winked* at her?

She glanced over one shoulder, then the other, then looked back at him, but there was no one else he could have meant.

A blush crept up her neck. Why did he do that? How dare he? She was just a musician, hadn't he seen her perform? How dare he flirt with her?

The man, now smirking outright, raised his glass as if to greet her, which threw her into even greater confusion. Did they know each other? She was certain she'd never met the man before in her entire life. Then he turned to his companion, an older gentleman with a wig, silk breeches and stockings, who was leaning on a stick and looking bored as he listened to the blond man talk.

Now that particular gentleman seemed vaguely familiar. Why was that? It took her a moment to register his identity. Didn't Karl say earlier that he was dressed in an old-fashioned style, just like she was? Excitement filled her. If so, then this *must* be Monsieur de Talleyrand...

As she tried to organise her thoughts about what she knew of the French statesman, her gaze drifted to the palm trees by the window, where a tall, dark-haired gentleman stood, staring at her as if she were a ghost.

Their eyes locked.

There was a stern, pale expression on his face, his jaw was set, and his eyes, his eyes...oh, heavens, his eyes!

They penetrated her very soul.

Her heart fluttered wildly and she began to tremble.

Who was he? And what did that look in his eyes mean? There was shock, anger...agony? No one had ever looked at her like that before. She was certain he was a stranger. Then why did she suddenly feel like bursting into tears?

Dazed, she began to drift towards him.

Someone grabbed her arm and pulled her back. "Helena. Hector has disappeared." Lena blinked and looked up into the familiar watery blue eyes of Adam Klein.

"Adam. What...what is the matter?" She blinked at him as if waking from a dream.

She glanced at the window again, but the man was gone. Had he been a mere figment of her imagination? It was hot and stuffy in the room and she'd downed that glass of champagne too quickly, leaving her dizzy. But surely, she couldn't be drunk from just one glass of champagne?

"Helena. Are you well?" There was a look of concern on Adam's face.

"Yes, yes, I am merely...dizzy." She shook her head to clear her brain. "What is the matter?"

"Hector. It appears he has run off," Adam said tersely.

Lena came to her senses. "Hector?"

"He's disappeared."

"He can't have gone far." Her eyes swept the room.

Theo arrived with the others in tow. "Where is he, Les? Surely you must know something. You two are always in league together."

Les shrugged. "I don't know. I was bored, so I kept myself busy counting the crystals in the chandelier. One moment he was here, the next he was gone."

"That little rascal," Theo muttered. "I'll tan his hide."

"What are we to do now?" Mona whispered. "We have to play again soon."

"Theo, go with Mona and search the rooms on the right. Les, Adam, and I will go to the left. We'll meet back here in ten minutes."

"Where could that boy be?" Lena's eyes swept the room.

"When it comes to Hecki, always follow your nose, Mama." Theo stuck his nose in the air and sniffed. "The smell of fondant, chocolate, and marzipan definitely coming from yonder room over there," he said with conviction, pointing to the next room.

Indeed, a lavish buffet had been set up there. True to

Theo's prediction, Hecki was standing next to the cake buffet, his mouth smeared with chocolate. He was in the process of plucking the brandied cherries from each dish and popping them into his mouth.

"Hector Arenheim," Lena exclaimed, relieved and annoyed at the same time. "How can you leave us like this in the middle of the performance?"

"All thish shocolate ish sho goood, Mama," Hecki hiccuped. He grinned, then popped another brandied cherry into his mouth.

"Good heavens. Are you drunk? How many of those cherries have you eaten?"

"Many," Hecki grinned. "Very many. Couldn't shtop."

"The boy's as drunk as a fiddler," Adam said. "It takes but a handful of those brandy-soaked cherries to get a little boy like him roaring drunk." He shook his head.

This set Hecki off into a whoop of laughter. "Haha, drunk as a fiddler, haha!"

"For heaven's sake, child." Lena bent over the boy, worried. "What are we to do now? Quick, bring a glass of water," she told Adam, who immediately left to do so.

Theo arrived with Mona. "So this is where he is. Stuffing his face with sweets."

Les's eyes grew round and he, too, began to surreptitiously help himself.

"Don't touch the brandied cherries!" Lena exclaimed. Heaven help them if Les, too, ended up drunk.

Adam returned with a water glass and Lena lifted it to Hecki's mouth. He drank it with thirsty gulps.

In the meantime, the other children stuffed themselves with sweetmeats.

"We haven't had any supper, Mama," Theo defended himself as he bit into an eclair.

Lena looked around nervously. "Children, we are employees, not guests. I am not at all sure we're allowed to help ourselves here." She threw a furtive look around her shoulder, then she grabbed a piece of almond cake, a macaroon, a raspberry tart, and a piece of chocolate cake, folded them into a napkin and pressed them into Mona's hands. "Quick, take this."

In the meantime, Hector bowed to everyone in sight. "*Küss die Hand, gnä' Frau*," he said gallantly, bowing to all and sundry, including the palm tree in the corner.

The ladies tittered. "Isn't he charming?"

"You were the performers from earlier," a low male voice said behind them.

Lena whirled around.

Hector beamed. "Yes we are, mon-monsieur. Did you likesh our music?" And then he turned pale, hiccupped, made a face, and vomited on Monsieur de Talleyrand's buckled diamond shoes.

Chapter Five

JULIUS, DUKE OF ALDINGBOURNE, CAST A WEARY glance around the room. Everyone of rank and name was gathered here tonight. All the statesmen, monarchs, ministers, and nobles who had anything at all to say politically on any subject.

Metternich had pulled out his pipe and they'd all followed his tune when he finally decided to play it. Tonight, he had decided that they would all gather here, in his magnificent palace. So here they were.

Politically, of course, it was another matter entirely.

Julius had expected this, so he did not see this as an occasion for entertainment, but for work. He would use it as an opportunity to talk to the representatives of the other delegations. He already knew that Metternich expected a tête-à-tête with him in one of his secluded cabinet rooms. Then there was Talleyrand, who, judging by his expression, seemed to be in a state of perpetual ennui, and the Tsar, who was expected to appear later in the evening.

Talleyrand, however, was not to be underestimated. It was not without reason he was considered one of the most successful diplomats the world had ever seen. Tsar Alexander was another matter entirely. Vain, explosive, and volatile like a grenade, he was not to be trifled with. Then there were the Prussians and their demands. He'd seen Castlereagh in a heated debate with the King of Prussia.

Julius furrowed his brow. It was going to be a difficult evening.

He'd arrived with Evie at a fashionably late hour, clad in a black tailcoat, a silver waistcoat, and breeches, all complemented with a crisp white cravat.

"You look sinfully handsome," his sister had told him admiringly. "If you weren't my brother, I'd set my cap at you. You must be careful, for many a Viennese lady will want to put you in her pocket."

"Let them try," he'd retorted.

Evie had laughed.

"You look very decent yourself, imp," he'd said, pulling one of her curls. That was an understatement. His sister was no beauty, but she had a charm and a vivacity about her that enchanted men more than physical beauty ever would.

He would have to keep a close eye on her.

And dash it all, he thought with increasing irritation, it eluded him why he should do so, when that was really the role of her betrothed, Hartenberg.

After circling the cramped salons, he'd managed to lose Evie in the crowd. Metternich had immediately cornered him and they'd had a lengthy discussion about the Polish affair. After an hour, Metternich slapped his shoulder. "Do not let me monopolise you, *cher ami*," he said. "Be sure to partake of the exquisite buffet that is available in the green salon." He lifted a finger and a footman approached with a salver of champagne coupes. He offered one to Julius. "To an indissoluble friendship between our countries," he said pompously.

Julius lifted his glass and drank. He took a second glass and drained it, too. The room was really too hot.

A lady crossed his path. She drifted towards him, soft baby ringlets framing her face. Her rosy lips pouted.

The Duchess Wilhelmine von Sagan.

"Your Grace? You look so…morose." She tinkled a laugh that sounded like silver bells. "I trust you are enjoying yourself?" She touched his arm gently.

"It is tolerable."

"Oh, you English. Always so…cold." She ran a manicured finger up and down his sleeve. Bending close to him, she whispered, "One cannot help but wonder what it would take to melt all that coldness."

One of his eyebrows rose.

The Duchess was a beauty. The entire world knew that she was Metternich's mistress. The poor fool was head over heels in love with her, and she was playing her merry game with him. What was she up to now? He'd wager a fortune that it was merely to make Metternich jealous. If she thought Aldingbourne was easy prey, she knew him very little, indeed.

He picked her hand off his sleeve. "Careful, then, madam, lest you get a frostbite." He left her gaping after him.

"I saw that," another female voice whispered into his ears. "A hit. A cut direct." She chuckled and a cloying cloud of perfume enveloped him.

Not again. Would these women not leave him alone? Had the ladies in London been as openly aggressive in their pursuit as the ones here? It was becoming quite a nuisance.

Irritated, he turned to the Princess Bagration. She was the Duchess of Sagan's most bitter enemy. They lived in the same palace—the Palais Palm—and were in fierce competition over who was the most beautiful, most celebrated society hostess in Vienna. Both were beautiful. Both were accomplished. Both were Metternich's lovers. Were they now setting their sights on him? Him and Tsar Alexander, if the rumours were true.

An irritated furrow appeared between his brows.

"If you'll excuse me, madam," he snapped. "I believe Castlereagh is expecting me."

He wasn't, of course, but it was a convenient lie.

The sound of strings and a piano drifted in from the adjoining drawing room. This orchestra played well, he noticed. Then he paused as the musicians came into view. A tall, lanky boy played the cello. A petite girl played the viola. A man played the violin. There were two young page boys with wigs turning the pages earnestly. He glossed over them.

Then the pianoforte took over. Julius appreciated good music. That was one of the advantages of being in Vienna, for the music here was exquisite. There was no doubt about it, this was fine music, played professionally. The other night he'd attended a performance of

Beethoven's Fidelio, and every fibre of his being had identified with the dark, heavy music.

His eyes wandered to the woman behind the pianoforte—

—He did not hear the sound of glass crashing on the marble floor as the champagne coupe slipped from his fingers, and every drop of blood in his entire body drained from him.

The pianist flinched for an infinitesimal second, but quickly gathered herself and continued to play.

At the end of the piece, they stood and bowed.

Aldingbourne was incapable of forming a coherent thought. Time had stood still. The woman was nothing special. Petite, slim with strawberry blonde hair. Big, brown eyes like a doe. A fine, wide mouth that curved upwards at the corners. A delicate nose, a charming dusting of freckles over it. His eyes moved to her right cheek.

A small, heart-shaped birthmark.

He inhaled sharply as the world around him began to tilt. He grabbed the windowsill behind him to steady himself.

Catherine.

His first inclination was to go after her, but an inner voice, the voice of reason and logic, stopped him.

No. It was impossible. It couldn't be. It was a coincidence.

He stayed by the window and watched her close the pianoforte, talk to the other musicians, and approach the fireplace, where she paused.

From that angle, he saw her sharp profile. The way

she moved her head, the way she walked. The gesture of her hand.

Anguish and confusion shot through him. He broke out in a sweat even though he was shivering with cold.

No.

This was impossible.

He closed his eyes, bottled up the feelings.

Impossible.

The woman who looked like Catherine ambled into the adjoining room. She paused at the door. She was wearing a gown from the previous century, which gave her a strange ethereal, out-of-time look, an aura of the supernatural.

Julius decided to follow her from a safe distance, determined to stay hidden from her. He wanted to watch her. To ascertain from a distance who she really was. To verify that she was not a figment of his imagination, but a being of flesh and blood.

He followed her around the room, unobserved. She glided among the people like a ghost, indeed, seeing everyone and everything, but no one else seemed to notice her.

Eight years ago, Catherine had died in a terrible accident. His world had been shattered that day.

Unless, of course, she hadn't.

As unbelievable as that was.

Eight years after her death, she appeared as a musician in Metternich's salon, playing the pianoforte.

Who *was* she?

How was this possible?

He remained by the palm tree, a steep frown creasing his forehead. Was this truly his Catherine?

She raised her eyes—and met his.

The look in her brown eyes was familiar and clear.

He forgot to breathe.

An eternity passed in a second, a second became an eternity.

Then, a man stepped up to her, grabbed her by the arm, and in the blink of an eye, her lithe figure disappeared into the crowd.

He breathed heavily.

Perhaps it had all been a mirage, a trick of an overly imaginative mind. After all the talk of Evie's, and his lack of sleep, this was the result. He was seeing things.

"Julius, did you see?" Evie sidled up to him, bubbling with excitement. "Did you see her? She is here! The same woman I was talking about the other day. Let us go and greet—"

"No."

"But Julius!" A moment more and she would be jumping up and down with both feet in frustration like she used to do as a child when she didn't get what she wanted.

"Do not, under any circumstances, approach her and speak to her. Do not let her know you're here. Do you understand?"

"But Julius!" This time it sounded like a whine.

He gripped her arm so tightly it would probably leave a mark. "I want to observe her first without her noticing me. I need to see what she is like. I need proof, first. Please cooperate, Evie. Don't let her see you."

"Fine," Evie grumbled. "I'll do as you say. But it is so very dull. It doesn't make any sense at all. If you want proof that she is indeed Catherine, you will have to talk to her. That is the only way."

He gave her a cutting stare that visibly wilted her. "Very well," she muttered. "I shan't say another word."

He wanted to look for her, but once again a Prussian diplomat approached him and tried to draw him into a debate. He replied in monosyllables, his gaze searching the room for her. He dimly noted that there was a hubbub in the green salon where the buffet was. By the time he could extricate himself from the conversation, strains of violin music had resumed in the other room.

Another gentleman approached to introduce himself. "If you will excuse me," Julius interrupted the man mid-sentence and went into the music room.

As she played each piece, Julius was convinced that she was a mirage, a figment of his imagination. Catherine had always been an excellent pianist. It had been her sole passion. Could this possibly be the same person?

After their performance, they bowed. He tried to follow them, but now he was detained by Talleyrand, who attempted to draw him into a debate on the Saxon question. As soon as he was able to extricate himself from the Frenchman, he searched every salon, but she'd already left.

Evie and Julius were silent on the ride back to their residence, each lost in their own thoughts.

The Forgotten Duke

The normally talkative Evie excused herself as soon as they arrived at the mansion.

Julius gently caught her arm. "I feel I have rather shamefully neglected you this evening. I was so very busy." He avoided mentioning the apparition of Catherine.

Evie played with the fringes of her scarf. "Yes. I confess it's rather dull when everyone endlessly talks about politics."

"I forgot to tell you I have arranged for you to have a companion," the Duke said. "So you're no longer isolated."

Evie nodded and gave him a small smile. "That is very considerate of you, Julius. Thank you."

Julius walked briskly to the study, sat down at the table, and stared at the blank sheet of paper. Then he penned a missive, sealed the envelope, and rang the bell.

When the footman appeared, he handed it to him. "With expediency to England. It is urgent."

"Yes, Your Grace."

Julius sat back and steepled his fingers. Exhaustion of a kind he had never known before overwhelmed him.

If this woman was indeed Catherine, the implications were beyond anything he'd ever dared to think, to dream. The logical part of his brain rebelled most violently against the idea that the woman he had seen was indeed her.

What was needed were facts.

There had to be proof.

Indisputable proof that she was Catherine.

Chapter Six

Hector had thrown up several times in the carriage, then fallen into the sleep of the dead. After the fiasco with Talleyrand, they had left him in the servants' quarters with Mona watching over him while they finished their performance. The next morning, the poor boy had a headache.

"I will never touch alcohol again for the rest of my life," he groaned.

Mona placed her hand on his forehead. "Let this be a lesson to you, Hector Arenheim. This happened because you got greedy. How many of those cherries did you eat?"

Hecki pulled a face. "I picked them off the cakes first, and then I saw a bowl of them and ate them right out of the bowl. They were so delicious I couldn't stop. I also drank some of the liquid. How could I have known that they were evil cherries?"

"Oh, Hecki." Lena shook her head. "Does your head still hurt?"

"Like the very devil," the boy groaned.

Lena had been torn between embarrassment for her son, concern for his well-being, and the fear that Talleyrand would have them all thrown into prison for having ruined his expensive shoes. To her immense relief, the gentleman had a sense of humour. "It reminds me of the time I drank my *nounou*'s cherry liqueur which she kept hidden in her cupboard," he said, a smile playing on his lips. "I was about the same age as that boy and rendered incapacitated for an entire day. How long ago that was, and yet I remember it as if it were yesterday…"

"But your shoes, monsieur," Lena wailed. "Please allow us to have them cleaned."

"What, and have me run around in my stockings in the meantime?" he chuckled. "Never fear, madam. My servants will attend to it." He lifted a finger and a footman came running.

"You are too generous to overlook this," Lena had told him.

"At least this otherwise tedious and dull evening has seen a touch of excitement, even if it was at my expense." His eyes had twinkled merrily.

Later, Lena confided in Theo and Mona. "Perhaps all this performing is folly after all. Because not only are these people highly eccentric, but they keep late hours, which is difficult for the little ones, and I am beginning to doubt whether in the end it will have all been worth it." She had kept the secret agreement she had with Agent August to herself, only mentioning that this opportunity had been presented to them unexpectedly at the last moment.

The Forgotten Duke

"They paid you, didn't they?" Theo asked, suppressing a yawn.

She opened the purse to show him the coins she'd been given before they left.

"Well, then it was worth it," he said, a mischievous grin spreading over his tired face. "Even if Hecki nearly caused a diplomatic scandal. I wonder whether the *Wiener Abendblatt* will run a story on this tomorrow. I can see the headline now: 'Even children vomit on French diplomacy!'"

"Theo!" Lena groaned. "Please don't even joke about that."

He laughed. "As much as I dislike the French, I must admit, I rather like this Talleyrand. Seems to be a good sport."

Lena agreed.

They hadn't arrived at home until three in the morning, and now everyone was still asleep, even though it was midday.

She brewed herself a cup of coffee and sat down at the kitchen table to write the missive for the spy. The instructions were to document everything she'd seen and heard that evening.

She chewed on her pencil, then began to write. The image of the man who'd been staring at her arose in her mind. She nearly dropped the pen.

Who was he?

And why had he stared at her like that?

Had she just imagined him? He'd disappeared in the blink of an eye.

Shaking her head as if to rid her mind of these images, she continued writing her report.

SHE MET August in the early morning hours at the lamppost outside the house and discreetly handed him the missive. He tucked it away swiftly and pulled out a small leather pouch, which she gratefully accepted. Not only was food for the week secured but the rent as well. Lena heaved a sigh of relief.

"I know you've detailed everything in the letter, but just out of curiosity—who did you encounter there?" August pushed his hat back so she could see his clear, sharp eyes.

Lena told him about the interchange between Castlereagh and the King of Prussia.

He nodded. "Their difference in the matter is well known. Who else?"

"Talleyrand." She cleared her throat, hoping her face did not betray anything about Hecki's mishap. "He was speaking with another gentleman I couldn't identify. He was of medium height, very handsome with dark blond curly hair, and a slightly receding hairline." She recalled with indignation how he'd winked at her. She frowned. "He was rather preposterous and arrogant."

And then there was the other, darker gentleman. Lena felt a chill down her spine merely by thinking of him. For some reason, she didn't want to mention him to August.

"I wonder who he could have been," she murmured.

August smiled knowingly. "Medium height, dark blond curly hair? Was he very charming?"

She felt a flush creep up her cheeks. "I wouldn't know."

August chuckled. "Of course he was. They call him the 'Adonis of the Drawing Room.' He is quite popular among women. Did he seem to recognise you?"

Lena threw him an astonished look. "How did you know?"

August smirked. "We know everything. That, my dear Frau Arenheim, was Prince Metternich—the man to whom our head of police reports. The man for whom, ultimately, you are spying."

With a grin, he tipped his hat and sauntered down the road, whistling a tune.

Lena stared after him, utterly flabbergasted.

LENA WENT to the market with Mona. Together, they planned to prepare the children's favourite meal: plum dumplings, lovingly rolled in buttered breadcrumbs and sweetly powdered with sugar. It was a delight to the senses.

"We must buy a lot of plums, Mama," Mona said enthusiastically. "The boys always have a competition to see who can eat the most. I want to eat at least three myself."

She had both hands in a bowl of potato dough when there was a sharp knock at the door. She heard the scuffling of footsteps in the house as one of the children hurried to open it.

A moment later, Theo appeared in the kitchen. "Mama, there is someone there to see you."

Lena looked up with a frown. "Who is it? I'm in the middle of making dumplings."

He shrugged. "They didn't say. They look like very fine people, though. I think you should talk to them. I put them in the parlour."

Lena dropped the dough into the bowl and wiped her fingers on her apron. She took it off, stepped out into the hallway and opened the door to the parlour.

Her eyes swept across the room to where two gentlemen stood by the fireplace, their top hats laid aside. She could instantly tell that they were people of Quality. Both men turned and stared at her.

One was of average height, dressed in a simple but well-tailored brown suit. His countenance held an air of open friendliness. When his gaze fell on her, his eyes widened and his jaw dropped.

But it was the other gentleman who truly captured her attention.

He was tall, impeccably dressed in beige pantaloons paired with a dark blue coat. His neckcloth, spotlessly white, was expertly tied around two stiff shirt points. He held a walking stick in one hand and gloves in the other. Dark hair framed his features, which, while not exactly handsome, exuded an air of arrogance and icy aloofness.

A tremor ran down Lena's spine.

"You," she stammered. It was the same gentleman who'd looked at her with such a penetrating stare the previous evening.

Their eyes locked. Once more, the man's gaze pierced

her soul. His jaw clenched and his lips thinned. He stood as still as a marble statue. He was also as pale as one. The only movement in his entire body was the ticking of a vein in his right temple.

Lena forgot to breathe.

At first she did not notice the third occupant, a lady sitting quietly in an armchair. She was elegantly attired in a fine walking dress, a cashmere shawl draped over one arm, her bonnet adorned with feathered plumes. She stood abruptly.

"Oh!" escaped Lena's lips.

The lady tripped forwards, grasped her hands and shook them as if she were a long-lost friend.

"I am so delighted to see you again!" She beamed at her.

Heaven help her, it was the mad Englishwoman.

Aware that she had bits of potato dough stuck under her fingernails, Lena pulled her hands away and hid them behind her back.

"When we met earlier, you said your name was Helena Arenheim?" the lady said.

"Yes, that is correct."

"It is clear you do not remember any of us. A shame. I am Lady Evangeline Stafford-Hill." She looked at her expectantly. "Does the name sound familiar?"

Lena shook her head. She was acutely aware of her own simple, washed-out blue cotton dress, and the jam stains on the sleeve. Her hair probably resembled a bird's nest. She rubbed the tip of her nose self-consciously, not realising that in doing so, she left a smudge of flour on it.

The English lady's mouth broke into a delighted grin.

"I would like to introduce you to someone." She took a deep breath and said, "This is my brother, Julius, the Duke of Aldingbourne." She gestured to the arrogant-looking gentleman.

A Duke? He was an English Duke?

She had no idea how to behave when one was presented to a Duke, English or otherwise. What was one supposed to do? Hold out one's hand to be kissed? Bow? Curtsy? And if so, which one, and how deep?

Lena ended up performing a mixture of both, a crooked curtsy-bow. "How do you do?" she murmured, hoping that she had done the right thing.

He opened his pale lips once, twice, but no sound emerged.

"And this is his secretary, Mr Emil Mortimer," the lady continued, pointing at the younger man in brown.

"Good heavens." The younger man stared at her with eyes so wide they looked like they would pop out of his face any minute. "How can it be? How is this possible?"

Lena did not know what to make of his reaction. She clasped her hands behind her back and wished them all to Jericho.

But the expression on the Duke's face was becoming increasingly worrying. He looked distinctly ill. Perhaps he needed some fresh air. Lena was about to suggest he sit down when he finally spoke.

"Catherine," finally broke from his pale lips.

Oh, no, no, no, no. Not again.

Lena backed away as the man dropped his stick and gloves and proceeded to descend down on her with unnerving determination. She backed away. "This is a mistake," she stammered as she bumped into the armchair.

As she turned to flee, his hand shot out, grabbing her arm with a steely grip and pulling her towards him. Abruptly, she found herself pressed against his chest—solid as marble, yet radiating heat. Dazed, she blinked, trying to process the sudden proximity.

"By all the saints," he breathed.

Lena looked up at him, bewildered, as he gently cradled her face between his hands, studying it intently. His finger traced the mole on her right cheek so delicately that goosebumps erupted across her skin. Her heart fluttered uncontrollably.

A waft of his cologne entered her nose. A masculine smell of cedar and musk, earthy and wooden, warm and... familiar. She paused, catching her breath, her chest tightening. A wave of emotion washed over her, an ache, a sadness she didn't understand. Glimmers of something flickered at the edge of her consciousness, yet out of reach.

She gasped. "Who are you?"

"The question is, who are you?" the Duke replied, his voice rough with emotion. "Are you an actress? An impostor chasing title and fortune?" His grasp tightened on her chin, the other still cupping her cheek. "Are you real?"

Lena's mouth dropped open. "I—What?"

"Julius." Lady Evangeline groaned. She covered her face with her hands and shook her head. "She can hardly be an impostor chasing after your title and fortune when it was us, specifically me, who chased her to begin with." Turning to Lena she said, "I apologise. What must you think of us. It is the shock of seeing you again after all this time. Julius!" she hissed. "Apologise."

The Duke opened and closed his mouth several times, then said with a hoarse voice, "You're right. That comment was unnecessary and uncalled for. I apologise."

Lena grasped the armchair for support. "You're mad. You're all mad." Her entire body trembled.

"If I may say so, I do not believe she is an impostor, Your Grace," Mr Mortimer interjected, dabbing at his forehead with a handkerchief. "She appears to be quite—authentic. I wouldn't have believed it if I hadn't seen her with my own eyes, though she clearly does not seem to remember any of us."

"I told you so!" Lady Evangeline exclaimed triumphantly. "Didn't I, Julius? I told them I saw you in that street, but Julius wouldn't listen. You can't imagine the schemes I concocted to find you and bring you two together, and now look, it's happened entirely by chance. It is fate lending a hand. You appeared suddenly at the Metternich soiree, playing like an angel, and Julius finally saw you. He dropped his champagne glass and almost fainted. Then you disappeared again. You must stop doing that, it is a most vexatious habit. With Mortimer's help, we were able to track you here." She clapped her gloved hands together, beaming.

Lena shook her head with determination. "Oh, no. You are mistaken. My name is Helena Arenheim, as I have repeatedly tried to tell you. Who is this Catherine you insist I am?"

The Duke dropped his hands to his sides. "My wife," he replied, his tone dull.

Chapter Seven

Some moments in life were so absurd that laughter was the only natural response. She tried to stifle it at first, so as to not disturb the gravity of the situation, for the room had fallen as silent as a deserted chapel. It escaped anyhow, an undignified and most unladylike snort. Right into the Duke's face, too.

Lena couldn't help herself. She laughed until tears streamed down her face and her sides began to cramp. She collapsed into the armchair, clutching her ribs. It wasn't amusement, but a hysterical, nervous release. Soon enough, her laughter turned into something that sounded more like sobs.

Lady Evangeline stared at her in surprise, at first, then laughed with her.

"I fail to see what is so amusing," the Duke growled, clearly put out.

"Me, your wife?" Lena spluttered between gasps, her voice trembling. "Me, a duchess? That's impossible! I have no memory of you or of any marriage between us."

The truth was, she didn't remember anything at all.

"You truly do not remember?" His face turned to stone.

"We are here to discuss the possibility that you are the Duchess, yes," Mr Mortimer interjected, his tone businesslike. "We must investigate, since we're uncertain. Although if you were to ask me, things are fairly clear."

Lena struggled to regain her composure. "I beg your pardon," she said, wiping her eyes with the corner of an apron, "but surely you must agree that it's unusual for a husband to embark on an investigation of his wife's identity."

"Not at all," he bit out. "Given the circumstances, it is a perfectly reasonable thing to do."

Mr Mortimer cleared his throat. "Her Grace having, ah, departed from this world eight years since."

Lena tilted her head to one side, her mouth dropping open. "Departed?" When the impact of the meaning hit her, her eyes grew as round as saucers. She looked at the Duke, horrified. "I am terribly sorry. My sincerest condolences, but I did not comprehend. You mean to say your wife is dead?"

The Duke looked out of his depth. "That was our assumption until you suddenly appeared."

"Oh." Lena sobered. Then she sat up as straight as an arrow as understanding dawned. "Oh! Forgive me for being a tad slow. Do you truly believe I am your dead wife?" She pointed her finger at her stomach.

"At first it was only me, but now there are three of us who recognise you," Lady Evangeline chimed in with satisfaction. "This can no longer be a coincidence."

Lena shook her head. "You are making a mistake. I am deeply sorry about your wife, truly, but I am not her." It was a phrase she would continue to repeat the next half hour, as if she were speaking to a brick wall. The three of them continued discussing her as if she were not even in the room.

"It is entirely incomprehensible to me, but she is the spitting image of the Duchess." Mr Mortimer stated. "But this of course begs the question—if she is the Duchess, who is buried at Aldingbourne Hall?"

All eyes turned towards her. Lena squirmed uncomfortably.

"A twin separated at birth?" Aldingbourne said after a heavy silence.

Lena rolled her eyes.

"I concur with Lady Evangeline that this must be Her Grace, the Duchess of Aldingbourne, Catherine Stafford-Hill." Mr Mortimer asserted. "The hair colour. The eye colour. The complexion and the height. Everything is identical."

"Yet her character and demeanour seem different," the Duke observed.

"True," Lady Evangeline put in, "but that is the only aspect that seems different. She has the same talent at the pianoforte, if not more. Her talent has developed, and she plays quite masterfully. And there are certain gestures. Look! How she holds her head as she does now, slightly tilted."

"And she has the same birthmark on her cheek." Three pairs of eyes were fixed on her face.

"I daresay many people have birthmarks on their faces," Lena muttered, self-consciously rubbing hers.

"Yes, but not many have that heart-shaped one, right where people used to place a patch when patches were still in fashion. You used to say you were lucky to be born with it, and that you did not need patches. Don't you remember?" Lady Evangeline pressed.

Lena shook her head.

"Don't you remember anyone at all?" The lady's voice took on a pleading tone.

Mr Mortimer joined in. "Do you really not remember me, Your Grace? Or Lady Evie, or your husband, the Duke? You and Lady Evie were friends. You were married to the Duke for three years. How is it possible you don't remember any of this?"

A feeling of helplessness flickered through her. "I really don't know what to say," she whispered. "My only conclusion is that I am not this Catherine."

Even as she spoke the words, doubt beset her. What if she was, and she'd forgotten it? What proof did she have that she was not Catherine?

"We need to get to the bottom of this." The Duke leaned forwards, piercing her with his stare. "How did you come to be here? Have you been here in Vienna all along? Why don't you remember any of us? What happened in the last eight years?"

Lena opened her mouth to reply but was interrupted by a sudden bang on the door. It swung open and a boy with short, stubbly hair and spectacles stumbled into the room.

"*So ein Mist!*" he swore, followed by a string of other unsavoury swear words.

"Achilles Arenheim, have you been eavesdropping?" Lena asked sternly, her arms crossed over her chest.

"Hecki pushed me," the boy said as he straightened his glasses and looked around curiously. "We didn't mean to eavesdrop, but it's hard not to overhear certain things, and then you started laughing."

The other children filed into the room.

"We really weren't eavesdropping, Mama," Hector said earnestly as he looked curiously at the guests.

"Mama?" the Duke echoed weakly. His eyes were fixed on Hector, his face devoid of all colour.

"Good heavens," Mr Mortimer exclaimed for the second time that day.

Chapter Eight

"Better and better," Lady Evangeline breathed.

The Duke finally found his voice. "This is your... son?"

Lena placed a protective hand on the boy's shoulder. "Yes. This is Hector." She nodded at the boy with the spectacles. "Achilles. Then Theseus and Harmonia."

"The whole Greek pantheon," the Duke murmured. "And you, of course, are the beautiful Helena. How could it be otherwise?"

Lena blushed.

Turning to the boy, the Duke asked with a strained voice, "Hector, how old are you?"

Hector returned his regard with steady curiosity. "Almost eight, sir."

"Eight." The Duke closed his eyes as if in pain. "Of course you are."

"Julius," Lady Evangeline whispered, her face as pale as his. "He's your mirror image."

There was a beat of charged silence. Then pandemonium ensued. Theo, the eldest, was the most vocal. "What is this? What's happening, Mama? Who are these people?"

"What did she just say? My English isn't that good," Les complained.

"This lady says," Mona pointed at Lady Evangeline, "that Hecki looks like him." Her finger moved to the Duke.

The Duke's knees finally buckled and he collapsed into a chair. "And the other three?" he asked with difficulty. "Are they yours, too?"

"Of course," Lena replied. "They are my stepchildren, but they are like my own flesh and blood."

"Stepchildren." The Duke, an eloquent diplomat and feared opponent in the English parliament, visibly struggled to find his next words. "You have a husband?"

"Er, no. Simon Arenheim was a widower. I took on the role of the children's mother, but we were not in a relationship. To keep people from talking, Simon suggested I take on the family name."

The relief that washed over his face was unmistakable. "And how exactly did you end up in this family?" he pressed.

"Begging your pardon, sir," Theo interrupted with a scowl. "But who are you?"

Mr Mortimer introduced them.

Theo's eyes widened. "You mean he's a real English Duke?"

"Indeed, he is," Mortimer confirmed.

"*Famos*," the two boys said in unison.

Theo scratched the back of his head. "And, for some obscure reason, I seem to understand that you're saying Mama's your wife and Hecki's your son? Or is my English so bad that I completely misunderstood?"

"You understood correctly." The Duke nodded curtly.

"What makes you so certain that she is your wife?" Theo pressed.

"We were about to investigate the matter when you burst into the room," the Duke replied.

"That is correct," Mr Mortimer pushed his spectacles up his nose. "We were about to examine the evidence, such as the uncannily similar appearance, the birthmark, and the gestures that are identical to those of Her Grace, as well as the fact that there are three of us to confirm it. We were about to discuss the most puzzling discovery that Her Gr—I mean, Frau Arenheim"—he stumbled over the name—"does not seem to remember anything. Not even us."

"There is one more thing," the Duke said with a frown. "Another birthmark." He turned to Lena. "You have another birthmark, don't you?" His gaze bored into hers.

She could deny it and end it all with a simple lie. Her life would go on as it did before. She could continue living with her children as she did before, simple and carefree, contained in a bubble of happy, blissful ignorance. Not caring, not knowing about what had happened in the past. She did not need to know. She didn't *want* to know. She just wanted to live and enjoy life. Here in Vienna. With her children. Without change. Ever.

She ran her tongue over her dry bottom lip.

"Don't you?" he repeated, his voice almost gentle.

She opened her mouth to deny it.

And she knew instantly, with a miserable punch to her stomach, that she couldn't lie.

She gave an almost imperceptible nod.

Lady Evangeline squealed. The children jumped and talked at the same time.

The Duke's expression was completely indecipherable.

"Where?" Theo shouted.

The Duke raised a pale hand and silence fell immediately. "Evie, go with Cath—I mean, Frau Arenheim to another room and let her show you the birthmark. You must see it with your own eyes. Then return to tell us where it is. I will confirm or deny whether it is identical to Catherine's."

"That's a fabulous idea." Lady Evangeline grabbed Lena's hand and pulled her out of the room. "Let's go."

LENA LIFTED her dress along with her shift and showed it to Lady Evangeline. Her other birthmark was on her stomach. It was a flat, brown, perfectly round disc the same size as her navel.

She tried to downplay its significance. "Of course, people have all sorts of birthmarks on their bodies, so who's to say this is the ultimate proof that I'm the lost duchess?"

Lady Evangeline leaned over to examine it closely. "Certainly, I too have birthmarks, one on my left shoulder and one on my hip. The one on my hip has the shape of England. However, that's beside the point. The point is that Julius knows it's there." She smirked. "I dare say only the most devoted husband would remember the exact location of his wife's birthmark after eight long years. Especially—" she glanced at Lena's stomach "—when it is in a location as intimate as this."

A fiery heat rushed into Lena's cheeks. She didn't want to think about how the Duke knew the birthmark was there. She refused to think about it. Just as she'd refused to think about so many other things the past eight years...

"Do you really not remember anything at all?" Lady Evangeline's voice was pleading. "We spent much time together at Aldingbourne Hall. You were the perfect duchess. I daresay you were happily married, Julius and you. At least you seemed to be, in my eyes."

Once again, wisps of something drifted up into her consciousness. A throbbing pain shot through her head like lightning. She winced and lifted her hand to shield her eyes.

"I—I really don't know."

Lady Evangeline looked at her for a moment in silence, then sighed and nodded. "Very well. Let us return."

They returned to the parlour, where the Duke was pacing in front of the fireplace. The children watched him in silence, following his every move. Les and Hecki sat cross-legged on the floor, Theo in a chair, and Mona in the armchair. Mr Mortimer looked up in obvious relief when they entered.

The Duke stopped pacing. "You saw it?"

"Yes." Lady Evangeline nodded. "It's circular, about this big," she indicated it with her fingers, "and located—"

"Just above her navel," the Duke said in unison with her.

"Thank the heavens," Mr Mortimer breathed. He pulled out a handkerchief and dabbed at his forehead. "I thought I would not survive the suspense. It is now officially established that you are Her Grace, Catherine Stafford-Hill, the Duchess of Aldingbourne." He made a formal bow.

The Duke, pale but with a determined set of his jaw, made a movement as if to reach out to her, but withdrew and clasped his hands behind his back. He rocked on his heels; his eyes boring into hers as he gave a curt nod. "Yes." That was all he said.

"Now what?" Theo asked, looking from one to the other. "I have so many questions." He spoke for all of them.

Now what, indeed?

A sick feeling churned in her stomach as it dawned on her that there really was no point in denying it any longer. She had to face the truth. She finally had to face her past.

Hecki jumped up, looking around wildly. "What does that mean?"

All eyes were on them, on Hector. The other matter that required resolution. Lena drew Hector into her arms protectively.

"I am not certain," she whispered into his hair. She had to protect this child at all costs. Her head started to pound and she felt weary, so weary.

Mr Mortimer cleared his throat. "Regarding the child's paternity—" He interrupted himself. "Perhaps it would be more appropriate to discuss this without the children present?"

Hector pulled away from Lena and glared at him. "I'm not leaving."

"I'm staying put, too." Les crossed his arms. "Hecki is my brother and needs my support."

"Nobody's going anywhere, Mr Mortimer." Theo placed a protective arm over both Hector and Lena. "We're a family. We remain together."

"Yes." Lena nodded. "We remain together."

"I refuse to skirt around the matter." The Duke's eyes never left the boy. "Let the children stay. Although, the question must be asked. Who is this boy's father?" His voice was heavy.

His question was met with silence.

"Well?" His voice was sharp.

"Simon Arenheim was his father, of course," Lena said helplessly. Simon was there when Hector was born. Simon had helped raise him. Simon had always been there for Hector. He was his father.

Hector clenched his hands. "Simon was my papa, but he wasn't really my father. Not like he was Les's, Theo's, and Mona's father." He turned his scowl on Lena. "You always said that it didn't matter because what mattered was who raised me, and that was Papa Simon. Isn't it true?"

Yes. She'd always told him that. Hector had always accepted the explanation. He'd never questioned it.

Until now.

Hector's question hung in the air like a live grenade, filling the room with a tense, charged silence.

"Your Grace?" Mr Mortimer prodded, looking expectantly at Lena for more.

"He means you, Mama," Theo put in.

Her shoulders slumped. "The truth is..." She swallowed. "I don't know," she finally whispered. She rubbed at the throbbing in her temples.

Hector directed his next question directly at the Duke. "If Mama is your wife, are you saying that you are my father?" His voice rang clear across the room.

Lena closed her eyes, feeling as if she was trapped in a dream.

At first, the Duke did not seem to want to answer. Then finally, he said in a thick, gravelly voice, "It seems to be a distinct possibility."

Everyone began to speak at once.

"Well, there it is," Theo muttered.

"This is a grave misunderstanding," Lena repeated.

"One must examine the evidence," Mr Mortimer said weakly.

"I knew it, I knew it!" Lady Evangeline clapped her hands.

Hector had gone white as a sheet and said nothing at all.

The pounding in Lena's head had increased as if the musicians of an entire orchestra were thumping their tambourines in her head. "Silence!" she snapped.

The Forgotten Duke

To her surprise, the room fell indeed silent.

She pulled herself up, walked to the door, and opened it. "I beg your pardon, but enough is enough. This situation is upsetting the children, and I won't have it. Please leave." When it came to protecting her family, Lena had no qualms about throwing an English Duke out the door by his collar. Even if he was supposedly her forgotten husband. Even if he might be Hector's father.

"I admit that all this must be rather overwhelming for you all," Lady Evangeline chimed in apologetically. "And we haven't exactly approached the whole thing with delicate sensitivity."

"But there is so much left to discuss," Mr Mortimer protested.

"Enough." The Duke cast a searching glance at Lena. "We have indeed overtaxed you. You appear unwell and in need of rest. We will no longer impose our company on you. Let us resume the matter another day."

He picked up his hat, stick, and gloves, and as he walked past her, she smelled it again, that strangely familiar scent. What was this? It made her want to cry.

Lady Evangeline began to say something, went to the door, came back and threw her arms around Lena, and, before she could recover from the surprise, she too left along with Mr Mortimer.

Lena was left alone in the parlour with her children.

Hector's face darkened. "He's not my father," he declared and stormed out of the room.

Chapter Nine

LATER THAT NIGHT, LONG AFTER THE HOUSEHOLD had settled into silence, Theo knocked softly on the door. "Mama, it's me. Can we talk?"

Lena opened the door, her eyes tired but alert. She had just returned from Hector and Les's room. Hector had buried himself under his blanket, refusing to speak. She'd sat on his bed in silence for a while, stroking his thick, dark hair, which was so similar to the Duke's. Then she dropped a kiss on his averted head and returned to her room with a sigh.

Theo stood barefoot in the corridor; his pale face scrunched into a worried frown. A rush of affection welled up in her as she looked at the boy who had been forced to grow up so quickly, stepping into the role of head of the family. It hadn't been easy for any of them since Simon died, but it had been especially hard on Theo, who had always tried to put on a brave front.

"Come in." She drew her shawl tighter around her shoulders and stepped aside.

Theo sat on the edge of her bed, a deep furrow in his brow. "I keep thinking about what happened today."

"I know." Her voice sounded as tired as she felt. "It's the most unsettling thing."

His gaze drifted to the intricate patterns on the drawn curtains. "I was just thinking. Wondering, actually."

"What were you wondering?"

"About that time...in Scotland."

Lena's breath caught. She knew exactly what he meant. "Almost nine years ago..."

"The accident," Theo continued. "If Papa hadn't found you...if he hadn't treated you..."

"...I would have died," she finished, her voice barely audible.

"You were almost dead, Mama. You were unresponsive for weeks. Then, somehow, you woke up."

Lena gently touched his cheek. "And yours was the first face I saw." A small smile tugged at her lips. "You were such a cheeky twelve-year-old."

Theo covered her hand with his. "But you couldn't remember anything. Not your name, not where you came from. That's why Papa gave you a name: Helena. When no one came to claim you, Papa took you in. You became our mama. You returned the happiness to us that we'd lost when my mother died. We were—we still *are*—happy."

"Yes," she whispered, forcing a smile as tears welled in her eyes. "I am your mama." Her voice grew firmer. "And I wouldn't want to be anyone else."

Fear gnawed at her heart—the fear of losing everything, of her family crumbling away, of the Duke who threatened to take it all from her. Already, the foundations of her life were shaking, the walls of her sanctuary cracking.

She shivered.

Theo swallowed hard. "When you saw them today—those people who might be your old family—you didn't remember anything? Didn't you feel anything? Nothing at all?"

Lena hesitated, then shook her head. "No. I have no memories of being a duchess. He could have been a shoemaker claiming me as his wife, and it would have meant the same to me."

"But the birthmark...not only one, but two of them, and there were three people who recognized you, who claimed you. And Hecki...Mama, you can't just ignore all that."

A dull ache began to throb in her temples.

"I want to ignore it," she whispered.

"They were your family first," he pressed on. "They lost you. All those years, they thought you were dead."

The silence between them grew heavy, like a weight neither could lift.

Then he spoke again, mercilessly. "They loved you too, Mama. Maybe as much as we love you now. Maybe even more."

Her hand trembled as she raised it, as if to ward off his words which were a dagger to her heart.

"What will you do now?" Theo's question hung in the air.

She looked at him, her eyes filled with helplessness. "I don't know." Her voice broke. "I simply don't know."

The best thing, Lena decided the next morning, was to keep it a secret. If she could just ignore it, perhaps it would fade away, lost in the routine of daily life. The faster she forgot all about this and moved on with her life, the better. The Duke would disappear, together with his claim on her and Hector, and she could live happily ever after with her family. She vowed that nothing—no one—would take her away from her children. Theo's words lingered at the edge of her mind, but she pushed them aside with determined resolve. She simply refused to think about it. That was the plan.

But this was Vienna—Metternich's Vienna, to be precise—and it was permeated by a spy-network so dense that not a fly could pass through without being caught in its web. "One cannot sneeze without Prince Metternich hearing about it," one visitor was said to have lamented. Thus it was highly unlikely that the Duke of Aldingbourne's personal visit to a most unfashionable suburb of Vienna, namely that of the General Hospital—complete with a morgue and a lunatic asylum—would go unnoticed.

"So he finally found his way there," Baron von Hager, head of the secret police, commented, as he read the dépêche through his monocle. "Took a while longer than I thought it would. What did they discuss?"

Agent August had to confess that he did not know.

Hager threw down the missive impatiently. "More intelligence, Agent August. More intelligence! What are we paying you for?"

Agent August raced back to the Arenheim home, heels clicking against the cobblestones. He was now sitting at the kitchen table, to which he had invited himself. He had knocked at the kitchen door and found Frau Arenheim furiously making plum dumplings.

"Well?" he asked.

Lena held a plate with dumplings under his nose. "Here, have some. They really are quite good."

August pushed the plate aside. "You have to tell us what he was doing here for an entire two hours and fifteen minutes. What did he say, wear, do, and eat?"

"Who?" Lena's eyes widened in mock ignorance.

"The Emperor of China," August growled.

"I haven't seen an emperor here." Lena pierced a fork into a dumpling and bit into it. "It's really good. Are you certain you don't want any?"

"If you're trying to butter me up by feeding me, it won't work," he said as his stomach growled. "Here are the facts: the Duke of Aldingbourne, his sister Lady Evangeline and his secretary Mr Emil Mortimer visited your home yesterday at one in the afternoon and left at three fifteen. What do you have to say about this?"

She pondered on the matter as she licked the sugar from her fingers.

"You know," August said with a sigh. "You can prevaricate and evade as much as you like, but sooner or later we will find out the answer. If Hager discovers you're not cooperating, everything will be null and void, and you'll be of no use to us." He leaned forwards. "No more musical opportunities. No more easy money. With that in mind, don't you think it would be better if you just told me directly? 'Twould save us all some trouble."

LENA LOOKED at the man sitting at her kitchen table with a steep frown on her face. Strands of greasy black hair hung into his forehead, and he looked younger than she initially thought he was. Possibly around her own age. She thought about what he'd said.

August was right; sooner or later the truth would come out anyway. Better they heard it directly from her. Secondly, if they indeed knew everything about everyone, couldn't that be of use to her? The secret police had all the information at their fingertips.

Lena pursed her lips. "You may have a point. Very well. I will tell you what happened." She pointed the fork at him. "But in turn, you will help me to uncover the truth of the matter."

"Uncovering the truth is what we specialise in," August said, crossing his arms, then he listened in silence. He was so absorbed in her story that he'd involuntarily picked up a fork and ate not one, but two plum dumplings.

"What do you think? A mad sort of tale it is, is it not?" Lena said as she finished.

He rocked his head back and forth. "I'd have to check my sources. What I know about the Duke of Aldingbourne is as follows." He ticked them off with his fingers.

"It is true that he is a widower. There were no offspring, at least not that we know of. He has never remarried and with the exception of you, shows no interest in women or chasing lightskirts. In this he differs greatly from the other visitors to the Congress." August curled his lips in disgust. "You wouldn't believe the bed-hopping that's going on, especially between the Princess Bagration, the Duchess of Sagan, Metternich, and the Tsar. Metternich enters the palais, visits the Duchess on the right, then leaves her apartment a few hours later to go to the door on the left where the Princess lives."

Lena's mouth fell open. "Really? Tell me more."

"For example..." He lifted his fork, ready to spill more gossip. Then he frowned and stopped, shaking his head. "What am I doing? I digress. This is not a gossip session over a cup of coffee. Read the papers tomorrow, it will all be in there. Back to the topic at hand. You said the Duke was your husband."

Lena wrung her hands. "That's what he claims."

"Hm. He recognised not one, but two birthmarks, you say. His secretary and sister identified you as well. That seems to me sufficient evidence that you are his wife." He tilted his head to one side and narrowed his eyes. "Do you really not remember him?"

Lena crossed her arms tightly. "No, I don't. What if it's all a coincidence?"

"A coincidence, really?" He leaned forwards, his eyes gleaming. "Do you know how his wife died?"

She shook her head. She had thrown them out before the Duke had had a chance to tell his story.

"The Duchess of Aldingbourne died in a carriage

accident in Scotland. Somewhere near the border. Wasn't that where you, too, had your accident?"

A chill ran through her. She shivered as her breath caught in her throat.

"In Scotland," she whispered. "A carriage accident."

"Yes. A massive coincidence, isn't it?" Satisfied, he leaned back and helped himself to a final dumpling. "None of what you told me is news to me."

She sat up straight. "What do you mean?"

"I mean to say that we already knew about all this," he said with a full mouth, waving his fork around.

Lena fell back into her chair. "Are you saying you knew about me possibly being the Duchess before you even approached me, asking me to spy for you?"

August grinned. "Naturally, Your Grace. The order came from the very top."

"The very top? You mean—" Lena took a sharp intake of breath. "Metternich." The man played with them like pieces in a chess game.

Her hand shook when she rubbed her forehead. "How on earth did Metternich know…"

"We know everything." August wiped his fingers on the tablecloth. "Whether you think you are the Duchess or not, whether you remember the man, or not, do one thing for us, please."

"And what would that be?" she asked warily.

"Play along."

She pressed her lips together. Then, after a brief pause, she said, "Why should I do that? What would I gain?"

"You might gain more than you think. A rich husband

for one, a noble one with a title." He laughed darkly. "You won't ever have to lift a finger to work again. You can drape yourself with diamonds, bathe in milk and honey, and eat caviar all day."

"I don't care for that," Lena replied stiffly. "That kind of life would be a lie if I don't remember him as my husband."

"A lie for Kaiser and fatherland. As his wife, you'd have direct access to a most influential Congress member at all hours of the day." He paused to reflect. "And at night, too, of course. It would be handsomely rewarded."

"It is unethical."

"Yes." He drummed his fingers on the tabletop. "But you'd do it for the children. Have you forgotten the poorhouse?"

Lena sat perfectly still.

"And lastly. There is something you have not considered. Wives are replaceable. They are easily set aside, particularly by men in that class. Why, then, should it matter whether you really are truly the Duchess? This isn't about you at all."

A heavy weariness seeped into her bones. "Then pray tell me who it is about if not me."

"You can protest all you want that you are not his wife, but if the Duke acknowledges Hector as his son, he'll whisk him away to England—with or without you. As his heir, Hector will be more valuable to him than all the diamonds in the world, and the law will be on the Duke's side. He won't need you at all, especially if you prove to be troublesome. Wives are—as we have already established—replaceable."

An icy dart of terror pierced Lena.

"But never fear," August continued with a cold smile. "We'll protect you no matter what happens, whether you truly remember him or not, whether you are the Duchess or not. It is very much in your interest to play along and be the Duke's good little wife, if only to be able to stay with your son."

He leaned forwards, his words heavy with warning.

All the blood had drained from her face, for he had just expressed her deepest fear.

Chapter Ten

Julius dropped into his armchair, feeling as if a regiment of Napoleon's army had blasted an entire battery of howitzers into him. The air was knocked out of him, his ears were ringing, and his head was light. For the first time, he understood how ladies felt just before they swooned. At that moment, there was nothing in the entire world he wanted more than to fall on the floor in a dead faint. It would certainly alarm his butler and the maid if they found him in that state. He was the Duke of Aldingbourne, after all. Cold and arrogant and unfeeling. Nothing and no one could disturb his composure. Dukes did not faint. What would the world come to if they did?

He poured himself a glass of brandy with a trembling hand, spilled half of it on the fine walnut table, downed it in one gulp, and poured himself another. The heat of the liquor burned through his veins, but it did not calm him in the least. It only dulled his senses and in the morning he would have a headache to boot. Cursing, he lifted the glass to smash it into the fireplace, hoping for some relief, but that would only wake his valet. He carefully placed it back on the table and rested his head in his hands.

She hadn't recognised him.
She hadn't recognised him.
She hadn't recognised him.

The thought bothered and nagged at him like rats gnawing at the wooden beams of a house, relentless and pervasive. Why did the thought that she didn't remember him shock him more than the discovery that his dead wife was alive?

There hadn't been a trace of recognition in her eyes. Neither now, nor at Metternich's soirée when he first saw her. He was a complete stranger to her. It was as if their three years of marriage had never happened. His identity as her husband was erased forever.

After the initial shock, he'd grappled with the acute sense of disbelief at what his eyes were seeing. Confusion and doubt had followed.

Now anger blazed through him, at her, at him, at God and the entire universe, and he feared he'd punch a hole in the satin-covered walls if he didn't find some sort of outlet. How could she have forgotten him so completely?

What the deuce was wrong with him?

By all the saints, it was a miracle! He should rejoice, for when had it ever happened outside of the realm of religion that the dead were resurrected?

He'd at first feared she was an impostor. Still, the woman had appeared sincere.

She had not sought him out to claim she was his lost wife. He had sought *her* out. She'd appeared shocked and, towards the end, terrified. Then she'd decided to throw him out of her house as if he were not a Duke, but a dirty peddler trying to foist faulty goods on a hapless housekeeper.

And the boy? What about him?

It seemed that not only had he found his wife, but he also had a son.

An heir to the Dukedom.

Everything inside him softened.

Hector. The boy—dark haired with light grey eyes—had a narrow face, a proud forehead, and a fine aquiline nose—features that were all too familiar to him.

The child was the living, walking image of a portrait of himself that was hanging in Aldingbourne Hall. Both Mortimer and Evie had reacted with the same recognition.

There was no doubt about it: the boy was legitimately his.

It was strange how certain he was about Hector. In the past, it had happened more than once that a Covent Garden doxy had approached him and claimed that her by-blow was his child, and he'd always denied it, firmly, arrogantly.

And now he'd claim the child as his own without a second thought, and it was strange. He knew, deep in his bones, that it was true.

There was no logical explanation for it.

It was the same kind of odd certainty he knew that this woman was Catherine.

Eight years had passed and she had hardly changed. She'd felt the same in his arms—soft, delicate, dainty. Her oval face, the gentle brows, the soft expression in her brown eyes were all as he remembered them. If there was a difference from the Catherine he knew, it was in her attire and hairstyle. The Catherine he remembered had worn only the most fashionable clothes and kept every strand of her hair immaculately in place.

This new Catherine seemed more dishevelled. Soft wisps of blonde hair escaped from her bun, and her dress was simple, slightly worn and stained.

All those familiar gestures and mannerisms—the way she raised her hand, the way she patted her skirt, the way her mouth quirked upwards to reveal a dimple on her left cheek, the mole on the right.

It was undeniably Catherine.

Yet she continued to deny it, and there was no glimmer of recognition in her eyes at all.

She did not remember him.

It was most disconcerting.

He had been astonished by how fluently she spoke German. Catherine was known to speak the language—her grandmother was Austrian, and she had studied it for years—but her pronunciation was almost native. Her English, on the other hand, had been slightly stilted as if she hadn't spoken it for years.

A sliver of doubt crossed his mind.

Her personality also appeared to have changed.

Catherine had been a quiet, reserved person. Almost timid, especially in his company. He'd forgotten how her nervousness used to irritate him, a constant caution lurking in the back of her eyes...as if she were afraid of him.

It had always made him feel like he was some sort of

monster, though he could never quite put his finger on why.

He frowned.

This Viennese Catherine, however, was an exuberant sort of creature who showed her emotions all too openly. She laughed with an abandon that was almost enviable. When she was sad, her brown eyes filled with tears, enormous and luminous, making him want to gather her in his arms and, and…

He shook his head.

And there had been anger. Her eyes had sparkled, and her cheeks had flushed. How she'd lashed out at him at the end, when she'd presumed her son in danger.

His hand shook as he drew it again and again through his thick hair.

She saw him as a threat. That much was clear.

And here was the biggest difference between the Catherine he had known and this new Catherine: she was a mother. Fierce and loyal and protective as only a mother could be.

He'd never seen Catherine like that. It suited her.

Suddenly, his head ached and he leaned back in his chair and closed his eyes.

He had to regain some sense of rationality in this matter.

One thing at a time.

He decided to send another missive to Aldingbourne Hall, asking to send them the identical miniature that had been made from the larger portrait that hung in the gallery, as well as another trinket that might be even more important.

Having made up his mind about the next course of action, Julius resolutely penned the letter.

"You have a visitor, Your Grace." Julius hadn't heard his butler enter the room and jumped at the sound of his voice at his side.

He looked up wearily. "Who is it?"

"Prince Metternich. Shall I tell him you are not at home?"

Metternich. Blast the man. The last thing he wanted to do now was to have another diplomatic debate.

"Show him in."

He ran his hand through his hair, once, twice, struggling to regain his usual aloof composure. It would not do to show the man anything other than that.

"*Mon cher ami*," the Prince said, strolling into the room as if it were his own drawing room. "You appear to be out of sorts."

Julius grimaced.

The Prince himself looked as if he had just returned from a ball: suave, charming, forever the statesman. Not a single hair was out of place. He smiled as he took in the brandy glass and decanter on the table. He pinched his nose with long, white fingers.

Try as he might, Julius could not like him. The man was handsome and perpetually smiling, but also cunning, manipulative and not to be trusted.

"A drink?" Julius waved a hand at the empty brandy bottle.

"I decline. I've had my fill for the night. If I am to

keep a clear head for the upcoming discussions tomorrow, I had better not consume any more alcohol." He paused. "With our Russian friend."

"Ah." Julius indicated a chair, and the Prince sat down, crossing his legs with an elegant movement. "I take it Alexander is being difficult?"

Metternich grimaced. "Exorbitantly so. This remains between us, but if you ask me, the man is unhinged. His character is completely unstable. Have you ever seen him throw a tantrum when he doesn't get what he wants?" He shook his head. "Worse than a toddler. The language he uses! I fail to understand why the public worship him so. As if he were some kind of god."

Clearly, Metternich was jealous.

It was no secret that Tsar Alexander was the darling of the masses, and he enjoyed every moment of it, too. No doubt it piqued Metternich's ego to see the ladies in the streets swoon whenever the Tsar made an appearance. Matters had not improved when Metternich's mistress, that Sagan woman, inexplicably began to flirt with the Tsar. The two were bitter rivals not only in politics, but also in the bedroom.

"My understanding is that you called this Congress to promote peace in Europe, not to turn this into a popularity contest," Julius commented. His rule was to stay out of the bedroom and stick to politics.

Metternich picked at an invisible speck on his sleeve. "Yes, that was the intention. Yet not everyone is as pragmatic as you." He looked at him thoughtfully. "Or is it indifference? A certain coldness that is not unbecoming can certainly be useful in certain situations."

A corner of Julius's mouth twisted into a self-deprecating smile. If he only he knew of the emotions that simmered beneath his surface. Right now, he felt like a dormant volcano, ready to explode at any moment.

"Get to the point, Metternich."

"The point, Your Grace, is that I need your help with the Russians. I can't get through to Alexander. He is worse than a child. He insists on Polish autonomy under Russian control, which is entirely unacceptable. It is clear that his main intention is brute territorial expansion, and he won't settle for anything less. A Polish state under Russian control will disrupt the balance of power we aim for. Already we have a stalemate, and the Congress has not yet officially begun."

Julius did not disagree, for this was also the British position. "I understand that Castlereagh had a meeting with the Tsar today."

"Yes. Castlereagh is too—what is the word I'm looking for? Stoic? Dry? He gives the impression of being perpetually bored. He comes across as utterly unsympathetic, and it infuriated the Tsar even more. What is it with you English and your penchant for understatement and aloof pragmatism?" The Prince got to his feet and paced, clearly frustrated.

"Why do you expect me to achieve what Castlereagh hasn't? Because I, too, have a penchant for, as you say, 'aloof pragmatism'."

"Yes, yes. But Castlereagh is a stubborn, ungracious fortress. He surrounds himself with an impenetrable stoniness that comes across as a lack of empathy. Whereas you, with your cold arrogance, have more style. You will provide a cool dose of realism that may not be unwelcome. Being Russian, he may find your Siberian coldness more palatable. It could be akin to a splash of cold water over the overheated, passionate head of the Tsar. A breath of cool winter air." He raised a finger as he waxed poetic. "The glacial iciness of—"

"I understand the gist of the matter, Your Highness," Julius interrupted. "You want me to speak to Alexander."

Metternich gave him a bright smile. "That would be the general idea, yes."

Julius drummed his fingers on the table.

Metternich sat back with his fingers crossed, watching him closely. "I would, of course, be more than generous to reciprocate by helping you with other, shall we say, more personal matters."

"Personal matters?" Julius echoed. "How so?"

Metternich merely smiled, and Julius thought he looked devious.

"There is very little that escapes my attention," he said, holding Julius' gaze. "I have a very extensive network of trusted agents. The amount of intelligence we gather is unsurpassed. It is detailed and usually very reliable."

"I am surprised you're so open about it."

Metternich waved a white hand. "It's no secret. Everyone knows about it."

"Yes, it is quite an extensive machinery of espionage you have set up for yourself there. Very much like a toy, yes? No doubt it must be of some use, if only to fill your spare time, to play with when you are bored." He shook his head. "I fail to understand where you even find the time to read all that intelligence, as you call it."

Metternich ignored the sarcasm. "Oh, you'd be surprised. It is quite fascinating, you know, of the things one learns about people. Besides, you will find that I am not at all reluctant to share...my toys."

A charged pause settled over the room as the two men held each other's gaze.

"I never mix the personal with politics," Julius said slowly. "It is a firm rule of mine and it has served me well."

"How very English of you, I am sure," Metternich replied with a yawn. "So very pragmatic. Yet you would be surprised at how useful it can be to bend those rules once in a while."

Julius leaned forwards, his eyes never leaving Metternich's.

The clock on the mantelpiece ticked.

"Helena Arenheim," Julius bit out at last. "What do you know of her?"

Metternich's mouth curved into a slow smile.

Chapter Eleven

It didn't help that they had to perform again that evening, this time in the Palais Auersperg. Lena noted with considerable relief that the British delegation was absent. This time, they left the two younger boys at home. The others received strict instructions to stay away from any brandied cherries, in fact to not even get in the vicinity of the buffet.

"The growling of my poor, starving stomach will drown out the music," Theo said, and Mona agreed.

They came, they performed, they received a round of applause, and that was that.

The days were also smoother. Agent August no longer hovered in the dark corners of the street, and now that they had some income, Lena was able to hire a laundry maid. That took a considerable burden off her shoulders.

Their neighbour, Emma, helped whenever she could, and Karl came every other day with a box of leftover fruit and vegetables that he could not sell at the market. That morning, he'd dropped off a box of apples, so Lena was busy all day making apple strudel, baked apples, apple cake, apple compote, and, because there was so much left over, she sliced them thinly and left them to dry on a newspaper spread over the ceramic oven.

All the baking and cooking helped her clear her mind.

It troubled her, everything that had happened with the Duke. She was worried about Hector, who'd withdrawn and not been up to his usual pranks.

Yet, they lived their life in their usual routine, as if nothing special had happened.

THE CHILDREN HAD BEEN PLAYING a boisterous game of musical chairs in the warm parlour, with the addition that whoever lost had to pay forfeits by coming up with a short impromptu performance. These moments, when she felt the support and love of her family, where she knew that she would protect them at all costs were the ones Lena enjoyed the most.

Theo jumped on the table and performed the *Schuhplattler*, a shoe slapping dance, banging his head against the ceiling as he did so, leaving everyone howling with laughter. Mona performed a pantomime from a Greek tragedy, turning it into a comedy, and Lena acted out a scene from her favourite poem, Goethe's 'The Erl-King', by attempting to be the elf king, the horse, and the child all at once. Hector, who had been in a terrible mood all day, picked a fight with Les because both insisted on choosing the same fable by Aesop. They ended up rolling around on the floor, wrestling with each other.

"Children, children." Lena sighed.

Theo intervened and separated the two by grabbing them by the collar and sending them straight to bed.

Lena stepped out into the front garden, fanning herself with her hands. Though it was late September, the month had been unusually warm. She inhaled the fresh evening air, leaning against the doorframe as she sought a moment of solitude. The quiet was a welcome reprieve, offering a chance to sift through the whirlwind of thoughts and emotions that had consumed her in recent days. She had tried to push them aside, but the image of the Duke kept resurfacing. It was impossible to ignore.

She wondered if he was attending the *Hofball* tonight at the Imperial Palace, a grand affair of glitter and glamour. The papers were full of detailed descriptions about who might and who might not be there. Thousands of people were expected to attend. They said it was fashionable not to dance, even though it was a ball. She felt sorry for the poor musicians who'd have to entertain a crowd of people who did not appreciate the music.

A tall shadow separated from the chestnut tree and Lena froze. Was the agent waiting for her again?

"August?" She squinted into the darkness. The light from the nearest lamp post was faint and distant.

"Who is August?" a deep voice asked.

Lena gasped.

The Duke stood before her, even taller than she remembered.

"Why are you here? Shouldn't you be at a ball or a soiree or some other event?" she babbled. She pressed her hand to her violently beating heart.

"Some other event?" he repeated.

"I mean, some important business concerning the Congress."

"This is important business."

She craned her neck to look up at him, but she couldn't see his face in the darkness.

She took a step back and bumped into the tree. "Look, sir. Your Grace. I believe it is in the best interests of everyone if we agreed to ignore this." Lena spoke quickly and quietly. "I believe it would be better for you and me, and certainly for the children." She knew her words were folly, but fear drove sharp spikes into her heart and forced her to voice these words.

"Impossible. I can't just ignore the truth."

She moistened her lips. "What if the truth is better left hidden?" She said it so quietly that it was barely audible.

With one hand, he tipped her chin up as he had done the other day. His thumb gently stroked the edge of her jaw and she shivered.

"Catherine was my wife," he said in a calm, measured tone. "We were married for three years before she met an untimely death."

A tremble went through her body.

He dropped his hands but continued talking. "For eight long years I considered myself to be a widower." His voice became hard. "Until I came to Vienna and saw the spitting image of Catherine, performing in

Metternich's salon. And you are asking me to just ignore it?"

He grabbed her by the arm again. "The same hair, the same figure, the same birthmarks. The same musical talent. Yet not a speck of memory of me or my sister. How can this be? Tell me. Unless Catherine had a twin, and nobody, including her mother, knew about it? How likely is that scenario?" His voice grew increasingly frustrated.

Lena averted her eyes and nervously picked at the skin of her bottom lip. The war raging within herself was terrible. She knew it was best to deny it all. To shrug her shoulders, to walk away, to tell him it was a mistake. Yet there was something about him that drew her to him, that kept her from fleeing.

"What was she like?" she heard herself asking. "Catherine."

"Catherine." His stare pierced her soul. At first she thought he would not reply, then he spoke. "She was beautiful and very young…and very shy. She had a quiet, reserved personality; she didn't talk much. She preferred the country to the city and enjoyed walks on our country estate more than attending balls during the London Season. She had a strong sense of duty and was always immersed in some charity work or other." He paused, staring into the distance. "Whether it was a soup kitchen, or a school, a hospital or an orphanage, Catherine would be involved. She knew the names of all of our tenants, including their children, more so than I did. She was afraid of horses, but loved walking, reading, and gardening. She had a wonderful voice and sang like a nightingale. She was also a virtuoso pianist." His gaze returned to her. "I sometimes thought that if she had not married me and become a duchess, and if her status and society had allowed her, she would have liked to become a professional musician." He paused before continuing. "She would have been very successful." He paused again. "As you are now."

Lena breathed heavily.

"She was much beloved as a duchess, and"—he swallowed—"as a wife."

"You make her sound like she was perfect."

"In many ways she was."

Catherine sounded as if she'd been a very different person from her. She could not identify with the image he had portrayed.

"What exactly happened?" Lena asked. She already knew, for August had told her, and a leaden feeling of dread sank into the pit of her stomach.

"News reached us of a terrible accident in Scotland involving several carriages. To this day, no one knows exactly what happened. Was it the bad weather and poor visibility? Or maybe it was the poorly maintained bridge? We will never know. What was assumed was that one vehicle crashed into another, causing such an impact that it overturned and careened off the bridge and into the river." He stared blindly into the distance. "We hoped and prayed that Catherine hadn't been in any of the carriages because her body wasn't found at first."

Lena went pale.

"Of the eighteen passengers involved, three died, and eight were badly injured." He drew in a shaking breath. "We found Catherine's body washed onto the shore several days later," he said with difficulty. "Identified only by the clothes she was wearing."

Lena pressed both hands against her mouth, not uttering a sound.

"We buried her in our family chapel."

"I am so sorry," she whispered in a thick voice. It was as if they were not talking about her, but someone else.

That scent emanated from him again.

Cedarwood and musk.

She knew it meant something. She could not deny it. Her breath caught and her eyes filled with hot tears. It shook her deeply, made her heart throb with a yearning she didn't understand.

She would have to tell him. It wasn't right not to. Her fingers trembled as she clasped them together, trying to steady herself. She opened her mouth to speak but faltered, the words refusing to come out. When she finally found her voice, it was barely more than a whisper. "I…I was there," she said, her eyes wide with fear as she forced herself to continue. "I was involved in the accident near Abbotsville."

His dark eyes burned into hers. "Yes," he breathed. "I know. Metternich told me."

"That man—!" she began angrily. "He is meddling where he has no business."

"In this case I am thankful for his meddling. He was doing me a favour. Go on. Tell me about the accident."

"The truth is, I do not recall any of the events. I do not know the woman you found who was wearing my clothes. Why would she do so? I do not know. I was found by the side of the riverbank with a severe head injury, considered dead, and placed in the side room of an inn where Simon was staying. He found me there and discovered I was not dead, but unconscious. I was merely wearing a simple shift."

He rubbed his forehead. "Was it the abigail we found and mistook for you? Did you change clothes with her, maybe?" She could hear the frown in his voice.

She shrugged helplessly. "Possibly. I do not know. What an odd thing to do, if that was the case. Simon thought that the bodies were stripped of their belongings by thieves. He thought that was what must have happened to me, too."

"And then, after they found you?"

"Realising I was not dead, Simon had me transferred to the house where he and his family were staying. He was convinced I must have been involved in the accident on the bridge. All I know is that through some miracle, I awoke in that house under his care, several weeks later." Her voice grew hoarse. "I have no recollection of what happened. I don't know why I was in that carriage and where I was travelling to. I do not recall my past, my name, my identity, nothing at all. It's all gone."

"I was with child," she continued. "It was nothing short of a miracle that I didn't lose the baby in the accident. Simon believed that I must have plunged directly into the water, instinctively tried to swim, but then struck my head against a rock. A fisherman saw it happen and pulled me out before I could drown. They called it a miracle when I woke up again."

"It's almost impossible to believe. Truly, it was a

miracle that you survived and that the child was not harmed."

"I owe my survival to God's grace and Simon's exceptional care. He was a highly skilled surgeon, deeply respected in his field. Not only did he nurse me back to health, but he also took me into his family. I became a mother to his children after the tragic loss of his wife two years earlier, leaving little Achilles in desperate need of care." A shadow of sadness fell over her face as she remembered Simon and how deeply he had loved his English wife. Simon had needed Lena just as much as she had needed him—and his whole family.

"Not long after, he received an invitation from his mentor to join a prestigious medical institution in Norway. We departed from Aberdeen for Bergen and Hector was born there."

"The trip would have been perilous," the Duke said with a frown. "When was it?"

"In early 1807."

"Just before the British-Danish conflict, then," he said.

"Yes. Had we waited longer, such a trip would have been impossible. Then, two years later, we travelled to Austria."

The Duke shook his head. "Madness. He carted an entire family with little children through the war-torn continent?"

"Simon utilised his diplomatic connections to secure safe passage to Vienna by joining an official delegation. He was the personal physician of the Duke of Würtemberg. It was a long and difficult trip, but we were quite safe."

The Duke nodded. "In late 1809, following Austria's defeat and the subsequent Treaty of Schönbrunn, there was indeed a brief period of reduced conflict that would have allowed such a journey."

"We travelled under the protection of this delegation, which provided us with the necessary diplomatic immunity and ensured our safety. Despite the occupations and the war, he was so happy to be back in Vienna. We built our home here. We were happy here. Then, nearly a year ago, Simon suddenly dropped dead at the hospital." Her voice shook. "A heart attack."

"My condolences. I wish I could have met him. He must have been an extraordinary man."

"He was," she replied softly. "An exemplary doctor and a deeply loved father. The children miss him terribly." She hesitated before adding, "Especially Hector. He thinks of him as his father, you know."

"I know," the Duke said, his voice heavy with emotion.

Just then, the front door creaked open. "Mama?"

It was Mona, peering into the darkness.

"Go," the Duke murmured. "We'll continue this conversation in the morning."

"Is that you, Mama?" Mona called again.

"Yes, I'm here," she answered, turning towards him. "I was just getting some fresh air."

"We want to play a round of cards, Theo and I. Do you want to join us?"

"In a minute, love." She turned back to say goodnight

to the Duke. He was already gone, leaving only shadows and the soft rustling of the tree where he had stood.

THE FOLLOWING MORNING, Lena gathered everyone around the kitchen table. They always held meetings like this during emergencies or when disaster struck. The last time they'd assembled like this was when their father, Simon, had died.

"We need to discuss this matter because it won't simply go away," Lena forced herself to speak calmly. "I also believe we should address everything openly. No secrets in this family, understood?"

Everyone nodded.

She took a deep breath. "Very well then, let's go over what's happened in the past few days. Theo, you're usually good at this. Please, go ahead."

Theo cleared his throat. "A few days ago, the Duke of Aldingbourne, his sister, and his secretary came to visit. They all claim that you are his wife, the duchess who supposedly died nine years ago, and that Hector is his son."

"I'm not," Hector muttered darkly.

"You naturally denied it. Here's the issue. First, you both bear a striking resemblance to the Duchess. Second, it's not just one person, but three, who see this similarity in both of you. Third, you have the same birthmarks."

"And there's the fact that we were both involved in the same accident in Scotland," Lena added quietly.

"I remember it well, since I was there," Theo continued. "Not at the bridge, but at the inn when they brought in the bodies. Father was busy tending to them."

"I remember it too," Mona said. "I was only nine, so the details are fuzzy. I do recall you lying in bed for the longest time, unconscious."

"Yes. When she finally woke up, she didn't remember who she was." Theo took a deep breath. "Logically speaking, one could argue that you could be the Duchess who lost her memory due to damage to the sensorium commune—the centre responsible for recollection."

Lena's voice trembled as she finally said what they had all been dreading. "It seems rather likely that I really am the Duchess."

The room fell silent.

"You may be his duchess, but he'll never be my father," Hector declared, crossing his arms.

"Hector," Lena said helplessly, "if he acknowledges you as his son, you're his heir. It's true that Papa Simon raised you. He'll always be your father in your heart, even if not by blood."

Hector scowled.

"What happens now?" Mona asked, voicing the question on everyone's mind.

"That's what we need to decide." Lena looked at each of them in turn.

"I say we ignore him and carry on with our lives. We don't need a duke," Hector suggested predictably.

"Having a duke in the family might not be so bad," Les chimed in. "Is he wealthy?"

"I don't know," Lena admitted.

"If he is rich, we wouldn't need to perform any more,"

Mona said slowly. "I'm not sure how I feel about that, though—I love performing. I sure wouldn't mind living in a grand mansion."

"What do you think, Theo?" Lena turned to him.

Theo stroked his chin. "I say...we test him."

"Test him?" Lena raised an eyebrow.

"Yes." Theo nodded. "Why are we acting as if being a duke makes him the centre of the universe? He should be the one proving himself worthy of us."

The others nodded in agreement.

"So, what do you suggest?" Lena asked.

A mischievous smile spread across Theo's face. "He should live with us—just like a regular person. No dukely privileges. Let's see how he handles that."

"You mean, he should live as one of us? A commoner?" Mona asked.

"Exactly. It's the only way to see if we're compatible."

"*Famos,*" Les said.

"I'm not sure he'll agree to that," Lena said slowly. "He's a busy man. He might not be able to do it."

"That's our condition," Theo insisted.

Hector folded his arms, mirroring Theo. "Yes, it's our condition."

Chapter Twelve

It wasn't often that Julius, Duke of Aldingbourne, received a curtly written summons to appear before people of lesser status than himself. One did not summon the Duke of Aldingbourne. It simply was not done.

Which was why he stared at the missive his butler had just delivered with a haughtily raised eyebrow and a steep frown on his forehead. To his servants and those who knew him, this was a well-known sign that the Duke was irritated and that it was better to slink away quietly and without comment. However, Herz, his butler, was Viennese. He hadn't been in the service long and lacked the quick wit to disappear when he should, and instead remained hovering over the Duke in a most irritating manner.

"Who delivered this?" Julius asked as he stared at the illegible signature at the bottom of the letter. It looked like the scratch of a crow's claw.

"A messenger boy, it seems, Your Grace," Herz replied.

"Was he dark-haired with a cheeky disposition, about eight years of age?"

"No sir. He was tall, thin, red hair sticking out like a crow's nest, about twenty-one. Cheeky disposition," Herz added as an afterthought.

Theseus Arenheim.

The boy needed lessons in penmanship.

And etiquette.

It was not yet ten in the morning, and the missive summoned him to an immediate morning call. The writer of the missive was obviously unaware that morning calls were traditionally held in the afternoon.

The Duke had a routine: rising at dawn, sitting down at his desk in his morning gown to answer letters and attend to the most urgent tasks, then dressing, having a quick nuncheon at noon, followed by morning calls. Lately, these calls had been long meetings with Castlereagh taking up the entire afternoon. The evenings were filled with tedious soirees and other entertainments whose primary purpose was not entertainment, but diplomacy.

Yet, here was a summons demanding his immediate presence at a house in the Spitalgasse, threatening to disrupt his entire day's schedule.

Normally he would have ignored such an impertinent summons, but for the woman who lived there, a woman he was certain was his wife. It was interesting, he thought, how his entire body tensed and his heartbeat quickened at the mere thought of her.

"Fetch Mortimer," he said to the butler.

His secretary appeared promptly.

"What is on the agenda today?" the Duke inquired as his valet helped him into his waistcoat.

"It will be a busy day, Your Grace." Mortimer opened a leather portfolio and read the agenda. "Breakfast with Castlereagh at eleven, lunch with Humboldt at one, and a meeting with Nesselrode at two. Then there is Metternich, who has called a meeting in the afternoon prior to a soiree in the evening. Lastly, Talleyrand has also requested a private meeting." He tilted his head sideways with a frown. "I am not certain how we are to fit that into today's schedule."

"Reschedule the first three meetings. Send a note to Talleyrand to arrange a meeting tonight before the Metternich soiree. Extend my sincere apologies to Lady Castlereagh for the last-minute cancellation, but an urgent private matter has arisen."

Mortimer gave him a quick, curious look. "Yes, Your Grace."

"I shall not be available until the evening. Take care of all business until then."

"Yes, Your Grace. May I enquire where you are to be found in case an urgent matter arises?"

"Nothing is as urgent as the matter I must attend to immediately."

"I understand. You are to be found at the Arenheim home, then. May I ask what you have decided in this matter?"

With an impatient movement, the Duke tied his neckcloth slightly less perfectly than usual—a sacrilege, but it couldn't be helped. He waved the valet away when he began to protest.

"I am ninety percent certain we are dealing with the Duchess. To alleviate the doubt of the remaining ten percent, we shall have to await the special courier from England."

Mortimer nodded. "I understand, Your Grace. Godspeed, Your Grace."

"And Mortimer—" The Duke turned before leaving the room. "See that I am not being followed."

The Arenheim home in the Spitalgasse was situated on the outskirts of Vienna, outside of the city walls, just behind the General Hospital. In the distance a massive, round tower rose into the sky: the Narrenturm—the tower of the lunatics. Right next to it was the morgue. It was the third time that Julius had visited the Arenheims, and it was only now that he took in the landscape beyond the house. Looking in the opposite direction from the hospital, a lovely landscape opened up in front, for the house stood on a hill that led down to a small river—the Alserbach—which meandered through the fields and vineyards beyond. The house was made of simple stone with ivy climbing up its walls, an arched wooden door, and small windows. Colourful flowerpots adorned the windows and the front porch, adding charming dots of purple and orange.

Julius rapped on the door.

The girl named Harmonia opened the door. She curtseyed awkwardly and said, "Welcome, Your Grace. We have been expecting you."

Julius entered the house, briefly wondering if they had any servants at all. They were waiting for him in the same drawing room where he'd first met them. There was an awkward silence when he entered.

His eyes went straight to her. She was standing in the middle of the room, wearing the same blue cotton dress, her fine blonde hair pulled back in a low bun, a composed expression on her face. Only her hands twisted together, gave away that she was nervous. She took a step forwards, then paused, her teeth catching on her lower lip, as if uncertain how to greet him.

In the end she merely nodded with a simple, "Good morning."

The other children were there too, staring at him.

She nudged Hector. "Say good morning."

His eyes lingered on the boy and, as on the previous day, he was shaken by the realisation that this could very well be his son.

The boy looked at him sullenly, then gave a curt bow and retreated as if he had the plague.

Theo cleared his throat. "Let us sit."

They all sat in whatever chairs were available. He sat in an armchair and crossed his legs.

Lena sat down as well, then immediately jumped up again. "Tea!" she exclaimed. "Do we need tea? That is what the English drink, correct? Or coffee? Since we are in Vienna?"

"Later, Mama," Theo said with a frown.

"Later will be fine," Julius said. His nerves were

beginning to strain. "I suggest we get to the core of the matter. What is it you have summoned me for so urgently?"

"Well," Theo said again, clearing his throat. "First of all, when the whole family is together, we will speak in German, for not everyone understands English well." He nodded to the younger boys.

As the Duke spoke German fluently, despite his English accent, he nodded in agreement. "Continue."

"The matter is as follows. We, that is, the Arenheim family, have given the whole situation a great deal of thought. All of us together." He waved his hand. "And we have come to the following conclusion."

The pause was dramatic.

"There seems to be every indication that it is more than likely that Mama, that is, Lena, is indeed your lost duchess."

Julius crossed his arms.

"Yet she remembers nothing of the fact, of you, of England, of her former life, or of how she came to be here."

Another dramatic pause.

"If Mama is the lost duchess, it seems more than likely that Hecki, I mean, Hector, is your son." The boy refused to meet his gaze and stared stubbornly at the vase to his right.

"Regardless of that, he is an Arenheim. As is Mama. No matter who she was before, she is and always will be our Lena. Our Mama."

The children nodded emphatically.

"We therefore have come to the conclusion that the

only reasonable course of action is to simply see whether or not you are amenable to our family."

He blinked. "I beg your pardon?"

"We need to see whether you are compatible with our family," Theo explained as if it were the most logical thing in the world.

"Compatible?" What the devil was the boy babbling about?

"He merely means to say," Lena finally said, "that since we are strangers, it would seem rather odd for us to be, er, suddenly acquainted, so we would first have to see if we really get along before we decide to pursue the, er, relationship."

"We?" he echoed. Normally he wasn't that slow in following a conversation.

"It's either all of us or none of us," Hector said belligerently. "You can't just take Mama and-and me away from our family." His voice trembled.

Theo glared at the Duke. "We won't let you take them from us."

The scales fell from his eyes. The realisation of how much of a threat he was to them struck him like lightning. His claim to Catherine and Hector would mean the disintegration of their family unit. The Duke's forehead knit together in a deep frown. So that was where the matter stood. Naturally, they were concerned about it. He hadn't even thought that far. But, good lord. Was he supposed to take on the whole brood?

Looking over at Lena, she nodded while putting an arm around Hector. "We belong together. All of us. I am a mother to these children, whether or not I am your duchess. My first duty remains to them. If you acknowledge me and Hector as your wife and son, you must know that you are also accepting Theseus, Harmonia, and Achilles. We will not be separated."

"And Marie," Les added.

"And Bello and Fips," Hector chimed in.

"And who are Marie, Bello and Fips?" Julius was entirely out of his depth.

"Our maid, dog, and bird."

"Good heavens."

Five pairs of eyes were fixed on him in expectation.

"Let me reiterate this to affirm that I have understood correctly. You expect me to take on the entire family, including the maid, your dog, and your bird."

The children nodded in unison.

"Yes. You see, we must first see whether you can be a proper father to us before we agree to accept you as one of us." Hector finally spoke up. He pushed out his lower lip in a stubborn line and met his gaze in a challenge.

For the first time in his entire life, Julius, Duke of Aldingbourne, was speechless.

Chapter Thirteen

THE PLAN WAS SIMPLE. HE WAS EXPECTED TO MOVE into their home as if he were their real father. Not just Hector's.

All of them.

"And then we will see if we can be a family together. Or not." Lena met his eyes and looked away quickly. He watched in fascination as a fine sheen of pink blush spread across her cheeks like a rose in full bloom.

Theo nodded. "That is our condition."

All five pairs of eyes were on him.

Now it was his turn to blush, and the telltale heat crept up his neck. Confound it. He hadn't blushed since he was a schoolboy at Eton. "You expect me to play the role of your f-father?" Dash it if he had to stumble over the word.

The children all shook their heads at the same time. "No. We just want to find out if you *could* be our father," Theo explained. "There's a difference."

He had no idea how to be a father, not even in a

hypothetical sense. He didn't think it would come naturally to him. He'd never had a real father figure in his own life, because his own father had been cold, distant, and absent. It had only been seventy-two hours since he'd realised that he might actually be a father, and the notion had confounded his reason and addled his senses. Judging by the way he was behaving now he evidently still hadn't completely recovered them yet. In his defence, most fathers had a considerably longer time to get used to the idea of fatherhood than he had. Now they wanted him to live with them to see if he *could*, potentially, be their father.

"As a sort of test, so to speak," he said aloud.

Everyone nodded.

"To see if I measure up to it."

Once more, they nodded.

It was absurd.

The Duke broke out into a sweat.

"And if I don't?" He crossed his arms over his chest to support himself.

Theo shrugged. "Then it won't work. It might be best for all of us to discover that now rather than later."

It was completely ridiculous, of course. Had anyone ever heard of such a thing?

"What if I have no interest in participating in this experiment?"

A chair scraped on the floor as Lena stood up, a stubborn tilt to her chin. "If you choose not to do this, Your Grace, then I am afraid we must break off contact immediately. Regardless of whether I really am your wife or not, whether Hector truly is your child or not. My loyalty is to my family and I must do what is best for them. We have discussed this and agreed that this is the best course of action. If you are disinclined to participate, then you may leave."

Julius stared at her, fascinated. He'd never seen his Catherine stand up for herself or others and fight with such stubborn determination. She lifted her chin and there was a stern glint of what might be called contentiousness—which was ludicrous. Catherine wasn't quarrelsome.

Never had he encountered such hard-headed negotiators. Yet, before signing a contract, one had to be informed of all the details.

"What exactly would this entail?" His voice was clipped as it was during his diplomatic negotiations.

"It would mean that you would live here, with us, of course," Catherine said, her blush deepening.

"And live our kind of life," Harmonia added.

"The life of the middle-class," Theo said.

"Not the life of a rich, privileged Duke," Achilles said.

"And what, pray, does that involve, in greater detail, if you please?"

"It means no servants, no fancy food, no fancy clothes," Theo said.

"And then we can decide whether you suit us or not." That was Hector.

"For how long?"

Hector and Achilles exchanged glances. "The longer, the better. Two years?" Achilles suggested.

"Out of the question."

The boy scowled. "Fine. Two months?"

Julius shook his head. "You seem to forget that I am here in Vienna on a mission. There is a Congress where my presence is required. I can't just disappear. I have duties to perform."

Catherine pulled at her lower lip thoughtfully. His breath caught. She had a tendency to do that whenever she was thinking, back then, as she did now. "That is a valid point," she said. "What time period do you suggest would be realistic? It would have to be long enough for us to get to know each other better, but also compatible with your schedule."

"The official start of the Congress involving the full participation of all states has been postponed until November. It will be difficult enough for me to negotiate time away from these matters until then. However, that is the best I can do."

"A month, then," Theo said, rubbing his upper lip.

"Yes."

"Mama? Is a month enough?"

Catherine nodded. "I suppose it will have to do."

Everyone else agreed.

"Very well. The idea has merit, for as you rightly point out, we are, after all, strangers who have been thrown together by a most peculiar quirk of fate. Though I know Catherine, I am a stranger to you, and if this is the means by which you can get used to the idea that we are married, then I will agree to it."

"And one more thing," she said. "I must insist that you do not call me Catherine. The name is strange to me. My name is Helena. To my family and friends, Lena."

Lena was a completely different person from Catherine. "Lena." He tested the name on his lips. "Very well. However, I too have a caveat."

"What would that be?"

"At the end of October, if there is no evidence to the contrary that you are not my wife and son, I will turn the tables on you, and you will come to live with me and take your role at my side. As my duchess." He gave her a challenging look. "That includes all of you as well." His gaze remained on Hector.

"Do you mean we all are to live with you in your palais?" Achilles's eyes grew round like saucers. "As children of a duke?"

"Provided you—what is the word you used earlier? Ah, yes. Measure up, I believe it was." He smiled coldly.

THEY WERE to begin the experiment immediately.

"Where do we put him?" Theo inquired. "He can hardly sleep in the drawing room."

"In Papa's bedroom, of course," Lena said.

"Never in Papa's room!" Hector cried. "He can stay in Marie's closet. Or sleep on the kitchen bench."

"Hector!" Mona exclaimed. "Behave. If he is to take on the role of the father, then he naturally has to stay in Papa's room."

Hecki grumbled.

Papa's room it was.

It was a small room filled with dark mahogany furniture and a small window covered with thick curtains. There was a narrow bed in it, a simple chest of drawers, a wardrobe, and a chair. There was a shelf with books on it, but they were mainly medical texts.

This had been Simon Arenheim's room, into whose shoes he was stepping. He must have been a man who lived a very simple kind of life. He'd been a surgeon, they said. Julius wondered what kind of man he'd been.

Just what kind of situation was he in now?

For an entire month, he would be without his valet, his butler, and his secretary.

The Duke sent the carriage back to fetch a trunk of his things, which Theo helped him to carry up to his room. He quickly wrote a letter and stepped out of the house to talk to the coachman. "Deliver this directly to Mortimer, and don't let anyone intercept the letter." He couldn't entirely trust the coachman, either. Who was to say he wouldn't open the letter and read it himself in the meantime? So far, he'd had no indication that the coachman wasn't loyal to him. It remained to be hoped that he was right.

When he returned to the room, he found Lena in it with a rag, furiously wiping the top of the dressing table.

"I merely remembered that the room hasn't been dusted in a while since Marie left, and I wanted to, you know, clean it." She cleared her throat again. "I thought I could do it while you were outside. Marie is our servant, but she isn't here because she's with her father. He's very ill. We don't have any other servants, I'm afraid. We can't afford them. Simon never had a valet. He could do things for himself. You know, shave, dress himself." She blushed once more.

She certainly talked a lot. That was another thing

that was different from her former incarnation. She fiddled with the string of her apron. "I hope you'll be comfortable here without servants. You must have many servants."

"I do." He thought of his valet, butler, two footmen, two chambermaids, a cook, a coachman, and his secretary. That was a total of nine people who saw to his daily comfort. "But never fear, I shall survive on my own. I am entirely capable of looking after myself." He paused. "Although I may need help with my boots, as they are rather difficult to take off."

Lena's face brightened. "I'm sure Theo will be able to help. All you need to do is call. We have no bells or anything here. If you want to talk to one of us, just call us."

He had some difficulty imagining himself opening the door and hollering into the hallway for one of them.

"It is a simple room," she apologised. "The dresser is here, and the wardrobe is there." She pointed to each piece of furniture as if it were not entirely obvious that they were there. "And well, that is all there is to it." She opened a drawer to the dresser and found some clothes inside. "Oh! I'll have it cleared out right away."

"Leave it," he said. "It doesn't matter."

She stood in front of him, not meeting his eyes. "Simon never spent much time here as he was out with his patients all day. Here is the study." She opened an adjoining door and stepped inside.

The study was as masculine an abode as could be. There was a desk by the window and another bookshelf. The fireplace was cold since it hadn't been lit in a long time. There was a slight smell of tobacco. It would do.

"What kind of man was Simon Arenheim?" he found himself asking.

Lena thought for a moment. "He was first and foremost a doctor." Lena went to the window and looked out. "He was a very talented surgeon. A good father. He loved music, travel, and learning new languages. He played the violin. He always said that if he hadn't become a surgeon, he would have been a musician. The children adored him. Theo wants to follow in his footsteps and become a physician because of him."

"I see," Julius replied, wholeheartedly wishing this Simon Arenheim to Jericho. "When did he pass away?"

"Simon was not young, you see. He should have retired long ago, but he refused. He worked all night in the hospital, and he must have overexerted himself. I wasn't there, but they said he just collapsed." She swallowed. "His heart stopped."

"I am truly sorry," he said, and as the words came out of his mouth, he realised how absurd they were, that he was offering condolences to his wife's employer? Friend? Lover?

The situation was, indeed, absurd.

Lena gave him a tremulous smile. "We all have to go sometime, and it was Simon's time to go. We are glad that it was quick and without much suffering. It was what he would have wanted." She hesitated before continuing. "But you have to understand, for the younger boys, especially Hector, this has been very difficult. This is no doubt the reason why he is acting the way he is towards you."

"I understand."

This would be harder than he thought. He wondered what he had got himself into and whether he had made a mistake coming here.

"Your Grace," she suddenly, hesitantly.

"Julius," he said. "That is my name. I think if we are alone together like this, we can dispense with the formalities." As he said these words, he remembered that Catherine had never called him Julius. He had no memory of her doing so. He had always been Your Grace and Aldingbourne.

"Julius," she said, looking up at him shyly.

Something painfully tightened in his chest. It was as if an iron fist was clenching his heart and squeezing it dry. What the deuce was that? Sadness? Longing? Regret?

He clenched his hands at his sides to prevent himself from reaching out and crushing her to him.

"Yes?" It came out rather hoarsely.

"I wanted to ask you something."

He cleared his throat, trying to steady himself. "Go ahead."

She took a deep breath, as if bracing herself. "Were we..." She bit her lip. Then she drew in a big breath and tried anew. "Were we...very much in love?"

An awkward silence hung between them, heavy and uncertain.

Finally, he spoke, his words weighed down with

emotion. "Before I answer that," he said slowly, "tell me—did you love *him*?"

Chapter Fourteen

Lena needed to know.

The guilt had been nagging at her, a relentless burn since the night he'd identified her as the lost duchess by confirming the birthmark above her navel. Her hand involuntarily crept up to the spot and rubbed it. Goosebumps pricked her skin at the mere thought that he even knew she had this.

It was...inconceivable.

His eyes sharply followed her every move. Eyes the colour of molten silver, sharp and cold, yet she'd seen them soften to a darker shade every time they fell on Hector. There was a wistfulness in them, a quiet longing, mingled with hesitation. She had seen the same look in the eyes of a poor boy once, standing in front of a confectioner's shop window displaying a colourful figure made of fondant and chocolate.

And just now, the same look was in his eyes.

When he looked at her like that, it took her breath

away, her mouth went dry, and her heart fluttered like a thousand butterflies.

He'd wanted to know about Simon, so she'd told him, but how could anyone who'd never met Simon understand who he truly was, what he had meant to her with just a few words?

Now he'd wanted to know whether she'd loved Simon.

Simon had been...Simon.

They had not been married. He had needed a friend and a mother for his children, especially for Les, who'd been so little. He had been her doctor, then a strong shoulder to lean on when she had no memory about her life, not even her name. He hadn't cared about etiquette and convention. He'd been her anchor when her world was again shaken when she discovered she was with child. He had provided a solution, suggesting she stay with them. Unconventional, yes, but it had been perfect for everyone. He had been a father to Hector and given him his name.

Had she loved him?

Of course she had. Who wouldn't love such a kind, selfless, caring man like Simon?

But they'd never been lovers, nor had they married.

And now this stranger stood before her. A powerful English Duke, handsome, haughty, and reserved. Intimidating and unlike anyone she had ever known. He claimed the most unlikely thing, that she was his wife. Then he wanted to know if she had loved Simon. How could she explain all this in a few words?

"We were not married," she said slowly, choosing her

words with care. "When Simon died, I was heartbroken. I miss him every minute of every day, and I wish with all my heart that he were still alive. He saved my life. He was my rock when I thought the darkness of my lost memories would swallow me whole. He helped me out of that hole, gave me a new life, a home, and a new name. I mourn him deeply as a very dear friend, not as a husband or lover. He was neither." She lifted her eyes to meet his. "Do you understand?"

He hesitated, then gave a single nod.

But now it was her turn. She had to know. With a wavering voice, she asked, "Were we very much in love?"

His silver eyes looked haunted.

She immediately pressed a hand against her lips and regretted the question. Just when she decided to tell him never mind, that he need not reply, he opened his mouth and said, "Yes." His voice was hoarse with emotion.

And oh, that look in his eyes!

She couldn't tear her gaze from his and felt an overwhelming sadness well up in her, because she could not remember a single thing about that love that had once been. A love that had come to her. A love that had been her very own. She'd forgotten all about it. She felt the bitter taste of guilt in her mouth, as dry as ash.

"I see," she whispered and hung her head.

He retrieved some trinket from his pocket and held it out to her. "I had it sent for immediately after the soiree at Metternich's two weeks ago. Castlereagh's special courier brought it back swiftly. It arrived this morning. Do you recognise it?"

It was a small, silver locket. He placed it in her palm.

A coat of arms was engraved on the oval plate, comprised of a lion, a stag, a tree, and a star. Above it, the ducal crown. *Veritas Vincit*, it said in Latin underneath.

"Truth conquers," Lena whispered.

It lay cold in her palm. She moved her fingers instinctively, opening the locket as if she'd known all along what was inside.

On one side was a delicately painted miniature of a lady in a blue dress. It was a young girl with a sweet disposition, her wide eyes brimming with innocence and her rose-petalled lips hinting at a smile. Her hair was swept up and fine ringlets framed her face.

On the other side was a lock of golden hair.

Lena gasped. Her hand instinctively went to her own hair. The resemblance was undeniable. The image mirrored her own features and the lock of hair appeared identical to her own.

"Do you remember?" he asked again.

Something hot pink flashed in the inner vision of her mind.

"I..." Her voice wavered. "I see...China roses?" She looked up in confusion.

"Yes." His tone was tinged with hope. "We were in a rose garden when you gave me the locket. It was an engagement present. Do you remember giving it to me?"

She stared at the locket.

"No," she whispered, hanging her head.

She did not notice the way his hand lifted and wavered in the air, reaching out to touch her, hesitating. By the time she looked up again, he'd dropped his hands.

"I am sorry," she said woodenly. What utterly meaningless words. What else could she say? She felt helpless.

He filled the room, tall, awkward, and silent.

He was a stranger she had once loved.

He was a stranger who had once loved her.

And she couldn't remember a single thing about him or the feelings they had once shared.

She cleared her throat, and it sounded terribly loud in the room.

"Well. I suppose we shall figure it out, yes?" she said with false cheerfulness and cringed inwardly. Heavens, that sounded awkward. "Eventually." She fiddled with the string of her apron, which she'd forgotten to take off when he'd arrived.

He looked at her with slightly widened eyes.

"I mean, that's why you're here." She rubbed a finger across the wooden surface of the dresser, as if to wipe away an imaginary speck of dust, just so that she could do something instead of standing in front of him like that.

He didn't say anything.

Why didn't he say anything?

She cleared her throat again. "So we can sort this out." She gestured wildly in the space between them. "This terrible mess. Together. Eventually." It didn't sound any better when she repeated it.

"Eventually," he repeated.

She nodded eagerly, relieved that he had finally said something. "Yes. It will all come together, won't it?"

He exhaled deeply, as if he had been holding his breath all the time. "I certainly hope so."

"Good!" She beamed at him. "Excellent." She rubbed her hands. "Wonderful."

"Helena."

Her eyes snapped up. "Yes?"

"Please trust me."

Her mouth formed an oval. "Oh. Yes." She chewed her bottom lip and her eyes darted around the room, desperate to avoid his glance. Heavens! She was alone with the Duke in the bedroom. He was a man. A stranger! Even if he was her husband. What an intolerable muddle it all was. At any rate, she certainly shouldn't be in the bedroom with him.

She paused at the door and took a deep breath. "I have another question."

"Please."

She could feel his presence behind her, warm and imposing.

"After all this—" She gestured vaguely with her hands "—I mean, after everything that's happened—after all this time, are we, erm...still, well is this, uh, marriage still valid?" The latter words tumbled out in a rush.

His face remained impassive. "I gather you did not die."

She thought for a moment. "It appears I did not."

"Nor did I."

She looked at him with wide eyes.

"Nor did we ever obtain a legal separation," he added.

She tilted her head. "We didn't?"

"We most certainly did not." His tone grew firmer.

"Though it is not pleasant, it must be addressed: I

The Forgotten Duke

have no intention of seeking a legal separation or pursuing any action based on the previous presumption of death. If I had remarried or you had wed Arenheim, the matter would have been different. Bigamy would have been a serious complication."

Her mouth dropped open.

"I have studied the law extensively and am well aware of the legal principles surrounding marriage. I will ensure that the courts in England remain uninvolved. Thus, since neither of us is deceased, and no legal separation was previously enacted, it is clear that our marriage remains both lawful and binding."

"Ah." It came out as a sigh. "How terribly efficient of you. If you don't mind, let's not discuss this any further. My poor brain can't take any more of this, and as we well know, isn't entirely reliable, so it's better not to overtax it. I have a tendency to forget certain things, you see. Such as the fact that apparently I have a husband."

She may have imagined it, but a flash of something resembling humour crossed through his steel-grey eyes. It left her flabbergasted, causing her to ramble on. "Let me see. Supper! Yes. You must be hungry. What on earth do English Dukes eat? You shall have to eat the same as the children. It can't be helped. The children must be starving. So let us eat at once. Yes. That is what we should do because that is what we always do."

She fled.

ALL THE CHILDREN were already seated around the table. When he finally appeared, their jaws collectively dropped to the ground.

She hadn't really thought this through, Lena concluded.

None of it.

"Good evening," he said, as if this were a formal soiree.

He'd changed his clothes.

No doubt that was what Dukes did, they changed their clothes three, four, five times a day, and most definitely each time before they sat down to eat.

True to that custom, he'd changed his clothes, only he wasn't wearing evening attire, but...a simple suit. The kind of regular, baggy, threadbare, and unfashionable thing that a costermonger would wear in the street. Instead of it taking him down a notch and relegating him to the lower classes, the lack of formality in his attire only made him look more approachable. More dashing. Slightly rakish, even.

He looked absolutely splendid in it.

It was true what they said, Lena thought dazedly. Dukes were born into their position and there was nothing they could do to hide it. Not even an atrocious suit. In fact, it made them look even better. How unfair was that?

He raised an eyebrow. "Is anything the matter?" He did not wait for a reply but sat down.

"Nothing," Lena said hastily, ladling soup into his plate. "This is *Fritattensuppe*," she explained. "We make it from pancakes cut into strips with beef stock. Have you ever tasted it?" Her eyes widened as it dawned on her that she was serving a Duke the kind of food the lower classes ate. "I daresay you haven't. It's made from leftover pancakes, after all." He'd probably never had to eat leftovers in his entire life. She'd boiled that little beef bone to oblivion until it was nothing more than a nub. Well, this would be an experience for him, then.

"I have not." He picked up the spoon.

Lena clutched the ladle. It was best to enlighten him in advance to avoid any kind of misunderstandings later. "We rarely eat meat, you know." There was a pause. "The truth is, we can't afford it."

"Sometimes on Sunday we do," Les chimed in, slurping his soup loudly. "Three Sundays ago Emma gave us a chicken, but it wasn't enough for all of us. We eat like a horde of locusts raiding Pharaoh's fields, Mama says."

The children proved the analogy correct by slurping their soup with enthusiasm. Hecki went so far as to lift the bowl and drink from it, when Lena leaned forwards and hissed, "table manners!" at him, with a sideways glance at the Duke who was spooning the soup with mechanical precision.

"It is quite delicious," he said formally.

"It's too salty." Theo grimaced.

"Maybe Mama is in love," Mona giggled. "They say that when a cook is in love, she oversalts the soup."

Lena rolled her eyes. "It is a silly German proverb, nothing more."

The Duke put down the spoon and looked at Lena in surprise. "You cooked this yourself?"

"Well, yes."

"Don't you have a cook?"

"Well, no."

"Not anymore," Theo explained. "Who knows when Marie will be back. Until then, we have to do everything ourselves." He propped both his elbows on the table in a gross breach of etiquette and grinned at the Duke. "Also because we can't afford more servants, you know. That means we have to cook and clean ourselves. Until recently, we even had to wash our own clothes in the river behind the house—"

"Good heavens," the Duke interjected, causing Theo to grin even wider.

"Fortunately, we can now afford a laundry maid. Never fear, you won't have to wash your undergarments and socks yourself after all."

"Theo," Mona hissed. "Stop mentioning undergarments at the supper table. It's not the thing."

Lena stood up to fetch the second course.

"Ooh, plum dumplings!" Hecki and Les exclaimed at the same time. "Our favourite. Let's have a contest to see who can eat the most."

Hecki reached out his hand to grab a dumpling, and Lena smacked his hand lightly with her wooden ladle. "Guests first," she said, pushing the plate towards the Duke, who stared at it as if he had never seen dumplings before. It was likely he never had.

"Go on, take one," she told him kindly. "They are plum dumplings and quite good."

He stuck his fork into a dumpling and put it on his plate.

"You have to put sugar on it," Les said. He took the sugar bowl and generously sprinkled sugar on his dumpling. "Like this."

"Not so much, Les," Mona said. "Sugar is horridly expensive, so don't be wasteful. Besides, not everyone likes sugar. I prefer to eat them without."

The Duke took a bite. "It's quite excellent." And he proceeded to eat the entire dumpling.

Satisfied that it was indeed good, they ate, chattering merrily throughout the entire meal, while the Duke quietly listened. Theo recounted what had happened in his anatomy lesson ("We were dissecting a corpse and it made a strange noise, like this, 'pouff', you should have seen how we all jumped back in shock!") while Les and Hecki took turns telling how great the military parade in the Prater had been ("but some of those soldiers looked ridiculous with that stupid feather on top of their hats. If I ever become a soldier, I will refuse to wear that hat."). Mona suddenly interrupted, "Mama, all the dumplings are gone. Nobody seems to have got the one with the onion in it. Did you not make any this time?"

It was a joke and a game that every time there were plum dumplings, one would be filled with an onion. There was usually a lot of hilarity and laughter when the unfortunate person bit into a spicy onion instead of a succulent plum.

Lena looked at the empty plate, perplexed. "I made one with an onion. As a joke. You all know you're not supposed to eat it." She paused. "Don't you?"

There was silence.

Then all eyes turned to the Duke.

Lena's eyes widened in horror. "Oh no. Don't tell me you actually ate it?"

"With all that sugar on top, too!" Hector laughed so hard, he fell out of his chair.

The Duke put the fork down with dignity. "As I said, the food was quite delicious."

Chapter Fifteen

HE OBSERVED THEM FOR THREE DAYS.

For those three days he remained an outsider, silently studying them, learning their habits and quirks, their customs and personalities. Only then would he have enough data to make informed decisions.

Evie was unaware of this arrangement. She had, quite suddenly, decided to visit a friend in the country.

"I haven't seen Pippa since we were children," she explained. "Besides, now that you have finally found Catherine, I imagine you'll be quite busy with her. Something tells me it's best if I stay out of the way."

He set down his pen with a frown. "Pippa? The wild farm girl who convinced you to jump from the barn roof into a haystack? You broke your leg."

Evie grinned. "I did not. I merely sprained my ankle. She wasn't a farm girl; she was just visiting her uncle's farm. Her father is a famous mathematician and natural philosopher."

"And why is she in Austria now?" he asked.

"Because she lives here. She returned to Austria before the war broke out. We've only recently been able to write to each other again. Since I would dearly love to see her, we agreed I'd visit."

He nodded. "Very well. You'll need to take along a companion. I believe Mortimer has already found someone suitable."

She pulled a face. "Very well, if you insist."

Evie had left several days before he moved into the Arenheim home. It was better that way. Much as he loved her, he needed her out of the way to have the time and space to sort out his affairs and his feelings.

After three days of observation, he discovered that certain things remained constant in this tumultuous household, and one of them was music.

Music woke him up and music lulled him to sleep.

It was the sound of the pianoforte, masterfully played, that would wake him at dawn. Catherine—that was, Lena—practised regularly for three hours.

Then, as she rose from the pianoforte, the sound of the viola took over as Mona practised in the drawing room for the rest of the morning. Meanwhile, the boys had gone to school; the older one to university. In the afternoon, the sounds of their violin and flute scales filled the house as they practised.

The Arenheims broke their fast early, with a rather strange drink they called coffee, but which turned out to contain not a single coffee bean but dried, roasted, and ground chicory roots. Lena boiled it in a copper pot to a bitter, earthy brew, and added milk and sugar. She served it with the hard, dark bread that the peasants ate, which was strangely aromatic and did not taste at all bad with butter and jam.

Lunch was a simple vegetable stew with the leftover bread.

Dinner was either dumplings or pancakes, or some other sweet Bohemian dish whose pronunciation he hadn't yet mastered. It was some kind of baked doughy substance with apricot jam in it, served with vanilla sauce. It wasn't bad, but, well, sweet. He'd never had so many sweet dinners in his entire life. He ate every crumb without complaining because Lena had made it with her own hands.

Lena was constantly in demand.

She was the heart of the house, the emotional centre. The mother.

He'd seen how Hector burst into the room, sobbing, and she'd picked him up and he'd clung to her as if he were but a toddler, and she'd carried him around the room, making soothing noises as he sobbed forth his story. He'd been feeding a stray puppy in the street that had insisted on following him unnoticed and it had got under the wheels of a carriage. Hector had held the little animal in his arms as it died. "It's all my fault," Hecki wept. "I killed it."

Lena had comforted him until his sobs subsided, and he hiccuped into her lap. Then he'd gone with Les, to give it an honourable burial. A few moments later, the mournful sound of Les's violin filled the room as he played a requiem.

Mona, too, had burst into tears, when, after many hours of practice, she couldn't get a certain passage right, and Lena had sat beside her, rubbing her shoulder and reassuring her that she was still as talented as ever.

Even Theo had burst into the drawing room one evening, just when he was penning answers to some letters that Mortimer had brought him, stalked over to Lena who was darning everyone's socks, dropped to his knees and burst into loud, uncontrollable sobs. He, the adult, had transformed into a child in a matter of seconds.

"I want to die." Theo buried his head in her lap.

"Oh dear, oh dear, oh dear," Lena murmured.

After much urging, he choked out, "She doesn't love me."

Lena listened to him patiently as he sobbed forth the entire sorry story. Something about a blacksmith's daughter named Rosalie whom he'd loved forever, thinking his affections were returned, only for it to turn out she was merely trifling with him. "She says I'm as poor as a church mouse and not g-g-good enough for her because she wants something better. Ultimately, she can't l-l-love me."

Lena sighed deeply. "Oh Theo. I am so sorry."

She really was quite remarkable, the Duke concluded. Instead of ranting about the girl's personality and how awful she was for rejecting Theo, she merely listened to the boy quietly, as if she understood his pain.

"I feel so stupid and ashamed," Theo confessed.

"Oh, Theo. Never be ashamed of love."

"Even if it is a stupid, unrequited love?"

"Theo. Love is never stupid," she'd insisted. "Especially when it is unrequited. Because then the heart has to gather all its strength to love even more so it can let go.

The Forgotten Duke

Even if it feels like your heart is breaking, you'll have loved the noblest love of all. One day, you'll find the right person who will be able to love you back equally."

She might as well have driven a dagger into his soul with those words.

Theo had sobbed even harder. "I can't let go, Mama. I simply can't. I don't want to. I won't!"

Julius had squirmed in his chair as an unwilling eavesdropper, grappling with his own dark emotions, understanding the sentiments only too well.

He found himself consumed by something akin to envy. He wished he could also let go, and sob and cry and bury his head in Lena's lap, like Theo had. Maybe she would rub his shoulders, as she was doing now, and hug him.

Dash it all.

He made an unsteady movement with his hand, nearly oversetting the inkwell.

In general, there was too much hugging and crying and laughing and fighting and an excess of freely exhibited emotion to which he was quite unaccustomed. He was in uncharted territory.

THEN THERE WERE other people who thought it was their right to interfere in their family affairs.

That neighbour, for one. Karl Bauer and his wife, Emma.

Karl, had, at first, peered at him suspiciously through two small, narrow eyes. "Who are you?" They'd been in the front garden, and he'd suddenly appeared at the other side of the fence, his arms on his hips, a pipe in his mouth.

"This is, um..." Lena had looked at Julius helplessly. They hadn't agreed on a story to tell outsiders about why he was here.

"Julius Stafford-Hill," he introduced himself. "A friend of the family."

The man stood in front of him with his legs firmly planted apart and his shoulders squared, assessing him from top to bottom. He crossed his arms. "English?"

"Yes."

"Why is he here?" he asked Lena, his eyes never leaving the Duke's.

"Well...because of the Congress, of course. He's also a friend of Simon's," she added.

Karl's suspicious expression softened, giving way to a broad smile. "In that case, welcome. Any friend of Simon's is also my friend." He extended a calloused, beefy hand and after a moment's hesitation, Julius took it. The man's grip was crushing, and Julius fought the urge to pull away.

"Care for a pipe?" Karl asked, holding out his own. Julius stared at the discoloured, roughly carved pipe with a chewed-up mouthpiece. He wistfully thought of his elegant briar pipe resting in a silver pipe dish on his desk back at his residence. He forced a smile and accepted it.

"Good tobacco," he commented after a slow draw. It was true; it was a surprisingly rich and potent blend.

Karl nodded approvingly. They stood side by side by the fence, passing the pipe back and forth between them in silence.

"Not much progress with the Congress, one hears," Karl said suddenly between puffs. "What with Talleyrand insisting on a place at the table with the Big Four. Has Metternich agreed yet?"

Julius's brows shot up. "Things aren't that simple."

"They never are."

"At the rate it's going, I predict the Congress will drag on much longer than anyone anticipated," Karl said.

"Possibly." Julius was surprised at the sharpness of Karl's observations. For a simple farmer who tended a vineyard and sold cheap cider at the market, Karl's observations were unexpectedly astute and revealed a far deeper understanding than most Congress delegates.

Karl Bauer, it turned out, was keeping an eye on the Arenheims. He provided them with fruit and vegetables, performed random repairs in the house whenever necessary, and his wife frequently cooked for the entire family. He looked unkempt and wore dirt-speckled clothes, but he was surprisingly conversant on politics and current affairs, expressing a sharp intellect that belied his humble background. This Karl was not to be underestimated, and Julius reluctantly admitted that there was more to the man than met the eye.

In the end, they parted on friendly terms.

Then there was this other fellow, Adam Klein, a musician who claimed to have studied under Beethoven himself. He played alongside them in their performances, completing their quartet as the fourth member. Like Karl, Adam Klein had met him with suspicion when they first met, his gaze sizing him up warily. Lena's firm introduction of Julius as a friend of Simon's, and a temporary guest in their home, left Klein no choice but to grudgingly tolerate his presence.

Lena, on the other hand, mothered everyone, including the neighbours, the stray dog Bello, the bird in the tree called Fips, and any beggar child who happened to wander by.

Once, he even caught her mothering him when she put a hand on his forehead to check his temperature. When he looked up in surprise, she withdrew her hand, blushing wildly. "You haven't said a word all day, so I wondered if you were ill. I can't have anyone ill in my house, because then we'll all fall ill, and Theo will insist on doctoring us, and then he'll get ill himself." She tended to ramble when she was embarrassed, and it appeared that she was often embarrassed in his company.

As if she didn't know how to behave in his presence when they were alone.

He regretted now that he'd answered her question in the affirmative. When she'd asked him if they had been in love....

He'd lied.

Chapter Sixteen

It had been an arranged marriage.

As was customary, their union had been decided upon by their parents when they were still children—or at least Catherine had been. He was nine years older and at that time more interested in roaming the countryside with his friends, hunting, fishing, and riding than being with his child bride, who, in her portraits, appeared to be a diminutive, well-mannered doll with corkscrew curls, dressed according to the fashion of the time.

He'd never questioned the arrangement. It was his duty to marry and provide the Dukedom with an heir, and he was expected to marry the woman who was chosen for him. Certainly, he'd had his bits of muslin by the side, for his child bride was one thing, and his mistress another. One thing was duty, the other was desire. No one in his class would have batted an eyelid, for this sort of arrangement was not only common and acceptable, but it was also expected of the men of his class. It was the way things were done. Julius did not give it a second's thought; he had had neither the time nor interest to court anyone else, and he regarded the entire Season as a nuisance. As far as he was concerned, the engagement was convenient. When he inherited his father's title at the age of twenty-six, they were expected to marry quickly. She was still too young, her parents had protested, barely seventeen.

He'd met Catherine at their official engagement a year later, a fragile, delicate slip of a girl, who'd looked at him with tremulous, nervous eyes. She looked as though a puff of wind would blow her away.

She was pretty enough, he'd decided. Good breeding, a good name, good manners. She could play the pianoforte, sing, and embroider well. She would bear him a son. In short, she would make an excellent duchess.

They'd taken a turn about the rose garden. It had been somewhat awkward. He wasn't the most talkative person, and she was painfully shy. It was clear as daylight that the girl was terrified of him. They had nothing in common. She never met his eyes. When she spoke, her voice was so low that he had to bend down to make out what she was saying. She blushed furiously as she pulled out a small trinket and handed it to him, stammering that it was to be his engagement present. It took her three tries to get the words out.

There had been something endearing about that. He'd taken the trinket, which had been engraved with his family's crest.

"You can open it," she whispered.

When he did, he found a surprisingly accurate miniature of herself inside, and on the other side several strands of gold. A strand of her hair.

It took him by surprise. This was a gift from a lover. He'd certainly never expected to receive such a trinket from his future wife.

"I'll always treasure it," he told her, and he'd meant it.

She glanced up at him shyly, like a fawn. Her lips had been slightly parted and looked like the dewy petals of a rosebud.

He'd kissed her then. He hadn't planned it, and he certainly hadn't thought about it. It hadn't been a gentle, tender kiss either, but a demanding, possessive one. For a moment he'd allowed himself to be lost in her intoxicating sweetness.

He felt her shrink and tremble, and the first sane thought that penetrated his foggy mind was that it was too soon, too fast, and she wasn't ready.

He let her go abruptly, and she looked at him with those fawn eyes as if he'd grown three horns on his head.

He'd suppressed a curse. Now he'd gone and frightened her with his brute handling of her. It was a miracle she didn't run.

He'd mumbled an apology and fled, leaving her standing alone in the rose garden.

Not an auspicious beginning to their marriage, he'd thought ruefully.

They'd been married a month later in the family chapel. She looked as white as porcelain, and her hand had trembled like a little bird in his. There was still that nervous look in her eyes, as if she feared he'd devour her on the spot.

Julius wandered away from the Arenheim home and stared across the distance over the river, ignoring the cold wind pull at his hair.

Had theirs been a happy marriage?

He'd been absent most of the time. When he was at Aldingbourne Hall, she had tried so hard to please him. She'd been such an obedient, dutiful little wife. But she'd been so much younger, in a different league; she hadn't been the companion he needed. She was always there, yet he'd barely acknowledged her existence.

Had he loved her at all during all that time?

The plain truth was that he had not. That was the thorn in his soul that kept him awake at night. He hadn't loved her enough.

Had he been fond of her, then?

Possibly. Like one was fond of a puppy that jumps into your lap and licks your hand. One pets it and gives it a treat. He'd done the same, quite literally, in that order. He grimaced, remembering how he'd patted her hand and given her a box of candied violets.

She blushed furiously and hadn't been able to meet his eyes when she'd taken the box.

"Thank you," she whispered.

He'd felt a flash of irritation. He'd dismissed her blushing, her persistent stammering, and her tongue-tied speech as mere awkwardness—symptoms of her youth, lack of personality, and inability to hold a conversation. Her nervousness in his presence he attributed to fear, which only annoyed him further. Yet why shouldn't she be nervous? Even men older and more experienced than her trembled in his presence. It was a way of commanding respect, something he'd mastered early on with his father as the ultimate role model. Cool, distant, feared. The Duke of Aldingbourne. With Catherine, it was different. He found it hard to tolerate that she saw him more as a duke than as a man, respectful of his status but intimidated by his personality.

He couldn't have been more wrong.

He'd understood nothing about her at all. Nothing.

A dark streak of anguish seared through him, followed by the old, familiar feeling of cold and leaden guilt pressing down on his chest.

He hadn't understood that she was suffering from a severe case of adulation and that she, in fact, adored the ground he walked on. It had never even occurred to him that she had been deeply in love with him.

He'd been completely unworthy.

He had been a blind, stupid fool, who hadn't seen or understood the treasure he was holding in his hands until it was too late.

So when she asked him the impossible question of whether they had been very much in love, what in the name of Zeus should he have said otherwise?

A "yes" might have been a lie, at best half a lie, but a "no" would not have been entirely accurate, either.

"Not yet"—should he have said that? In reference to when? The past or the present? What sense did that make?

Possibly, the more accurate answer should have been, "Maybe. If so, it was too late."

Chapter Seventeen

THE NEXT MORNING, BREAKFAST WAS A LIVELY affair. The boys were animatedly recounting the details of the fireworks in the Augarten that had taken place the previous night, when Lena suddenly interrupted. "Children, we have a performance in several days. It's the Peace Ball at the Metternich Palais. And, oh, let's not forget, tomorrow is the annual market fair in Nussdorf. Mona and I will be baking *lebkuchen* the entire day."

Everyone spoke at once.

"Oh yes, it will be a merry occasion," Mona exclaimed. "We'll take turns performing and selling biscuits. There will be music and dancing and plenty to eat and drink. There will also be puppet shows, travelling theatre troupes, and many stalls selling local crafts."

The Duke, who had been listening quietly up to this point, set down his coffee cup with a frown. "The Metternich ball is one thing. But do you really intend to perform at a common fair?"

Lena tensed at the Duke's cold voice, bracing herself for the inevitable conflict that would follow.

"Certainly. It has become an Arenheim family tradition. We go every year to provide the music." Theo crossed his arms and threw him a challenging look.

"You intend to stand on the street corner like any ordinary fellow and play? With the entire city gawking at you? While people throw coins into your hat?" His voice was laced with incredulity.

"We have a tin box," Hecki said. "After the performance, Mona goes around collecting coins. It clanks nicely when someone throws in a coin."

"Good Lord." The Duke seemed momentarily speechless.

"We certainly intend to perform. This is the most lucrative event of all, and our *lebkuchen* sells out to the last crumb," Lena explained, in case he did not quite understand the extent of the matter.

"You are not only performing, but also selling *lebkuchen*." His voice grew increasingly frosty.

"You make it sound like we're selling something revolting, like pig's innards." Mona pushed out her chin in a challenge.

"What's wrong with pig's innards? Pig's innards are good," Theo said. "Haven't had them in a while."

"Yes. We eat them with *sauerkraut*," Hector said. "My favourite."

"Or stuff them into blood sausages," Mona suggested.

"Or eat the stuffed stomach—with bread and herbs. It's delicious." Lena realised their conversation was missing the point when she caught the Duke's disapproving glare. She cleared her throat. "My point being, there is nothing whatsoever wrong with us taking part in the fair."

"Karl helps us sell while we perform," Les threw in, as if that somehow alleviated the matter. "And when we take a break, we sell them ourselves. We usually have a competition to see who sells the most."

The Duke shook his head. "That's out of the question."

Lena blinked at the Duke. "The competition? But why?"

"The whole thing." He gestured with a hand. "Performing in a market fair. Selling biscuits as if you were a simple farmer's wife." He flared his nostrils in indignation. "I am vehemently against it."

Theo grinned as he leaned back in his chair. "This is what we do. Father's grandparents were indeed peasants, did you know? We sell goods in the streets, haggle, and perform for the ordinary village folk. We will do anything for a coin thrown our way. It's in our blood."

"I do not approve," the Duke growled, "of having the entire world gape at you as you expose yourselves to all and sundry in the middle of a street fair."

"It's not as though it would be the first time," Mona set down her coffee cup so hard, the liquid sloshed on the table.

"How often have you done this?"

She shrugged. "Seven, eight times?"

"Good heavens. No thought at all regarding decorum and reputation?"

"Told you he's a disagreeable, crabby old stick,"

Hector whispered to Les, who nodded emphatically. "No sense of humour at all."

The twitching of the muscle in his jaw indicated that he'd heard that.

"Oh hush, Hector," Lena placed her hand on Hector's shoulders. She turned to the Duke with narrowed eyes. "What do you mean, 'decorum and reputation'? Perhaps we should discuss this in private, Your Grace." She felt a sudden belligerent spark ignite within her, followed by an irresistible desire to quarrel with him.

His eyes were wintry. There was a distance between them as vast and cold as a frozen wasteland. "There is no need for that," he retorted. "This concerns your entire family, so let us continue the discussion here."

She put her hands on her hips and glared at him. "Well, if you insist. But we won't let you take this from us. This fair is important. We have to earn our money somehow."

"If funds are an issue, rest assured I have plenty."

"No, that won't work," both Lena and Theo said at the same time.

"We don't want to be dependent on you," Theo added.

"Dependent. What nonsense is that?" A muscle jumped in his cheek. "Did we not agree that I am to join this family as a provisional member, which means that you, all of you without exception, are now my family. Is that correct?"

"Well, yes," Lena said. "I thought that was the general idea."

The Forgotten Duke

"As the head of this family, I can provide for all of you. No more appearances at fairs or anywhere else."

"Wait. Did we ever agree that you are the head of the family?" Theo stood up, planted his legs wide and placed his hands on his hips.

The Duke quelled him with a flinty stare. "I am the eldest. Therefore, I am the head."

"But—" Theo wanted to argue, but Lena interrupted.

"Let us not fight over this now." She turned to the Duke. "Your Grace, I thought we agreed that the idea of you living with us is that you get used to our way of life. That means you must allow us to let us earn our own living. It also means no financial support from you. In other words, we don't want your money."

"I will repeat, for the last time, that I do not countenance having my family on public display," the Duke said coolly. "I will not change my position on this."

Lena threw up her arms.

"He said 'my family'," Les whispered audibly to Hector, who scowled.

"Even Emperor Francis and his children perform," Mona pointed out. "What is the problem?"

"The difference is that Emperor Francis doesn't do it for a living, nor does he stand on a street corner like a beggar," the Duke countered.

Lena shook her head. "The issue, clearly, is earning money. Unheard of for an aristocrat." She got up to clear the table.

"Noblemen don't work, you see," Theo explained to the boys, who shook their heads with disapproval.

The Duke inclined his head coolly. "You may perform on an honorary basis, without receiving a wage."

"But that's unfair." Theo glared at him. "Why should we perform for free?"

His Grace's eyes narrowed to slits. "It is either that, or not at all."

"Tyrant," Theo muttered under his breath.

Lena pinched the bridge of her nose. This discussion was going nowhere. "Your Grace," she began, her voice firm, "you can't forbid us to perform. It's at the heart of who we are. However, your main concern seems to be that we make a living. I understand that this is unheard of for a member of the high nobility, and you have your family name to consider. We shall donate all our earnings from the fair to the local parish. We won't keep a single *Kreuzer* for ourselves. Let us perform. Think of it as a glimpse into our family life, struggles and all. Remember, this is only temporary. After that, we'll discuss further arrangements."

She knew that another letter to August, filled with colourful details, would secure some funds. They'd manage. A murmur of discontent rippled through the others.

"Very well," the Duke said curtly, but judging from his clenched jaw, he clearly wasn't pleased.

Chapter Eighteen

On the day of the fair, they were all assembled outside, but the Duke was nowhere to be found.

"He's not here, Mama," Hecki said as he jumped down the stairs. He'd banged on the Duke's bedroom door and found him gone.

"What can we do? We can't wait for him to return." Lena was irritated at the Duke's inflexible attitude. She was adamant not to let this disrupt their day. "Let's go."

In the carriage, the children abused the Duke all the way to the fair, calling him everything from 'rigid as a stone gargoyle' to 'starchier than an ironed collar' to 'as humourless as the dead eyes of a trout.' When they all agreed that he was 'a tyrant worse than Nero', Lena lifted a hand to put an end to it.

"Children. He is an English *Duke*. With his rank and name, he is accustomed to rules and behaviour that are quite alien to us. No doubt, our way of life must seem more than strange to him. He is like a fish trying to adapt to life on land. While I don't condone autocratic behaviour, we must understand that this is what he is used to: giving orders and having people do his bidding."

"Maybe it is best that you don't remember too much of him then, Mama," Mona muttered under her breath.

"He's just like Napoleon. And look what happened to him: he got crushed by the allies!" Les piped up.

Hecki nodded enthusiastically. "Yes. We are the Allies! Let's banish him to Elba immediately."

Lena rolled her eyes and leaned back in her seat, while Hecki and Les planned all the ways and means of banishing the Duke to Elba.

The fair was a vibrant event, the streets and stalls filled with people, smells, sounds, and lots of eating and dancing. Arriving late, they had no time to check on Kurt and Emma, who had arrived earlier to set up their stall. They immediately went up to the small wooden stage and started to perform.

Lena and Mona both wore blue dresses with fitted, sleeveless bodices, white blouses, full skirts, and red aprons. White stockings and buckled shoes completed their look. The boys, meanwhile, wore red and white chequered shirts and *lederhosen*.

As Lena's pianoforte was too cumbersome to take to the fair, she played the recorder flute with the boys, while Theo played violin and Mona the viola. It was an unlikely combination of instruments, but strangely enough, it worked. They played cheerful pieces and soon people were dancing to their lively tunes.

In the middle of one piece, Lena almost dropped her recorder flute. Out of the corner of her eye, she saw a man standing somewhat apart from the crowd with his arms crossed. Surely it couldn't be him, standing there in simple leather breeches with suspenders, a linen shirt, and a short dark grey jacket—exactly the same clothes the farmers wore. A round hat with a wide brim shaded his eyes. After she blinked, once, twice, he was gone. Confused, she looked around, but the people had crowded around the stage and she could no longer see the man.

She shook her head. The Duke had been so much on her mind that now she saw him everywhere.

After the performance, Mona walked around with her tin box, collecting coins from the audience. A couple of young men, already drunk from too much wine, bumped into her and she dropped the box, spilling the coins on the ground. As she scrambled to collect the coins, one of them kicked the box away, forcing her to scramble after it, and just as she was about to grab it, one of them kicked it again, while the other picked up the coins and put them in his pocket. As she stumbled and fell on her knees, they burst out in raucous laughter as if it was the funniest thing ever.

"Stop it!" she cried, but one of the men just kicked the box again.

Lena, who was in the process of packing up the instruments, saw Mona on the floor scrambling for the coins and the two drunkards mocking her. Her mouth pressed to a thin, hard line, and she clenched her hands to fists. Then she turned to Theo. "There's trouble with Mona."

Theo didn't have to be asked twice. He leapt off the

stage and elbowed his way through the crowd, followed closely by Lena, her hands clenched into fists. Someone was attacking one of her children. She would not allow it. She was ready to swing at them in defence. She crashed into Theo's back, who had come to a full stop.

A small circle of curious onlookers had formed around Mona—the two men, and a third who stood wide-legged in front of them, bending a horsewhip.

"I said, pick them all up." A voice, cold and quiet, sent shivers of dread down their spines. The silence was thick enough to cut with a butter knife.

Lena pushed through the crowd and saw that the situation had reversed itself: The two men were on their knees, scrambling about to pick up the coins.

"And if I find that you have a single coin in your pockets that doesn't belong to you, I will..." He did not finish the sentence but flexed the whip demonstratively.

The men turned pale and scrambled about even faster.

"You should whip them anyway," a voice shouted from the crowd. "They're good-for-nothing drunkards who need to be taught a lesson."

"Aye, bullying such a pretty girl. 'Twould serve them right if you were to whip them," a woman agreed.

"Mona!" Out of breath, Lena reached the girl and drew her to her chest protectively. "Are you well?"

"I am now, Mama," Mona said. "He intervened just in time."

The Duke of Aldingbourne, dressed as a common peasant, towered over the two men on the ground, who were clearly terrified of him.

Lena gasped.

"I swear it's all the coins," one of the men stammered. "She can have all of mine, too." He added a handful of *Kreuzer* and emptied his pockets to show him that there was nothing left. "Please let us go. We will never do this again."

The Duke grabbed him by the collar. "If you do, I will know about it and come after you." He brought his face close to his. "I have connections with the secret police, you know."

Wide-eyed with panic, the drunkard began to blubber forth apologies. When he let him go, both men scuttled off and disappeared into the crowd.

The Duke picked up the tin box lying on the ground and shook it so the coins rattled together. "The show has ended. If you enjoyed it, your contribution is greatly appreciated."

People pulled out their purses and generously dropped coins into the box as the Duke walked around.

Lena and the Arenheim children stood by, jaws dropping.

"I've never seen anyone do anything so cracking fantastic." Les finally said.

Hecki nodded mutely and stared in awe at the Duke as he continued to make his rounds holding out the box, and the coins kept dropping, dropping, dropping. Then he reached Lena and stopped in front of her, shaking the box.

"This should be enough, don't you think? If you add more coins, it will overflow." He held the box out to her.

Lena took it. "When did you arrive?"

"Long before you, apparently." The Duke shrugged. "I came with Karl and Emma Bauer to help them set up the stall. We nearly sold all the biscuits before you arrived."

Lena uttered a puff of incredulous laughter.

"Wait." Theo had pushed himself forwards. "Did you just say you sold our biscuits?"

"Yes, he did, every single one of them," a booming voice said behind them. Karl beamed at the Duke. "We made good work of it, didn't we? Although it has to be said that it was really he who did all the work. He sold most of it while I helped our neighbour with his stall, which had collapsed on him. Julius was on his own most of the time, weren't you?" Karl clapped his hand on the Duke's shoulder.

"Business went well," he replied laconically.

"Business went well," Lena echoed, stunned.

"I see your performance has come to an end, too." He nodded at the children, who gazed at him with open mouths, as if seeing him in an entirely new light.

"Thank you for helping me," Mona said shyly.

A thundercloud passed over the Duke's brow. "And that is precisely why I so vehemently objected to you doing this in the first place." He put his arm gently around Mona's shoulder. "It isn't safe for young ladies like you to be out in this crowd alone. The two men are not the only drunks here. When the wine flows freely, there will be more unruly behaviour as the day progresses." He looked up directly at Theo. "Which is why you, Achilles, and Hector are to accompany her and remain next to her for the remainder of the fair."

"Yes sir," Les and Hecki said in unison.

"Can we buy some sausages? We're starving!" Les said.

Lena nodded. "Of course." She gave each of the children a few coins. "Spend it well."

"*Famos!*" They disappeared into the crowd.

The Duke watched Lena, and she imagined seeing a fleeting look of tenderness cross his face as he looked down on her. She blinked, looked away, looked back again, but now his face was neutral. She couldn't tell what he was thinking.

"And you?" she asked. "Are you hungry?"

He shook his head. "Frau Bauer has been feeding me all morning."

They made their way through the fair. "I didn't know you left with them this morning. I thought that maybe you'd gone to town to do some work."

"Adam asked me if I could help him set up the stall." He frowned as he took Lena's arm to help her over a puddle.

"I confess I did not think you had it in you, Your Grace," Lena said. "I think you have earned the respect of the entire family today. And Mona has begun to idolise you."

A smile flitted over his face so quickly that Lena thought she must have imagined it. "Nonsense. Now. Shall we have a look at those stalls over there?"

"They sell *lebkuchen*, too," Lena said. "But they must not be as good as ours, since there is still an entire basket full of them left. How did you sell them, by the by?"

He shrugged. "It wasn't difficult at all. I first studied

the price at which everyone else sold them, and then I decided to lower the price of ours. They went away almost immediately."

Lena laughed. "So that was your secret. You gave them away for almost free."

Once more, he nearly smiled. "Not for free. It would never occur to me to give away something you made with your own hands for free."

Their eyes met. Her stomach flipped. Her heart began to pound. Blinking rapidly, Lena looked away quickly.

"I'm glad you came," she said, shyly.

He nodded gruffly. "I'm glad to be here."

Chapter Nineteen

In terms of personality—Catherine, Helena, Lena—this woman remained an enigma to him. How could this vibrant, chaotic woman, now leaning on the kitchen table with her elbows, teaching her son—his son, by Jove! He had a son! He still did not comprehend it—with unruly strands of hair tumbling over her cheeks and lips, dressed in an ill-fitting, patched gown worn by servants—how could she possibly be the same timid, fragile little thing he had once married, who shrank away every time he looked at her?

Physically they were identical. That is, if one ignored the way they were dressed. Catherine would never have worn stained linen aprons. It was as if there was a stranger inside the body of Catherine. Her entire demeanour had changed.

Even though he understood the reason for it, it perplexed him to no end.

Lena usually met his gaze in a straightforward, calm way. He often found her looking at him, mostly thoughtful and puzzled and with the kind of caution one approached the ice of a frozen lake, as if she couldn't decide if she could trust it to carry her.

He wasn't used to that.

She blew her hair out of her face as she leaned over the table, leaning on her elbows, giving him a good view of her shapely bottom.

His body tensed, and he tried to look away but found himself unable to.

She was beautiful. She always had been, of course, but the years had added a sense of womanliness and quiet confidence that had been lacking when she was younger.

He swallowed.

"No Hecki. Not thirteen. You forgot to carry over the number, here. Try again." She pointed to a figure on the slate. She had chalk on her finger, on her nose, on her forehead, and ah! Now she was rubbing her eyebrows, smearing the chalk over those too.

He watched in fascination.

Their heads were close together, her blonde head, and the boy's dark one.

"No. Try again." There was a hint of vexation in her tone.

The boy petulantly threw the chalk down, breaking it in half.

"Hector!" she exclaimed.

"I did what you said, and it still doesn't make any sense. Explain it so I can understand!"

Julius stood up. The time for him as an uninvolved observer was over.

"Let me help."

Both looked up.

"No thank you," the boy said immediately. "I can do it myself."

"Oh, could you? That would be wonderful." She stood up and stretched her back, which must have been aching.

"Doesn't he have a tutor?" Julius stepped to the table and looked at the numbers scrawled on the slate.

Lena grimaced. "No. We can't afford it. In the past, Simon used to teach the younger boys. Hector and Achilles go to the local school here, and I daresay Herr Maier does his best, but there are thirty children in the class, the youngest being five and the oldest fifteen. I suppose it is a bit noisy."

"It's unbearable," Hector muttered, picking up the chalk and drawing on the kitchen table. "Lessons are either too easy or too difficult, and Herr Maier explains even worse than you do."

"Oh hush, I'm sure he's not that bad," Lena retorted.

"It's a waste of time. We're better off fishin—" He interrupted himself with a cough.

"Hector Arenheim. Never tell me you're skipping lessons to go fishing." Lena placed her hands on her hips.

"Almost every day." Les poked his head around the door, then quickly disappeared as Hecki threw a piece of chalk at him.

"Tattletale!" He shot up to run after him, but Julius clamped his hand on his shoulder and pressed him down into his chair.

"You stay here, and I'll be your tutor."

Lena nodded with approval. "Excellent. Behave

yourself, Hecki," she said before disappearing into the kitchen.

L ENA SAW the two dark heads together, the big and the little one. The deep, sonorous voice of the Duke vibrated as he explained the rules of arithmetic to the boy. The higher tones of Hector replied. She watched with mixed emotions.

A pang of tenderness flooded through her and vanished as quickly as it had come, followed by a quick jab of fear.

He wouldn't take Hector away from her, would he? He wouldn't tear her family apart. If August was right, he had the power and the right to do so. There would be nothing she could do about it.

But if he'd wanted to do that, wouldn't he have done it already, instead of agreeing to their experiment? Here he was, dressed in commoner's clothes, helping her son—his son!—with arithmetic.

She didn't know him well, but it struck her that he wasn't that kind of man. Her first impression of him was that he was arrogant and proud. He had a cold shield around him that was difficult to penetrate. He never smiled. He seemed to have a strong sense of duty and fairness. She hoped she was right, and that this sense of duty and fairness would prevent him from doing something as cruel as separating a mother from her children. To her, things were clear: if he wanted her or her son, he would have to take them all on. It was either all of them, or none of them.

He'd asked her to trust him. She found that difficult. There was so much about the man she didn't understand. The gaps in her memory frightened her, but so did the memories themselves. Random scraps, bits and pieces, uncoordinated fragments and flashes that made neither head nor tail.

It wasn't anything concrete, just a feeling, like when she smelled his cologne. She blushed at the thought of when, earlier this morning, he'd caught her sniffing at him like a dog when she thought he had his back turned to her.

She was almost obsessed by the scent.

It triggered a wave of emotions that were unfamiliar to her.

A delicious weakness ran through her legs and she leaned against the counter.

"Before we do that," he said, "you have to learn how to read the clock properly." He pulled out the fob with his pocket-watch, flipped it open with one hand, lifted it to his face and lowered his gaze. His profile was as sharp and commanding as that of an emperor's on a Roman coin.

The soup tureen crashed to the floor.

Both Hector and the Duke leaped to their feet. "Mama!"

"Are you hurt?" the Duke asked at the same time.

All the blood had drained from her face and she gripped the table for support. "Do that again."

"I beg your pardon?" A slight frown formed on his face.

"What you just did." She moistened her lips. "With the watch."

He lifted it. "This?"

She nodded.

"What did I do?"

"Put it back in your pocket, then take it out and look at it."

After a moment's hesitation, he complied. He tucked it into his pocket and drew it out with one fluid motion, flipping the lid open.

Lena closed her eyes.

She felt him warm and solid stepping up behind her, gripping her shoulders.

"What is the matter?"

She swayed under the overwhelming surge of emotions. "I finally remembered," she whispered.

"What?" His grip tightened slightly on her shoulders.

She looked up, meeting his eyes.

"You."

Chapter Twenty

It was a clear, sharp vision of colour, sight, and smell.

She'd just stepped out of a shop into a busy street, when a voice suddenly exclaimed from behind her. "Oh look, quickly, my lady, there's your betrothed." Was it her maid? Was her name Martha?

Her heart began to pound and her breath quickened in anticipation. She craned her neck and tiptoed forwards to get a glimpse of him, her very first glimpse, and then she saw him pulling up in a curricle, which was immediately surrounded by several other gentlemen. He stood up and pulled out his pocket-watch.

"A quarter to the hour," he said, "to the minute. That means I was one and a half minutes faster than Garford. I have won the wager."

Several pedestrians paused and murmured amongst themselves. "The Marquess of Drayton. Son of the Duke of Aldingbourne. Ten thousand pounds per annum and two estates, and he's not even a Duke yet. They say he is a rising star in Parliament, remarkable for his young age. Mark my words, he's on the path to greatness."

She'd felt a surge of pride that this was the man she would one day marry. How fine he looked, how tall and handsome! He was immaculately dressed in a dark blue coat and trousers, his beaver hat perched rakishly on his head, the flaps of his greatcoat swinging back as he stepped down from the curricle with a light foot.

He swept past her, not knowing who she was, for their betrothal had only been informally agreed upon by their parents, and they had not yet been formally introduced. Had he noticed her, he would have seen an awkward, pale fourteen-year-old girl in a brown pelisse and a bonnet that covered most of her face. She could have touched him if she had stretched out her hand, but he never noticed her. He disappeared in a house, followed by his friends.

She craned her neck to catch a last glimpse of him before the door closed.

"A most distinguished young lord," Martha said. "And so very handsome! How fortunate you are, my lady."

"Yes, I am very fortunate indeed," she said, pressing her hand to her chest as a wave of happiness swept through her. She would still have to wait three years for their formal engagement.

Lena blinked, disoriented, as if awakening from a dream and stared at him, noting that his face was now older, manlier. "The Marquess of Drayton?"

He looked at her sharply. "The courtesy title I had when my father was still alive." His eyes paused on

Hector. "He is the Marquess of Drayton now," the Duke said softly.

Lena covered her mouth with one hand as the realisation sank in that Hector, her Hecki, was, in fact, a lord. A marquess.

Oh dear.

"Is that all you remember?" the Duke pressed.

She gave a brief account of her memory, avoiding any mention of the emotions she had felt during the scene.

"It makes no sense at all. Being one and a half minutes faster than Garford? Who is Garford? And why were you faster? Whatever for?"

He rubbed his forehead. "Garford was a friend. It was a bit of a sport for us to race from our townhouse to White's, with others placing wagers on who would be faster. How peculiar, though." He knitted his brows together. "How could you have witnessed this? It must have been on Bond Street. What were you doing there? And if it involved Garford, it must have been decades ago, since he has long since moved to Ireland." He paused to calculate. "Hector. Help me with a basic mathematical problem to solve this conundrum."

The boy looked up, interested. "How?"

"If I ceased to be the Marquess of Drayton at the age of twenty-six, and your mother is nine years younger than me, how old was she then?"

"Twenty-six minus nine?" Hector stuck out the corner of his tongue as he calculated. "That is, er, sixteen."

"Seventeen. Your mother was at most seventeen years old during this event. Yet she mentions Garford, who moved to Ireland at twenty-four. He's my age. To narrow it down further, we can conclude this must have happened before he left for Ireland. How old would your mother have been then?"

Hector looked at him with incomprehension. "How should I know?"

"At most fifteen. Probably closer to fourteen." He turned to Lena. "That's a very early memory, indeed."

"Yes. Strange." She blinked at him, puzzled. "Why is it that I can seem to remember early memories and not later ones?" Her eyes widened as she suddenly understood. "Oh! It must have been my very first memory of you. The first time I saw you." She made a movement imitating him as he pulled out his pocket-watch. "This is why it made such an impression on me."

He knit his brows together. "While I remember the event of racing against Garford, I do not recall seeing you there."

"Well. I know somewhat more about young men by now. Would you have noticed a green girl standing in the middle of the road? We hadn't been introduced. I was one of many. I could have been anyone. I daresay you thought the same. You were with your friends and your mind was elsewhere." She knew immediately that it was true.

He was silent.

Hector scrambled out of his chair and ran out, hollering. "Theo, Les, Mona! Mama remembers him!"

The approaching footsteps heralded the children arriving in the room.

"How? What?"

"Do you remember anything else?" the Duke asked.

She thought for a moment, then shook her head. "Nothing." Not a single memory of their marriage. Try as she might, it would not come.

That troubled her.

"Never fear. I'll invent a device to make you remember," Les said. "Something to wear on your head that will stimulate your brain."

"Maybe you should see a doctor," Theo suggested. "A phrenologist even. Though I'm not entirely sure that field isn't a bag of moonshine. I don't think Papa thought highly of phrenologists."

"What does a phrenologist do?" asked Mona.

"He reads the shape of the skull and relates the bumps on the brain to mental abilities. It's not entirely scientific, but maybe he might have some suggestions on how to regain lost memories." Theo turned to the Duke. "Though I dare say you will play the most important role in prodding her memory. Do you have any objects that she might recognise?"

Once more he nodded. "I have already shown your mother a locket she gave me. It did not help her remember."

"Maybe you could recreate certain situations that might spur her memory on," Mona suggested. "They would have to be moments of significance. I don't know. Like a proposal? Or the wedding itself?"

"I'm certain that's not necessary," Lena intervened hastily. The last thing she wanted was to reenact their wedding to trigger her memory. How awkward would that be?

"I'll think of something," the Duke said.

Mona looked thoughtful. "Since it was the Duke's gestures which helped you to remember before, it is likely that the same might happen again. The best course of action is that Mama and the Duke spend as much time together as possible and repeat many of those things you did when you courted her, yes? This is the only way to jog your memory."

The Duke cleared his throat, his eyes flickering to Lena.

A blush crept up her neck. "Yes. I suppose you might be right." Not knowing where to look, she rubbed her neck and got up. "Well, there is much to do today. I have to meet Emma, and I must go to the market for flour. And eggs. And sugar. Though maybe not, I think there might still be some left in the pantry. Either way, I must see Emma." She realised she was rambling. "Children, make yourselves useful for the remaining afternoon." Without waiting for a response, she hurried from the room.

"Shouldn't he be going with you?" Theo called after her, but she'd already gone. "Strange, I thought we'd just agreed that you two ought to spend as much time together as possible." Then he shrugged. "Come boys, let's go see the military parade in the Prater. I hear the King of Prussia, the King of Denmark, Tsar Alexander, and our entire imperial family will be there."

"*Famos!*" The boys jumped up and scrambled out of the room.

Mona remained behind, sitting across from the Duke. Her eyes shone with determination as she leaned in closer. "Have you tried flowers yet?"

That evening, Lena sat at her desk, ready to pen her daily missive to Agent August. But tonight, her thoughts wandered, and her pen hovered aimlessly over the paper, splattering ink as she stared out of the window, her eyes unfocused.

Her mind was tangled. He wasn't the man she'd thought he was. Beneath that gruff, cold exterior lay a surprising kindness. She knew it for a fact. There was that look in his eyes, a fleeting softness that sent a flutter through her stomach every time she caught it. She wanted to understand him, get to know him, peel back the layers and discover the man he was beneath the facade.

She had been trying so hard to remember more, but the memories refused to surface. The only two memories she had of him were vivid, consistent and powerful in their emotions. The first was on St James's Street, where she had fallen hopelessly in love with him as an awkward fourteen-year old.

It must have been puppy love, of course. She'd been just a child. Lena pressed a hand to her heart. It still lingered there, echoes of powerful longing, the feverish sizzle in her blood. It left her breathless and agitated.

Then, later, the memory of holding the locket she had given him...as an engagement present.

They had been in a rose garden.

*Rose garden...*she scribbled involuntarily on the paper. Then, as if out of its own volition, her hand moved and wrote two more words.

She stared at them.

First kiss.

Where on earth had this come from?

Was the room hotter than it was before?

And what was that feeling again? Overpowering, overwhelming her.

Cedarwood and musk engulfed her.

It was true.

They must have kissed.

Lena's fingers wandered to her lips.

A dreaminess took hold of her, the same feverish sensation she'd felt as a fourteen-year-old.

Then she shook herself as if to free herself from the sensation. *You must compose yourself at once, Helena Arenheim,* she scolded herself. *These were mere memories. They were in the past. Things were quite different now.*

Besides, the rational part of her mind suggested of course they must have kissed. If they were married and Hector was truly his son, they must have done so much more than—merciful heavens!

Don't think about it, don't think about it!

Lena jumped to her feet and her chair fell backwards. She fluttered around her room, fanning herself.

Why hadn't this occurred to her earlier?

Of course they must have been fulfilling their conjugal duties. That was the natural course of things, established since Adam and Eve and the dawn of creation. No cause whatsoever for maidenly blushes and this cringing embarrassment that had taken hold of her.

It wasn't hot in the room; it was positively scorching.

She tore open the windows and dropped back into her chair, still fanning herself.

The Forgotten Duke

If only she could remember!

How utterly humiliating not to recall a single thing about the man with whom she must have shared the most intimate moments of a married couple's life.

She would never see the Duke in the same light again.

She drew in a sharp breath as an idea struck her.

No, she couldn't dare.

It was outrageous.

It was impossible.

She could never, ever do that.

Could she?

To see if it would jog her memory...

If only she had the courage...

To kiss him.

Chapter Twenty-One

THE BALL THE FOLLOWING EVENING COULDN'T HAVE been more different.

Metternich's Peace Ball was to be one of the grandest events of the Season. The rooms of the entire palais had been opened up. There were oriental tents and faux temples, a hot-air balloon and fireworks in the garden, and orchestras in every room and in hidden corners behind the hedges. There was a ballet, and people danced wherever there was space. The Arenheims were assigned to perform in a Turkish tent in the garden, which meant that the pianoforte had to be set up there.

Their performance went smoothly, as usual.

Lena had been worried that the Duke might be hovering nearby, scowling at them while they played, but fortunately, he was not. In fact, she hadn't seen him since they'd arrived, and as the night wore on, she began to wonder if he'd be putting in an appearance at all. It would be strange if he did not, with all the foreign dignitaries here. She'd learned to recognise them all by now and was eagerly soaking up the atmosphere of the place. There was so much information to take in. August would be pleased with her report that night.

They took a much-needed break, having played for hours. Adam had gone to organise some refreshments for them, and Theo had gone with Mona to have a look at the hot air balloon hovering above them on the other side of the garden.

Perhaps it was the mild night's breeze, unseasonable for October, or the scent of roses and Turkish Delight carried on silver platters by footmen.

Or maybe it was the hushed titter of two ladies deep in conversation, the sighs of, "You wouldn't believe the most beautiful trinket he gave me! Look. Isn't it exquisite? I had a locket made for him too. In London. At Garrard's in Albemarle Street. It is to be an expression of my sentiments, for I love him dearly…"

Lena gasped.

Images flashed in her inner eye. She was holding the commissioned locket that Mr Garrard had just given her, talking to her friend Elizabeth, who was with her in the shop.

Elizabeth! A vision of a pretty brunette appeared in her mind, who was smiling as she teased her. "Confess. You're head over heels in love with him already, aren't you? Yet you haven't exchanged two words with him. I can see it in your eyes, and in the way you blush, like you are doing now." She laughed softly. "Your cheeks have taken on the colour of beetroots."

She covered her cheeks with her hands. "He is so

dear to me. I love him so very, very much. Oh, Elizabeth. I am so happy! I cannot wait for us to be married."

"Lucky, lucky girl! Would that I, too, could marry for love."

The scene faded, and she remained standing beside by the hedge, staring foolishly at the little red lampion hanging from a branch.

That had been her. Her own words, her own voice saying, *"He is so dear to me. I love him so very, very much."* A wave of emotion so intense followed that it took her breath away. Was such happiness possible? Her stomach fluttered with the sensation of hundreds of butterflies. Her heart clenched deliciously as warmth spread from her chest encompassing her entire being, lingering and burning like golden embers.

Her knees grew weak as water.

Shaken, Lena dropped onto the small marble bench beside the hedge, her breath coming in uneven gasps.

There was no doubt about it.

She'd been madly, deeply in love with him.

This hadn't been a passing infatuation.

This had been a love as deep and profound as she was capable of. With every fibre of her being.

And now?

She blinked, disoriented, as she took in her surroundings once more.

Of course, that had been back then. That had been the memory of her being in love a very long time ago. She no longer felt like that.

Did she?

She'd heard of love that had died. Of love that had

run its course. Of love that petered out. Yet what about a love that was simply...forgotten?

What happened to that love? Where had it gone?

Did that love still exist somewhere? Did it continue to burn deep within the soul without the soul being aware of it, or had it simply fallen asleep, waiting to be awakened? Or was a love forgotten...simply gone? Vanished, puffed away like dandelions in the wind.

Lena did not know.

She'd loved him very dearly, once. She'd just now regained a glimpse of the memory of that love, but it had shaken her to the core.

She wanted, no, she had to find out if it was still there. She had to find the answer.

The sky above her exploded in a silvery shower of stars and light. She jumped and flinched at the loud explosion.

It was midnight.

The fireworks.

They were to wait until the fireworks were over, play for another hour, then they could go home.

He'd arrived late, having been detained by the Prussians who insisted on a conversation with him and Castlereagh on the future of Saxony.

There had been no movement on the matter at all.

After an hour of fruitless back-and-forth, he had excused himself to find Lena and the children.

Odd, how he'd come to feel so protective of them in such a short time. As if they really belonged to him.

"There you are, *mein Freund*," a very familiar, languid voice said behind him. "Hiding from diplomatic negotiators instead of facing them head-to-head on the battlefield, I mean, the ballroom."

Julius whirled around. A rare smile broke across his face as he saw the tall, lean figure of a man with golden curls resting against a precarious trellis of roses, arms crossed, and a mocking grin on his lips.

"Careful, Lindenstein, your weight will bring the structure down. It doesn't appear to be that sturdy." He grasped his arm and they embraced, slapping each other on the back like long-lost brothers. "I thought you were out of town. How refreshing to see a familiar face for a change, even if it is merely your hideous grimace."

"I was indeed out of town, enjoying myself tremendously with my ladybird. I was ordered back, most inconveniently, just when we'd reached a most critical juncture in our relationship. Been in a devil of a temper since. What can one do? Must obey the pater's order. Best to appease the old man, as we haven't been seeing eye to eye lately. You know how it is." He grinned at Julius. "*Verdammt*, it's good to see you here on my turf. It's about time. Must show you all my favourite haunts. Places hidden from prying eyes. Is Atherton here too?" He looked around. "Would be more fun if there were the three of us, even better with Hartenberg, the four of us together like the good old days."

"No. Was informed the other day that the marchioness has just given birth to a baby boy, so there is nothing in the world that would cause Atherton to currently leave England."

"Lucky devil. What about Hartenberg? Lady Evie? Aren't they supposed to get married?" He pointed his two forefingers at each other and twirled them around.

"It's complicated. Hartenberg's in Italy with his troops. Evie is visiting a friend in the country. She tired of the festivities already after a week."

"Understandable. I've had it up to here—" he drew a line at his head "—with all the fuss they make in Vienna these days." He grimaced. "It's only bound to get worse —" He interrupted himself as his eyes fixated at a spot behind him and his jaw slackened.

"Aldingbourne," he said weakly, "I'm really not well, you know. Am suffering here," he placed a hand over his heart, "from what I believe may be diagnosed as a particularly severe case of lovesickness. Because I am on terrible terms with the *pater familias*, I have been suffering from migraines and have been in a general, terrible sort of temper lately. Now it appears my mind and eyesight are sadly affected as well." He leaned forwards and squinted. "No, do not turn around, my friend." He clasped an iron grip on Julius's shoulder to prevent him from turning around. "But tonight the theory that ghosts indeed walk the earth has been proven correct. Either that, or I'm stark raving mad."

"If you are not well, sit down, and I shall fetch the physician."

"To the devil with the physician." Lindenstein closed his eyes, opened them again, blinked, and shook his head. "I am about to give you the shock of your life, dear friend. For over there, my eyes behold...Catherine. The ghost of your duchess."

Julius turned to see Lena standing next to the hedge, her eyes raised as she watched the last remnants of the fireworks flare up in the sky. A powerful emotion coursed through him, leaving him shaken. "Ah. You are not mad. It is a long and interesting story. It is indeed Catherine. Come and meet her."

HER EMOTIONS STILL IN A WHIRL, Lena stood by the hedge with clasped hands. She had to talk to him again. This time more honestly, about her feelings. That was difficult enough, but in her case, it was even more complicated because she had to talk about the memory of the feelings.

Was that thumping in her heart, that sizzling sensation, a mere memory, or was that what she truly felt for him now? Or was it simply because she thought it was what she *should* be feeling now?

She shook her head. Oh, how confused she was!

She was definitely overthinking it.

Best to find him and talk to him.

And say what exactly?

"Lena."

She jumped and looked up. Speak of the devil. The Duke was right over there, tall and handsome as sin in his evening clothes, walking straight towards her as if she'd conjured his presence just by thinking about him.

Beside him was a man, a golden-haired Adonis, staring at her as if he'd just seen a ghost. "But she looks like the image of Catherine." He reached out to touch her arm. "No ghost." His grip closed over her arm. "Most definitely not. This is very much solid flesh, if I'm not mistaken."

"Hands off, Lindenstein," the Duke growled. "She's still my wife, and I don't like people touching what's mine, even if you are my friend."

A shiver ran through her at these words. As if she really belonged to him.

"Wife? You truly are Catherine? Holy saints above in heaven. It is not an illusion? But how? Why?"

Lena looked at the Duke helplessly.

"Catherine, also known as Helena Arenheim. This dolt here is an old, dear friend of mine. He goes by the name of Lindenstein." He paused, then added softly, "You were once acquainted, too."

"Acquainted. Surely, we were more than that. Friends, weren't we? Are we still?" His hands went to his head. "Before you died. Which, it seems, you did not. Now she looks at me like she doesn't know me. I am confused."

The Duke gave a brief summary of what had happened—the accident, the amnesia, the chance meeting with the help of Evie.

Lindenstein collapsed on the marble bench. "What a story! It's a miracle. You truly do not remember him? Or me? Nothing at all?"

"Some of my earlier memories are returning in fragments, without rhyme or reason. I'm sorry, but no, I don't remember you." She shook her head regretfully.

"We need to discuss this further." He looked up and glanced at the ballroom entrance where several footmen were gathered, receiving instructions from the butler. He frowned in consternation. "But not now. They are looking for me. I must leave before they find me. We will talk. We will talk!" He pointed at Lena, nodded at the Duke, then disappeared between the boxwood hedges.

Lena found herself alone with the Duke. Suddenly shy, she forgot her resolve to talk to him. "I must go too." She turned to leave.

"Stay," he murmured, his hand reaching out to brush against hers, sending a shiver down her spine.

"But I have one more performance, and the others..." Her words trailed off as his grip tightened gently.

"Dance with me," he whispered, his voice husky. The strains of violins playing a waltz lingered in the air. The grip in his hand tightened ever so slightly, drawing her closer until she stood before him, their eyes locked. He placed his hand on the small of her back, a light pressure leading her into a slow turn.

They danced between the hedges, the night air thick with the scent of roses and the melody of the waltz. She was light on her feet, easily following his steps, humming softly to the tune.

As they danced, a memory washed over her, vivid and undeniable. A memory of another ballroom, and his arms holding her close. A memory of a heart overflowing with an almost painful joy.

She opened her eyes and met his gaze, a soft smile gracing her lips. In a sudden, sweet rush, she took his face in her hands and kissed him.

The dance stopped abruptly. He froze. Then, when she thought he wouldn't respond, he pulled her in, pressing her tightly against him, the warmth of his body enveloping her. A wave of comfort washed over her. It was all so familiar; him, the way he felt against her, the way he smelled.

Once more, a golden warmth blossomed in her chest, a flicker of something she thought had been extinguished. Could it be? Was the love she thought lost still glimmering deep inside her?

The realisation hit her, leaving her breathless.

He released her gently and stared back at her with an unfathomable expression in his eyes. A silent question hung heavy in the air.

He released her abruptly, stepping back as if the connection between them had never existed. "The Prussian and French delegations are waiting for me." The cool night air blew between them. "I have several meetings to attend before I can retire. I believe you mentioned you have one more performance."

His tone was stiff and formal. Lena shivered. Self-consciously, she smoothed her hands over her dress. "Yes." She glanced around, feeling disoriented. "The performance." She'd completely forgotten about that.

"We shall meet at home, then." He gave her a curt nod, turned and walked away, leaving Lena to stare after him.

SHE REPLAYED the kiss in her memory over and over again, wondering whether she had made a terrible mistake. She had wanted to see whether her memory had been true, so without thinking, she'd grabbed his face and kissed him. She'd been right about the kiss triggering memories. The locket, the rose garden, the ballroom, the dance, Elizabeth, their first kiss—oh! That kiss. It had all come rushing back to her, overwhelming her, while at the same time wrapping her in a feeling of homecoming after a long journey.

How could she have been so impulsive? The poor man had clearly been caught off guard and had had no idea what to do, so he'd kissed her back, out of politeness...Her entire body was burning with shame, and she felt like crawling into a mouse hole. No wonder he was all cold and polite afterwards. What must he think of her?

Lena paced in her room, waiting for the Duke's return two hours later. When she heard his footsteps in the corridor, she slipped out of the door and caught him just before he entered his bedroom.

"Lena." He nodded at her. He'd discarded his coat and tugged at this neckcloth.

"I know it's late, but I was wondering if we could have a moment to talk." She gestured helplessly.

He followed her into the parlour. The fire was still burning, and she stepped in front of it, rubbing her hands, although she was not at all cold.

"What do you want to talk about?" He rubbed his jaw. He looked pale and there was a strain about his eyes.

"About...earlier." *About the kiss*. She gave a quick shake of her head and rushed on. "I wanted to let you know that some memories have returned. It happened twice. Once, just before I met Lindenstein. And then when we waltzed." *When we kissed*.

He clasped his hands behind his back. His face showed no expression at all. "What did you remember?"

She rubbed her hand along the mantelpiece. "Earlier, I remembered the locket and a conversation I had with a friend in the jewellery shop where I had the locket made. I remembered Elizabeth."

He nodded. "Lady Wilton. She is married now and has three children."

Lena placed her hands on her cheeks. "Elizabeth—married! Of course she would be," she murmured more to herself. "She always wanted children. How glad I am for her!"

A smile trembled on her lips. "What I wanted to say, actually, was that I remembered a conversation we had and, and—" She stumbled over the words. She stepped forwards and resolutely took his hands. "I remembered that I was very fond of you." The last few words rushed out of her.

It was an understatement, but she couldn't bring the word 'love' over her lips. Did he understand? The echo of her confession hung heavily in the air.

When he remained silent, she looked up and saw his jaw was set in a grim line. "Are you certain that your memory was not deceiving you?" His words hung harshly between them.

Lena dropped her hands. "Deceiving? How so? It is predominantly the feelings that I seem to remember. I am certain my feelings do not lie."

He squared his shoulders, and he seemed to retreat within himself. It was as if he'd pulled up an invisible wall around him that she could not breach.

Turning slightly away, he said, "A word of advice. Do not put too much faith in the truth of your feelings. You may find them to be fickle, or worse, untrue."

She blinked. Before she could ask what he meant, he turned to the door. "If you will excuse me. It is late and I am rather tired." With that he left.

Lena remained behind.

What had that been about?

She rubbed her nose in confusion. She'd thought he would be glad that her memories were returning. Why did she have the feeling it was the opposite, that he did not want her to remember? She had almost, not quite, but close enough, declared that she loved him. 'Fond' wasn't nearly the same as 'love', but she'd summoned all her courage and told him that she remembered that she'd liked him.

Rather a lot.

So why did he have the demeanour of a man who had been told like the world had just ended?

Truth be told, his behaviour had changed since that moment they'd danced in the garden. Since she'd kissed him. When she'd looked at him and realised that her feelings were no longer forgotten.

She pressed a hand to her heart.

They were still there, those precious feelings.

Her eyes filled with tears, not because she was sad, but because she was endlessly relieved that she'd remembered her love for him.

But he had withdrawn immediately. As if shutters had closed inside him, creating an invisible barrier between them, leaving her utterly confused and a little hurt.

Why was he pulling away, and what was she supposed to do about it?

She snatched up the poker and thrust it into the glowing embers of the fireplace with a frustrated motion, sending a shower of sparks shooting upwards like tiny fireworks. She leaped back, avoiding the fiery spray.

Was that it? Was he retreating because he, too, was afraid of getting burned?

She dropped the poker with a clatter to the hearth and rubbed her eyes tiredly.

If only she could understand the man!

Chapter Twenty-Two

She seemed to be remembering only the happy memories. No doubt there had been those, too; those rare moments when she'd been happy.

Yet it would only be a matter of time before she remembered the other memories as well. When she had not been happy. Those had to be the overwhelming majority.

When they'd danced in the garden, that must have triggered one such memory. He should never have asked her to dance to begin with. He hadn't thought at all, which was unusual for him.

That kiss!

It had been so long ago since they'd kissed.

He'd acted purely on the impulse of the moment, out of the desire to feel her in his arms again. It had been one of those moments when all sense of time and place had been suspended. The air had been thick with unexpressed emotions, and he'd allowed himself to surrender to the moment.

A fatal decision.

He'd known it was a mistake when she'd raised her face to kiss him, her eyes brimming with the exact same expression Catherine had.

He hadn't understood it then. What a thick-headed dunderhead he must have been not to see that what had been in her eyes was love.

He understood it now.

An icy arrow of terror had shot through him.

Suddenly, she was no longer Lena, but Catherine, as she had been then. Catherine, with that look of adoration in her eyes. Catherine, whom he held in his arms.

She had always loved him.

He had loved her far too late.

She had left him.

And from then on, the whole tragedy had unfolded.

He realised with sudden clarity how foolish he had been to assume that giving her the locket and helping her to recover her memories would solve all their problems, when the opposite was true. They would unearth corpses that would best have been best left buried and forgotten. They would pick up right there where they'd left off, with all the pain and heartache and suffering.

She only remembered the happy memories now. How long would it take her to remember all the rest?

The temptation to give in to that sweet look had been too great. So, he'd distanced himself, physically and emotionally. The look of hurt confusion on her face had pained him.

But it was for the best, he told himself, running an agitated hand through his hair.

It was for the best.

FEELING a strong urge to get away from the Arenheims, he'd spent the whole day at Castlereagh's domicile, which pleased Lady Emily Castlereagh, who fluttered about him, filling his ears with anecdotes and detailed descriptions of what she had worn to the masked ball the night before. "The ladies wore regional costumes, to represent different countries. I believe the Duchess of Sagan woman wore a Carinthian costume, which did not suit her at all. It was very simple and, if you ask me, she looked like a peasant. I decided to opt for something different. Who do you think I finally decided to impersonate, Your Grace?"

Julius almost barked at her, "I haven't the damnedest idea." Instead, he pulled himself together and offered in measured tones, "As Boudicca, mayhap?"

Lady Castlereagh giggled, and the sound of her laughter grated on his nerves. "Oh no, but close! I decided to go as a vestal virgin. Everyone stared at me, admiring my beautiful and original costume."

"They were staring at my Order of the Garter which you had pinned to your chest," Castlereagh put in dryly. "No doubt people wondered why I would let you wear it on such an occasion." He looked at her with fond amusement. "But no more frivolous talk of balls and costumes. If you will excuse us, my lady, Aldingbourne and I must discuss the matters on the agenda for tomorrow's meeting with the Tsar."

Lady Castlereagh pouted, but Julius was relieved to change the subject.

He returned to the Arenheim home late that afternoon, exhausted and well aware that he had broken his agreement to spend the day with them. He'd needed to get away, needed time to think. Maybe he could renegotiate the whole arrangement before she remembered more and the entire sordid story came to light.

Maybe the right course of action was to bestow upon them a generous annuity and to just leave them be. His footsteps came to a slow halt and his hand froze as he reached out to open the front door of the Arenheim home as that thought sank in.

Leave Catherine to her new life and her new family.

Leave his son, Hector.

A dull pain in his chest told him he was too selfish to do that. He could never do it.

Thus, he entered the parlour with a thunderous frown on his forehead, and came to a halt at the entrance.

The scene he saw before him rendered him speechless.

An all too familiar gentleman sat on the sofa, legs crossed. A wisp of dark blond hair that escaped his receding hairline brushed across his high forehead. He was speaking to an attentive audience, his finger raised for emphasis. No doubt, this was one of his favourite pastimes, Julius noted sourly—to hear himself speak. Next to him was his audience: Lena, sitting rather close, indecently close, her skirt brushing his trouser leg, her hands folded, facing him and listening intently.

He entered quietly and closed the door without disturbing the couple.

"I beg of you, what am I to do, madam?" Metternich said mournfully and continued without waiting for an answer. "She will not receive me. She is either indisposed, or out walking or shopping. She won't even acknowledge my letters! And oh, the letters I've written! At least six hundred of them, if not more. I arranged the splendid feast last night only for her, you know. I had a special place made for her in a private nook, a trellis of roses surrounding us for privacy. I had those roses delivered all the way from Naples! Yet she managed to elude me all night. We exchanged no more than nine words, I counted them all: "Good evening, Your Highness," and "It is a beautiful night." Nine meagre words! I tell you. When I wanted to dance with her, she claimed her feet ached. I didn't sleep all night. In fact, I haven't slept for weeks." His pale face and dark rings under his eyes appeared to confirm this.

A gloomy shadow crossed his face. "But when it came to dancing with her former lover Prinz Alfred of Windischgraetz a moment later, her feet seemed perfectly fine."

Lena made a sympathetic noise.

"I beg you, madam. What does it mean? Does she not know how dearly, how passionately I love her? Does she not care? What am I to do?" He buried his head in his hands and sobbed.

Julius crossed his arms and leaned against the mantelpiece, suppressing a sigh. Metternich's unhappy love affair with Wilhelmine von Sagan was well known, and it was no secret that the duchess' interests lay elsewhere. The Prince had been pining for her quite publicly.

Lena made clucking noises and patted his arm in a motherly fashion. "Well, if you're asking my advice, Your Highness, here is what I think."

The Prince pulled out a handkerchief and dried the corners of his eyes. "I am all agog to hear what words of comfort a sensible, warm-hearted woman like you might have to soothe the pain in my heart."

She grimaced. "I am afraid it will have to be a bucket of ice water, Your Highness. It appears that the lady in question is simply not...how shall I put this delicately? She may find herself unable to reciprocate with the same emotional depth that you are experiencing."

He stared at her bleakly. "You are saying she doesn't love me."

"Well, um...er. The truth is...yes."

"But...why?"

Lena shook her head. "With all due respect, Your Highness, that's not the right question. The right question is why *your* affections are so involved with this lady, when, forgive me for saying so, but you are married, are you not?"

"To my Lorel, yes. She is a good woman and has been most patient with me." He pursed his lips. "I daresay she loves me most dearly. My children are a delight." His face brightened. "I sometimes suspect I missed my vocation when I went into politics and became Austria's foreign minister. I should have become a nanny instead. I would have been quite good at it, too. Whenever I can, I play with my children in the nursery. My family is my only joy in times like these."

Lena stared at him, aghast. "You have a loyal wife and wonderful children. Then why on earth are you hankering after a woman like the Duchess of Sagan, who not only does not return your affection, but chases after that good-for-nothing Prince Alfred?"

He looked at her sheepishly. "Because she is as beautiful as a goddess, intelligent, and wise. She is the unofficial hostess of this Congress. She says she no longer wants to be my mistress, hidden away shamefully in the shadows, but to take the place of my wife." A steep frown appeared on his forehead. "But divorce my Lorel? Never."

A strange look crossed Lena's face. She rubbed her head as if it pained her. "It's just...I don't know why I feel so passionate about this. It really is none of my business what you choose to do and who you choose to associate with, Your Highness. I really should not say anything at all about this, so forgive me for being so bold for voicing my opinion anyway. I feel very strongly that when you are married, you ought not fall in love with other women. You should not have mistresses at all. It's not right. The thought of it...it pains me. Here." She thumped her hand against her heart. "There. I've said it." She leaned back in her chair and blinked rapidly as if suppressing tears.

Julius clenched his hands so tightly his knuckles were white.

"What bourgeois sentiments you have." Metternich looked at her with concern when she did not reply. "My dear Mrs Arenheim. I have not upset you, have I? With all my silly talk. That was not my intention."

She pulled her mouth into a wobbly smile. "It is the way of the world, isn't it? I shall say no more on the matter." She had pulled out a handkerchief to wipe her nose when she looked up and her eyes met Julius's. "Oh!" She jumped. "When did you get here?"

"Aldingbourne." Metternich rose from the sofa. "When did you arrive? We didn't notice you there."

"Pardon my intrusion. You were so absorbed in your conversation with my wife that I was reluctant to interrupt." He pulled himself up stiffly. "I would have introduced you to my wife earlier, but I see you have forestalled me, as you seem to be acquainted already. Quite intimately too, if you are already seeking my wife's advice on matters of the heart." His voice had an edge of steel.

Lena looked at him with wide eyes. He'd said 'my wife' three times, hadn't he? Just to make sure to hammer the point home. A muscle jumped in his cheek. Julius bared his teeth at the Prince.

Metternich flicked a non-existent speck of dust away from his sleeve. "I came here to seek you out for a conversation of a more private nature, away from prying eyes and ears." He seemed oblivious to the irony that his well-oiled spy network was currently eavesdropping on all of Vienna and that he was the mastermind behind it all. "I found you away, but your charming wife was here to keep me company instead. She is not only beautiful, but an excellent conversationalist and has been giving me the

The Forgotten Duke

best of advice." He lifted her hand and kissed it. "I shall take your words to heart, madam."

She nodded. "I hope you do." Looking at Julius, she asked, "I will see that you are not disturbed. Would you like some coffee and biscuits?"

"Thank you, but no. His Highness is a busy man. I am certain he will have to leave imminently." Julius declined the offer with a motion of his hand.

"Yes, please." Metternich sat down again and crossed his legs. "Coffee and biscuits would be most agreeable. Now, Aldingbourne. As to what I wanted to discuss with you. What the devil are we to do about the Tsar?"

Chapter Twenty-Three

For several days that followed, the Duke was seldom at home, as though he'd forgotten his agreement with the Arenheim family. He no longer joined them for breakfast and supper, always claiming to have important meetings. Lena had no doubt that this was true, but she suspected there was more to it. It was rather more likely that he was deliberately avoiding her. He had retreated behind the aloof mask of the distant, unapproachable Duke once more.

Just as Lena had resigned herself to the notion that it had all been for naught and that their experiment had failed miserably, out of the blue things shifted once more. Suddenly, he showed her a completely different side of himself that she hadn't seen before.

It was, quite frankly, maddening.

But she couldn't make herself be cross at him. It seemed he was making a considerable effort to bond with Hector. That much was clear. He studied arithmetic and history with the boy, took him for walks, and talked to him whenever possible. Hector had let go of his initial suspicion of him, and it appeared that, even though he might not yet be fond of him, he had come to accept him.

Then, one evening, the Duke returned with a kite.

A kite!

"They were selling them at the market. I thought the boys might like it," he said almost bashfully. "Shall we try it?" He held it out to Hector. "The weather is sufficiently blustery outside today." He left with Hector and Les, heading to the meadow by the river, and from her kitchen window Lena watched the three of them try to get the kite up in the air, which wasn't so easy at first.

Then there was the time when he came back from a walk with Hector, carrying a basket full of roasted chestnuts.

"Good heavens, did you bring home the seller's entire stock?" Lena asked.

"I did, indeed," he replied, looking rather pleased.

Lena placed her hands on her hips. "But I thought we'd agreed that you wouldn't use your money to buy us anything."

"He didn't," Hector put in.

"It was hard-earned, in fact," the Duke explained.

"How so?" Had he finally discovered that working wasn't such a terrible thing after all?

"He saved the chestnut lady's little daughter from a carriage that almost ran her over, and as a thank you, she gave him the whole basket. May I have one?" Hector didn't wait for an answer and helped himself to one.

The Duke made no comment, but quietly peeled a chestnut and popped it into his mouth.

The man really was a mystery.

Then there was the episode when she'd struggled to hang up the sheets in the courtyard. The wind kept blowing the wet cloth into her face, and it was a chore to attach it to the string hanging in the yard.

When her neighbour called, she'd left them in the basket to hang them up later.

When she returned, all the sheets were gently flapping in the breeze.

No one had done it.

Hector and Les were out playing with their kite, Theo napping, and Mona was practising her viola. The Duke, whose bedroom window overlooked the yard and who might have observed her struggling with the sheets, said nothing when she demanded at suppertime who it had been.

A duke? Hang up laundry? Lena shook her head. What nonsense. He would never stoop so low as to hang laundry. It was unheard of.

"Maybe it was a *Wichtelmännchen*, Mama," Hector said as he slathered a piece of black bread with butter and bit into it. Those little mythical creatures who did good deeds in the house when no one was looking.

Since it couldn't have been the Duke, it must have been those little helpers, indeed.

Yes, things had shifted quite drastically with the Duke. He no longer missed breakfasts or suppers and now he was around the house far more often than Lena would have preferred. He seemed to fill every room he entered, and she found it nearly impossible to focus on her tasks whenever he was near. The memory of the kiss still lingered between them, yet neither of them ever mentioned it. Sometimes she wondered if she had imagined it altogether.

It was most maddening, indeed.

Then there was Theo.

He deposited a container in the middle of the table while they were having dinner.

It was a glass jar with a suspicious brown liquid in it and a shrivelled object floating eerily inside.

Everyone screeched.

Even the Duke dropped his spoon into his soup with a splash. "By all the saints."

Lena nearly dropped the soup tureen she'd been holding and only held on to it at the last moment.

"Theseus Arenheim, what is this hideous thing that you have planted in front of us?"

"A hand." He smirked. "From a corpse."

Hector mimicked the motion of vomiting into his soup bowl.

Les pushed his spectacles further up his nose and leaned forwards to study the body part with interest. "*Famos*. Did you cut it off yourself?"

"Theo, that is the most revolting thing I have ever seen in my entire life!" Mona exclaimed. "Take it away at once!"

"Why? What's so revolting about a hand? Most of us have one." Theo lifted his hand as if playing an imaginary violin. "Do you know how many veins we have in our hands? Hundreds," he announced with satisfaction, without waiting for an answer. "A complex network of deep and superficial veins. This particular specimen, a donation, I might add, allows us to study it in great detail. We had the most interesting anatomy lesson with Professor Barth today. I am almost convinced that I want to specialise in this field myself."

"What other body parts did you study?" Les asked.

"Legs." Theo grinned. "It was a male leg, in case it matters."

"I wonder, if it had been a female leg, if it would have come complete with stockings on," Mona mused aloud. "Would you have had to take them off before cutting into it, I wonder? Considering you are all men, I mean."

"Harmonia!" Lena groaned. Not only was the topic of conversation scandalously inappropriate, but they were talking about undressing a woman's legs. Whether it was a corpse's or a living woman's leg, with or without stockings, it simply wasn't the thing to discuss at supper. What must the Duke think? Not to mention the children's behaviour...

Hector propped himself up on both elbows as he slurped his soup, Les abandoned cutlery altogether and drank straight from the bowl; Theo had brought in a piece of a corpse, which now sat on their supper table between the soup tureen and the milk jar. Then Mona insisted on talking about women's legs, of all topics. Lena hardly dared to look at the Duke. He hadn't said a word all evening aside from the shocked expletive he'd uttered earlier, but impassively proceeded to eat his soup, which was overly salted, as usual.

Rubbing her eyebrow, she desperately sought to change the subject, but Mona intercepted her. "It is a legitimate question, Mama, considering the price of stockings these days. It would be a shame to ruin them by cutting into them."

She had a point.

"To answer your question, naturally the bodies are first stripped of their clothing." Worse and worse. Theo prepared to describe the intricate process of undressing a corpse in minute detail. "Now. As for female bodies. Most come in naked—"

"Theo!" Lena shrieked.

"What?"

"You can't talk about that now."

"Why not?"

She leaned forwards and hissed with a sideways glance at the Duke. "In case you've forgotten, we have a duke sitting at our table."

Theo dismissed him. "Oh, him. I don't think he'll mind."

One of the Duke's eyebrows lifted. "I am still sitting here," he observed, but no one heeded him.

Lena's mind worked feverishly. Stockings. Price. A better subject than naked female bodies, dead or otherwise. Lena jumped on it. "It's true. Stockings are horribly expensive," she babbled before Theo could continue his elocution on naked female corpses. "I was looking at the shop window of Schönberger's the other day. There was a lovely pink pair with such pretty embroidery. I wanted to buy them, but..." She sighed. "You cannot imagine how much they cost. I was so shocked, I nearly dropped the violin." She looked around to make sure she had their attention. "Guess how much they wanted for a pair of pink silk stockings? The winner gets an extra helping of *Apfelstrudel*." It was a game they sometimes played.

The children enthusiastically jumped at the opportunity. The distraction worked. Lena sighed with relief.

"Five *Gulden*?" Hector offered.

"Eleven," suggested Les.

"Nineteen?" Mona said.

"Since we are talking about a purveyor to court," Theo said, "I assume a pair of embroidered silk stockings might cost more than that. I say twenty-nine."

All heads turned to the Duke.

He folded his arms across his chest. "I say less. Twenty-five."

Lena wondered, fleetingly, if he'd ever gone shopping and knew the price of stockings, and if his lower number was to let Theo win. If so, it was inordinately kind of him. She flashed him a quick smile. "Fifty. Fifty *Gulden* for a pair of silly stockings. Isn't that price shamelessly exorbitant?"

Theo whistled.

Mona shrieked.

Hector and Les grumbled.

"Good brother that I am, I'll share the *Apfelstrudel* with you, never fear," Theo said, satisfied that he had won that round.

"You may not collect your prize until you have removed that body part from the table," Lena insisted. "It's robbing me of my appetite."

Theo did so promptly.

"Well, this has been a most...enlightening evening,"

the Duke murmured after they had finished supper. "If you will excuse me. I have some work to do."

Lena fiddled with the cords of her apron. "I'll see that you're not disturbed by my brood of barbarians. You must think we have no manners at all, discussing female body parts and legs—" She floundered hopelessly, succumbing to an embarrassed coughing fit. "Your Gr—that is, of course, Julius."

Then something incredible happened, leaving Lena completely stunned.

The corners of his mouth turned up, and the cold steel in his eyes melted to liquid silver as they looked at her appreciatively.

The Duke of Aldingbourne smiled.

Chapter Twenty-Four

THE DUKE WAS NOT AT HOME. EARLIER, HE'D mentioned needing to return to the town to meet with Castlereagh and the British delegation for an important meeting. He had seemed apologetic and reluctant to leave.

A courier had arrived later, delivering a dispatch into her hands, which she found strange.

"You must deliver this to him personally," the courier urged.

She turned the packet over in her hands, wondering what it could be. Normally, his mail was handled by his secretary.

Deciding to leave the packet in his room, she knocked on the door, just in case he was inside. When no one answered, she went inside.

The room no longer felt like Simon's. The Duke had been staying there for some time now, and his presence was palpable—his books, his clothes, his essence seemed to fill every corner. Considering that he had to fend for himself without any servants to tend to him or clean his room, it was surprisingly orderly. The bed was neatly made, and a few personal items were arranged carefully on top of the bureau. A small stack of books lay by his bedside. Curious, Lena picked one of them up.

So the Duke read in bed. Interesting.

'The Conduct of the Great Negociation at the Treaty of the Pyrenees' by William Temple. No surprise that his reading matter would be a dull treatise on diplomacy. It would certainly put him to sleep quickly. She picked up the other book, which was titled 'Pride and Prejudice, by the Author of Sense and Sensibility, Vol I.'

She flipped through the pages. This was an actual novel, light and satirical, certainly not the kind of thing she'd expected from a Duke.

She turned the volume in her hands and fleetingly wondered what the book was about before she put it back.

Her eyes travelled through the room and landed at the dressing table on a small flask with the name of the perfumer Floris on it.

She unstopped it, closed her eyes, and inhaled deeply.

Cedar and musk filled her nose.

It filled her senses, flooding her with warmth, a painful yearning that was almost unbearable. Tears welled up as she gripped the furniture to steady herself, her breath coming in quick, shallow gasps.

Her hand shook as she replaced the stopper on the flask. In doing so, she accidentally brushed a small pile of books and letters, causing them to tumble to the ground.

She bent to pick them up, her fingers closing around a small leather journal.

Flipping through it, she immediately recognised the handwriting.

She stared at it. Why did he have this? Why was it here? Had he read it?

Of course he had.

Turning it in her hands, she realised that there was no need for her to read it.

Not anymore.

With deliberate care, she placed the notebook back on the table and rearranged the letters as they had been before.

Oddly her movements were calm now. Even odder was the sense of calm settling within her, as if something had clicked into place.

She walked over to the window and stared out as raindrops slid down the glass.

THAT DAY, she'd gone to the dressmaker. Not because she needed more gowns, but simply because there was nothing else to do, and her friend Elizabeth had asked her to accompany her. The bell had rung and a tall woman in a carmine walking dress had entered, lifting her skirts as she gingerly stepped over the threshold to reveal a delicately booted foot.

Elizabeth gasped when she saw her. "Good heavens."

Catherine blinked at her in confusion. "What is it, Elizabeth?"

"Nothing," Elizabeth said urgently, grabbing Catherine's arm and leading her further into the shop. "Here, look at this fabric. Isn't it beautiful?"

But Catherine had turned to look at the woman. Her dark hair tumbled around a narrow, elfin face, and her eyes were limpid and blue. She wasn't beautiful, she was breathtakingly stunning. "Who is she?"

"No one. No one at all. Look at this silk. Isn't it exquisite?" Elizabeth thrust a bolt of yellow silk under her nose.

The woman caught sight of them and ran her gaze down Catherine, sizing her up. Sneering slightly, she turned to the shopkeeper and said, "So this is who he's married. A little green girl, none too pretty."

Catherine froze, shocked at the stranger's rudeness. No one had ever dared speak about her like that in her hearing.

"Don't listen," Elizabeth whispered, placing her hands over Catherine's ears. "Don't look. She'll be gone soon."

The woman had cast one last sly smile at Catherine before sweeping out of the shop.

"Did you see her? Isn't she utterly gorgeous?" another customer, a buxom lady in a purple walking dress, said in a loud, strident voice to her companion. "Violetta Allan. The famous opera dancer. She's the Duke of Aldingbourne's mistress. He is said to be madly in love with her..."

The blood drained from Catherine's face. "It's not true, is it?" she whispered to Elizabeth, who was shaking her head vehemently.

"Lies, lies, all lies."

But the strained expression on her face told Catherine that it was true.

Later, as they rode back to Aldingbourne Hall, Catherine stared out of the window, unseeing, the raindrops pattering on the glass. "Does everyone know?" she'd asked in a flat, monotone voice.

"No, of course not." Elizabeth did not meet her eyes.

"Please, Elizabeth. *You* knew."

Elizabeth winced.

"Since when?"

Elizabeth dropped her head. "It is well known that Miss Allan is his mistress," she finally admitted. "She has been for quite some time."

Catherine's gloved fingers toyed with the strings of her reticule, tying them tightly around her finger until it hurt.

"I see."

Elizabeth hesitated before speaking again. "It is, of course, perfectly normal for men like the Duke to have mistresses." She made a helpless gesture. "Horrible as it is. We are expected to look the other way and pretend not to know."

"Yes," Catherine replied, her voice wooden. "I know."

Elizabeth shifted uncomfortably before taking Catherine's hand. "I am so sorry," she whispered.

There was nothing to say to that.

The carriage turned into a wide alley and Aldingbourne Hall came into view—tall, stately, and cold.

"But if my husband were ever to have a mistress, I wouldn't stand for it," Elizabeth suddenly burst out.

"No, you wouldn't," Catherine echoed. Then she looked sadly at Elizabeth. "But what if he loved her more than you? What then?"

Elizabeth's shoulders slumped. "I don't know. I don't think I could bear it."

Catherine nodded slowly.

Neither could she.

Chapter Twenty-Five

It was most confounding.

He'd been determined to put some distance between them but found it impossible.

She was constantly on his mind. Not the Catherine of old, the pale, silent creature who had drifted through Aldingbourne Hall like a sad ghost, but the lively, untidy Lena who constantly talked and laughed and had stains on her washed-out gown and who couldn't stay still for one moment.

When she spoke, he couldn't tear his eyes off the expressiveness of her face, the way her lips moved, how her eyes crinkled at the corners. The way her hips swayed sent a flush of heat through his body. And when she did the most incredible things he'd never imagined the Duchess Catherine was capable of, like cooking, baking, sweeping the floor and hanging out the laundry and darning socks, he found himself unable to tear his gaze away.

Who was this woman?

From his bedroom window, he'd watched with amusement how she'd wrestled with the heavy, wet sheets in the courtyard earlier. She'd pulled her sleeves up to the elbows, revealing bare arms, arching to stretch her back as she wiped loose strands from her forehead. Suddenly, he'd felt the urge to kiss her again, to press her against him and devour her lips.

That kiss at the ball had been too sudden, too swift, and too short.

It left him confused.

What was even more confounding was that that urge hadn't left him since.

Then, he saw her throw the sheets back into the basket and leave, no doubt having been called by one of the children.

Without thinking, he'd gone downstairs and hung up the sheets.

It hadn't been an easy task, but since he was taller, he had been able to reach the rope more easily than she had.

He'd suppressed a smile seeing the look of bafflement on her face when she'd returned to find the job done.

And now...he was sitting in the carriage returning to the Arenheim home, staring in consternation at the slim package on his lap. What devil had driven him to spend the greater part of the morning in that stocking shop, wading through countless stockings—women's stockings, mind you, not men's—trying to find that one particular pink pair she'd wanted so much?

Of course they no longer had it.

The shopkeeper had nearly despaired. He'd pulled out every single pair of stockings he had in stock, but it wasn't the one. Then the man had hit on the idea of sending a footman to the workshop where they were made to obtain a pair.

While he'd been waiting, he'd picked out four more. One in pale blue, one in light violet, and one in cream with golden embroidery. Then a pair for the girl, Mona, in pastel yellow, so it didn't seem quite so obvious that he'd gone out of his way to buy stockings only for Lena.

With all these stockings on his lap, Julius wondered if he'd lost his mind. It wasn't the first time he'd been prompted to do something completely out of character ever since joining the Arenheim family.

The other day, for example, he'd gone out to fly a kite with Hector and Achilles.

Once again, what devil had made him buy one in the first place? It hadn't been a very good kite, either, just a cheap one made of thin, blue paper.

Seeing the boys' eyes light up had been worth it.

They'd gone to the meadow by the river, and Julius had watched in amusement for a good hour as the boys had tried to get the kite to fly. After he'd helped them and it was up and flying, Julius had felt a sense of...satisfaction and contentment. He hadn't felt that sense of satisfaction that intense in any of the successful diplomatic negotiations that had gone his way.

He, content?

That was a feeling completely foreign to him.

Then a strong gust of wind had come up, and the kite had soared higher, tangling itself in the branches of an oak tree.

He still could not reconstruct the exact events of how he had ended up climbing that tree to retrieve the kite.

He still couldn't believe he'd actually climbed a tree.

He hadn't done so since he was Hector's age.

But he'd done it. It was with great satisfaction that he'd handed the kite to Hector, who'd looked at him with a whole new look in his eyes. "You don't seem to be a bad sort after all," his son had said, with a tone of grudging respect in his voice.

He'd been speechless.

His son now saw him in a completely different kind of light.

His son. He'd looked down at the child, seen his tongue protruding from the corner of his mouth as he rolled up the string, his hair dishevelled, so much like him, and he'd felt, for the first time, a painful squeezing in the region of his heart and an inexplicable desire to see that light in the child's eyes again.

For the first time in his existence, Julius, Duke of Aldingbourne, wanted to be a father. Not just any father, but a good one. He'd wanted to be the father he himself never had.

And this realisation shook him to the core.

He was feeling altogether too much, he decided, as the carriage drew up in front of the Arenheim home.

He wasn't sure how to take that.

As Lena stepped into the hall to greet him, his heartbeat increased.

She wore a pale green muslin gown, and her hair was

tied back in a loose chignon, with strands of soft hair escaping from it. He watched her lips, and indeed, she pursed them to blow away the strands of hair, as she always did.

He swallowed.

She gave him a strained smile.

"I was in town." It was an obvious thing to say, but all his diplomatic eloquence had left him, and for the life of him, he couldn't come up with anything better. "I brought you this." He handed over the box.

She cocked her head inquisitively, then her eyes widened. "Never say. Stockings?"

He cleared his throat. "I thought they were needed."

She opened the box and stared at the contents. "And there is a pink pair, too..." she murmured more to herself. When she looked up, her eyes were bright.

He looked away. Was she crying? Dash it.

"It's merely stockings," he said gruffly. "Nothing special."

"They must have cost a fortune. I thought we agreed —" She interrupted herself, gave a quick shake of her head as if she'd changed her mind about what she was going to say, then merely whispered, "Thank you."

"The yellow pair is for Mona."

"She'll love them."

Why was she standing there, staring at him with that odd look in her eyes? He couldn't quite interpret it. It felt as though she was assessing, judging him. He shifted his weight from one foot to the other.

"Thank you, Julius. This was very thoughtful of you."

Every time she said his name, a flush of pleasure ran through him.

He gave a curt, embarrassed nod.

"There's a visitor in the drawing room," she continued. "Waiting for you."

"Not Metternich again?"

She shook her head. "Come and see."

Chapter Twenty-Six

THE GOLDEN-HAIRED ADONIS WHOM SHE'D MET AT the ball had arrived without warning and made himself at home in her drawing room. The children were out, as was the Duke, and Lena, still reeling from her newfound memories, was at a loss as to what to do with him.

He'd thrown his stick on the sofa, peeled off his gloves, tugged at his neckcloth, and collapsed into the armchair in front of the fireplace with a groan. She frowned as their eyes met.

"Join me, Catherine," he'd begged. "Regardless of whether you remember me or not. I am in need of a friend. I am at my wits' end. What am I to do?" He buried his head in his hands.

"First of all, coffee." She'd brought in a tray and handed him a cup. "Now, tell me everything."

And he had.

"I have fallen in love with someone whom I am not supposed to love," he confessed. "It is a great secret that I have carried around with me like a millstone around my neck." He gave another tug at his neckcloth. "It's suffocating me not to be able to talk about it."

"There is nothing wrong with loving someone," Lena had countered. "Most of us do at some point in our lives, I dare say."

"Yes. But I am not 'most of you'." He leaned back his head back against the armchair.

"What exactly does that mean?"

He hadn't answered, but merely sighed a sigh that seemed to come from the depths of his tortured being. "It means that some of us can't love the way the rest of humanity does." He stared morosely into the fire.

She tilted her head with a frown. "You can't love like the rest of humanity? That doesn't make any sense at all."

"Shouldn't," he amended. "Maybe the correct word is 'shouldn't.'"

She shook her head. "Equally nonsensical."

"I am in love. With a girl." His teeth worried at his bottom lip. "She is the granddaughter of a mathematician and scholar of natural philosophy. He's an Englishman who through some quirk of fate ended up living in Austria. Far up in the Alps, where fox and hare say goodnight to each other, like we say in German."

Lena bent forwards, listening intently. "Yes? But that sounds charming."

"Charming?" He tore his eyes open in horror. "She is outrageous. She dresses like a boy. Her hair is short. She's not beautiful. She spends more time in the stables than in the house and carries with her a whiff of manure everywhere she goes. She has straw in her hair. She eats with her fingers. She has a heart bigger than the universe, an intelligence that rivals her grandfather's, and she is better at arithmetic than I am. She weeps when she sees a dead fly. She is kind to a fault and altogether wonderful, and I want to marry her." He stared at Lena with horrified eyes. "By Apollo. I didn't just say this out loud, did I?"

Lena smiled serenely and folded her hands. "Like I said, she sounds charming. I think you should marry her. Does she love you?"

"Heavens, no." His shoulders slumped. "She thinks I am a good-for-nothing dandy and a rake who is incapable of putting two sentences together, which might actually be true, come to think of it. She hates me. Which is probably for the best." He heaved a sigh.

"Well then, I suppose you'll have to woo her."

He shook his head. "There is no time. Besides, if word ever got out that I'm courting an English mathematician's daughter..." He suppressed a shudder.

Lena frowned. "I don't understand. Is she socially inferior to you?"

Lindenstein opened his mouth to answer, when there was some banging outside, and the boys stumbled into the room.

"You won't believe what just happened, Mama," Hector said breathlessly. "We saw the Tsar ride by in the Prater, and he waved at me!" He stopped short when he saw Lindenstein. "Oh!"

"Not only that," Les said, stumbling in right behind him, "we also saw—oh!"

Theo came in. "You won't believe who we just saw—oh!"

The three boys stood in the room, mouths agape.

"Mama?" Lindenstein got up from his chair and looked at Lena with raised brows. "Did I understand them correctly?"

Hector pointed his finger at him. "He—he—he—is…"

Les took his spectacles off and cleaned them on his shirt, put them back on and proceeded to stare at him with owlish eyes.

"Are you who I think you are, or are you who I think you might be, but are not?" Theo demanded.

Lena blinked, confused. "Who do you mean, Theo?"

"He is—" Theo began.

"No one. No one at all," Lindenstein interrupted hastily, waving his hand in denial. "I'm definitely not who you think I am. That is completely out of the question. I am no one. A complete nonentity."

"Are you sure?" piped up Les, staring at him with his head tilted sideways.

"Absolutely. Unquestionably."

"Because I thought I just saw someone who looked remarkably like you riding with Emperor Francis at the parade of the emperors—but you are right, it must be a figment of my imagination, a trick of the mind." Theo continued to stare at him with bulging eyes. "I must most definitely be wrong. Members of the imperial family don't just turn up in our cramped little drawing room and drink coffee with Mama as though they'd been best friends for ten years or more." Theo collapsed into the chair as though his knees would give way.

"You are absolutely correct. They would never in their wildest dreams think of doing that, they would never stoop so low, they are far too proud and arrogant to do so; so let us all agree that I can't possibly be who you think I am." Lindenstein crossed his arms over his chest.

Lena looked from one to the other, a puzzled frown on her forehead. "I have no idea who you are talking about, Theo. This is Lindenstein. An old friend—of, er, the Duke of course."

Lindenstein pointed his fingers at the three boys who were still gaping at him. "And these are your sons? My arithmetic may be bad, but I don't think it's that bad. How can you be his mother? You would have been about five or six years old to give birth to that one." He pointed at Theo.

Theo jumped up again and made a crooked bow. "Allow me, Your Imperial Highn—"

Lindenstein broke out into a loud coughing fit, drowning out Theo's words.

"Theophil Arenheim is my name, son of Doctor Simon Arenheim, musician and keen student of medicine. Helena Arenheim is our chosen mother. That rascal over there is Hector Arenheim, and the one with the glasses and the hair like a hedgehog is Achilles. Make your bows," he hissed to the boys, who followed suit and bowed crookedly.

Lindenstein waved them away. "Yes, yes, no need to bow. There is no need for ceremony. Back to what really matters." He turned to Lena. "How did you become their mother?"

"It's because Mama has lost her memory, you see," Les explained.

"That explains everything, of course." Lindenstein

nodded solemnly as though all was crystal clear. Theo told him the story.

"I vow, the drama in this household is more interesting than anything they could put on in the Burgtheater. Fascinating! Catherine, who is now the fair Helena. Poor Aldingbourne." He shook his head. "I suppose that explains why he's been beside himself lately."

Lena perked up. "He has? In what way?"

"He seems rather distracted. Aldingbourne and distracted! I never thought I'd say those two words in the same sentence, but there it is. Watching him work is painful. He sits down, reads for five minutes, jumps up, paces, sits down again, jumps up again…it is extremely tiring. I immediately suspected it was a woman." Lindenstein grinned at Lena. "But when I dared to suggest it to him, he nearly tore off my head. Say, what have you got there?" He walked over to Les, who'd pulled out a handful of marbles and started playing on the carpet. "I haven't played marbles since I was your age." There was a note of longing in his voice. "May I join you?" He dropped to his knees beside the boy.

"Yes, but no cheating." Les told him severely.

"What, me? I never cheat," Lindenstein said, and promptly started to cheat. Hector and Theo joined in and soon everyone was crawling on the floor.

Lena shook her head and stepped out to bring some more fresh chicory coffee.

Just then, the Duke returned and handed her the stockings.

"Well met, Aldingbourne," Lindenstein said cheerfully as he snapped a marble with two fingers, but it missed its target. He groaned as the boys cheered. "I seem to have lost. Would you care to join us for another round?"

Aldingbourne demurred. "Why are you here?"

"To visit your lovely wife." Lindenstein stood and dusted his trousers. "And to meet your children." He grinned. "They are your children now, aren't they? Lucky fellow."

Lena's gaze snapped over to the Duke, but he neither confirmed nor denied the statement, instead proceeding to busy himself with pouring a glass of wine from the decanter on the sideboard. "A drink, Lindenstein?"

The children played another round of marbles while the men sat in front of the fireplace discussing the political topic of the day. Theo sat between them, flushed with happiness to be included in their debate.

She watched the three men, absorbed in their conversation. The light from the fire reflected in the Duke's hair with golden-orange glints. As he spoke, his face moved in animation, a slight smile crossing it as he watched Hector, his face softening.

She made up her mind not to tell him.

It was simply better that way.

As if sensing her observation, he looked up and their gazes locked. He raised an inquisitive eyebrow. Her stomach flipped. A very old, very familiar shyness crept over her.

In the past, she would have blushed and looked away and spent the remaining evening in a corner, blindly plunging her needle into a piece of embroidery, yearning to talk to him but being afraid to.

No.

She was no longer that Catherine.

She was Lena now.

And Lena did what she wanted.

So, she allowed her mouth to curve upwards into a smile as she stood up and stepped towards the men.

They rose from their chairs when she approached, and she waved her hand. "Don't let me disturb you." Lindenstein offered her his chair, but she pulled another one forwards. "I prefer to sit here. Now tell me all the political gossip in great detail so I can pass it on to Metternich's secret police."

Theo nearly spat out his wine. Lindenstein roared with laughter, and an appreciative glint lit up the Duke's eyes.

Lena patted her skirt. "It is not a joke, you see. I was approached by an agent, and I agreed to spy for them on the condition that he acquired us commissions for musical performances. That is the agreement." She looked at the Duke apologetically. "I hope you understand that it is nothing personal."

The gleam of amusement in the Duke's eyes died. "In truth, now. You were spying on me?"

"Of course. I have specific instructions to report everything you say and do to Agent August, as he is called. I tell him everything. Absolutely everything. That you prefer to drink your coffee with two lumps of sugar, but no milk. That you were wearing a dark blue coat and grey breeches yesterday, and that your stockings were very fine and matched your outfit." Lena hoped that her flippancy would serve to lighten up the situation. The icy

The Forgotten Duke

look of fury in his eyes said that he was anything but amused.

Lindenstein, however, crowed with delight and slapped his hand on his thigh. "She is wonderful. Truly wonderful! I vow, if you weren't already married, I would marry you myself."

"No, you wouldn't, because you already have a girl waiting for you to marry. I expect an invitation to the wedding." Lena glanced at the Duke, whose face was still thunderous.

"Lighten up, my friend." Lindenstein patted him on the shoulder. "Everyone is into it, high and low. So what if one's own wife dabbles in a bit of harmless espionage? It's quite the rage these days, so you might as well get accustomed to it."

"Did you tell them anything of political significance?" he bit out.

"Of course." She stuck her nose in the air. "I am an excellent spy, you see. I told them, word-by-word, in the most exact manner, the conversation you had the other day. With Metternich."

Lindenstein laughed so hard he cried. "That's priceless! Oh, well done!"

"And tonight I shall do the same." She nodded to herself. "It will be a very long report, indeed. There is so much to tell! There will be a full description of the stockings you bought for me, and of Lindenstein playing marbles with the boys. It is a most pertinent piece of intelligence that Metternich must be informed of. As for politics, I have a shockingly terrible memory when it comes to names, and I sometimes tend to mix up things quite accidentally, of course. It is possible that I will write that you expect the British delegation, headed by Talleyrand, to be in unanimous agreement with the Prussians, headed by Castlereagh, and that Tsar Nesselrode of the French delegation wants to remain friends with the Austrian Emperor Wellington."

"In other words, you will write such a farrago of nonsense that they will not be able to make head or tail of it." Lindenstein grinned.

Lena folded her hands in her lap. "We understand each other perfectly."

The Duke did not smile, but the sternness on his face and the tension in his shoulders had marginally eased.

Lindenstein rose. "Well. I must say this has been one of the most entertaining evenings I've had in a long time." He shook hands with the children, who gazed at him in awe, and bowed over Lena's hand.

After the gentlemen had left, Lena turned to the boys. "And now. Tell me. Who *is* he?"

THE DUKE STEPPED out with Lindenstein and escorted him to his carriage.

"How are you coping with the situation, old friend?" Lindenstein asked abruptly. "And I don't mean the Congress."

Julius was silent for a long time.

"I suppose that silence is also an answer." Lindenstein clapped a sympathetic hand on his shoulder. "It must be a deuced difficult situation."

"She can't remember. If at all, then only fragments of

the memories that were strongest in her mind, the good moments, of course." A wind blew a lock of black hair across his forehead, not knowing it made him look younger, more vulnerable. "She has painted a rosy picture of our marriage, a distorted one. Only you, Hartenberg, and Atherton know how matters really stood. It was an arranged marriage." He shrugged helplessly. "There is not really much more to say about that, is there?"

Lindenstein's eyebrow rose. "You have always been remarkably stoic about it, something I have always admired about you. I certainly am incapable of accepting arranged marriages with stoicism. I, for one, am determined to resist this fate with both hands and feet."

"Your father is pushing you into marriage?"

"He is trying his best." Lindenstein scowled. "But let us not change the subject. We were talking about you and Catherine. It was an unequal marriage. She was too young, you were too worldly; she was an innocent with no idea of the world, while you were decidedly not an innocent." He flashed a quick grin. "You had no head for anything but politics. She adored you anyway. We all knew that."

"Feelings I never reciprocated," Julius said bitterly.

"Did you not? Never?" Lindenstein threw him a swift glance. "What a strange thing for you to say. I would stake my life on the fact that you were rather fond of her, though you certainly had your own way of showing it. I also wouldn't say that a man who was as devastated by the death of his wife as you were was someone who never loved his wife. It almost destroyed you. Hartenberg and I even went to England in disguise, risking our lives to pull you out of your hole. It was a marvellous adventure." A faint smile tugged at the corner of his lips. "We were almost caught by the French *and* the English—but that is another story. My point being, this is not the behaviour of a man who has never loved his wife."

Julius exhaled heavily. "That trip was the most idiotic venture you ever embarked on."

"You know us. We like to live dangerously. Coincidentally, we also had some highly secret missives to deliver in the service of the fatherland." He made a dismissive wave with his hand. "Now forget I ever told you that." He leaned forwards and peered at him closely. "Are you certain it isn't just denial? Protecting yourself behind a mask of guilt? It might be quite convenient to not have to examine one's feelings too closely." He studied his fingernails. "I am speaking, of course, from experience."

"Guilt? Nonsense," Julius said gruffly.

"I know you took on full responsibility for the accident."

"Because I was responsible for it."

"Nonsense. You were in London; she was in Scotland. How could you have been responsible for it?"

"She left me. I—I could have—If I had taken better care of her, she would not have been so lonely, so unhappy. She would have had no reason to leave me." It suddenly exploded out of him in choppy bursts. "She wouldn't have had any reason to run away from me. I failed to care for her, to protect her, to love her. I failed as a husband in every way, and it cost her her life. If I had tried but a little harder, she would never have taken that stagecoach to Scotland with a drunk coachman who catapulted the vehicle straight over the bridge. Of course it was all my fault. How can anyone say it wasn't?" His voice had risen almost to a shout.

"But now it turns out that all that did not really happen," Lindenstein continued mercilessly. "Yes, there was an accident, but she did not die. She just lost her memory, and you found her again. And now?"

"And now I haven't the faintest notion who she is, who I am, who we are, or what, in the name of all that's holy, we are meant to be doing." He breathed heavily. "She is content, has a new family that loves her, and I am the monster who threatens to destroy her life. Again. It would be better for all of us if I left them well alone and disappeared this time."

"Except you have a son and heir." Lindenstein refused to relent. "Not something you can easily ignore. You would be an enormous fool not to fight for your woman and your only son."

He clenched and unclenched his fists. "The truth is, Klemens, that... I am not sure she is still my woman. While biologically mine, I am not heartless or cruel enough to claim only Hector and whisk him off to England. I couldn't do that to them."

"Then you must claim them all." An impish grin sprang across Lindenstein's face. "You will be the father of four children overnight. Some men have all the luck."

Julius groaned.

Laughing softly, Lindenstein turned towards his

carriage, but swung back to him at the last moment. "Have you started to woo her?"

"Woo?"

"Yes, woo." He gave an exaggerated sigh. "I am not a native speaker of English, but I believe the definition is commonly known to be 'to court' or 'to win the love of someone'. Have you never done that?"

Julius' eyebrows knit together.

"Flowers? Chocolates? Poems?" Lindenstein ticked off each item with his fingers. "Written by yourself, of course."

"Poems?" Julius' face was a study in horror. "Certainly not. And flowers? That girl, Mona, suggested the same." He shook his head. "But why should I give her flowers when she has an entire rose garden at Aldingbourne Hall, which she planted herself?"

"Had," Lindenstein corrected. "She had an entire rose garden. I speak of the present. Nothing at all? Chocolates?"

"I don't see the point."

"You're as romantic as a dry piece of bone. A hopeless case." Lindenstein shook his head. "Though take it from me, women, all women, no exceptions, like to be wooed. I'd wager all your problems will be solved in a jiffy." He snapped his fingers. "I ought to follow my own counsel and do the same myself."

"Stockings," Julius muttered through gritted teeth.

"I beg your pardon?"

"I gave her stockings." A blush crept up his neck. "Mind you, I don't normally buy stockings. Only because she said she wanted them but thought they were too expensive and couldn't afford them..."

Lindenstein's teeth flashed as he smiled. "Not such a hopeless case after all. That's an excellent beginning, *mein Freund*. Now you must proceed from there. It's child's play." He slapped him on the shoulder and climbed into his carriage.

"Woo her," Julius repeated as the carriage departed. "Child's play. How in blazes does one do that?"

Chapter Twenty-Seven

THE BOX WITH THE LOVELY STOCKINGS LAY ON HER bed. She took them out of the box and ran her fingers over the fine material.

She had never owned anything so beautiful. They were delicately knitted, so fine one could hardly see the texture of the fabric. The embroidery stitches—twirls and leaves winding themselves up the leg—were the prettiest she'd ever seen.

Not all the memories had come back to her. She remembered with some certainty that he had not given her gifts very often.

A very long time ago, he'd given her a family heirloom, a wedding ring. She jolted upright. Her ring! She'd always worn a ring, hadn't she? Yet her hands were bare. When she'd awoken in the hospital in Abbotsford, there had been nothing at all on her body aside from a simple shift. She wondered what had happened to the ring. Someone must have stolen it, along with her clothes. Simon had never mentioned a ring. The lack of any personal belongings on her was the reason why it had been impossible to identify her.

Lena rubbed her forehead.

A heaviness settled on her heart.

He had known the truth all along, of course. He'd lied when she'd asked him whether they'd been in love. Maybe he simply hadn't known what else to say. It explained his sudden aloofness and why he'd pulled away when she'd told him she remembered her love for him.

Memories were deceptive, he had said. How right he had been!

While she had adored him as only a child could, an adoration that had later blossomed into love—he had not loved her back.

She rubbed the empty space where her wedding band had been.

Yes, she had loved him. Of that she was certain, but she'd also feared him.

It hadn't been a good marriage.

He'd returned to London soon after the wedding, leaving his young wife behind in the magnificent country house that was a glittering palace filled with gilded mirrors and marbled halls.

She'd been so lonely.

He'd always been polite to her. Courteous, as one was to a stranger. She'd tried so hard to please him, but it was difficult to please someone whom one hardly knew. He'd intimidated her, and in her eagerness to please him, she'd begun to fear him. Fear of seeing the look of impatience in his eyes. They'd been in different worlds. He, so much older, so far above her, and she, barely out

The Forgotten Duke

of the schoolroom with no idea of the ways of the world...

It was the music that had kept her company. Alone in the hall, she'd spent hour after hour playing the piano. It had almost become an obsession. There was nothing else that gave her pleasure. She'd practised and practised for hours, honing and sharpening her skills as a pianist. The only people who had ever listened to her were the butler, the housekeeper, and the other servants.

Up to that point, the memories were clear. Then everything was jumbled together like scattered pieces of a broken mosaic, refusing to fit into any coherent pattern. There were so many visions, scenes, disconnected fragments that seemed to make no sense. All these faces.

Good heavens, her parents!

She jumped up, wringing her hands.

Her mother, pale and tired, and her father, boisterous and loud and cheerful. Had Aldingbourne informed them that she was alive? They needed to be informed.

She probably ought to tell him, too, that most of her memories had returned.

Lena rubbed the back of her head as it began to ache.

Most, but not all of them.

She still had so many questions. Why Scotland? Why had she gone there? Why couldn't she recall why she had left? Was it because she'd discovered he had a mistress?

She clasped a hand over her mouth. Good heavens. Of course. She must have run away. Didn't she have a great-aunt living in Scotland? She must have run away to stay with her.

Her head thumped and ached and refused to retrieve

any more memories. Instead, there was the same empty void that had previously engulfed her entire mind.

She pulled on the new stockings, tied them with a matching pink ribbon and admired them.

Her first real present from him.

It must mean something, must it not?

She furrowed her brow in consternation.

But what, exactly, did it mean?

When they met in the hallway some time later, he did not meet her gaze. He tugged on his neckcloth with an impatient move, as if it suffocated him. Then he strode away to his room without a word.

Lena hurried after him before he could close the door. "I wanted to thank you again for the stockings."

He cut her off with a dismissive wave of his hand. "There is nothing to be thankful for. Harmonia has been thanking me repeatedly for the last half hour, and I must say it is getting tiresome. There is no need to repeat what is not worth mentioning."

"Well." She swallowed. He was certainly in a mood, wasn't he? Best to address the elephant in the room. "Are you still cross about me spying on you?"

His face darkened. "Cross? This is beyond mere annoyance, Lena."

"I assure you; it is really quite harmless. I am not stupid. It would never occur to me to pass on information that is really important."

"That is certainly to be hoped," he replied coolly.

"If all things fail, I could tell them about your kite excursion with the boys and how you got stuck in the tree. Les told me all about it." A corner of her mouth quirked upwards. "I'm certain Metternich will enjoy hearing about that."

"Is this all a game to you, madam?" His voice was tight. "Let me assure you, this is neither amusing nor a game. I do not appreciate being the object of scrutiny, my every move and word weighed and judged. I have gone through great pains to purge my household of potential spies and have prided myself on being quite successful, only to find my own wife at the epicentre, hired by Metternich himself." He blew out his nostrils in indignation.

"When I first took the job," she countered, her voice surprisingly steady, "I had no inkling of who you were or that we were even vaguely related. It meant nothing to me, so why on earth should I not do this?" She threw up her arms. "I needed the income. I have to feed my children somehow. Why not like this?"

He stared. "By Jove. I'd forgotten what it was like."

"What?"

"To have a wife."

Ice-cold heat rushed through her veins. She took a sharp intake of breath. "And what is that supposed to mean?"

He ran his hand through his hair. "Someone who needs constant care and protection, someone to think about all the time, someone with a mind and a will of her own, someone—" His voice trailed off.

"Who is a burden and a millstone around your neck."

She had no idea where that had come from, but there it was.

Their eyes locked. A flicker of something—sadness? pain?—passed through his eyes before they darted away. "This is...absurd," he said, a moment too late.

But the seed of doubt had been planted in her heart.

Maybe he wasn't really that delighted to have her back. Perhaps he had been content as a widower. He must have led a jolly life, not tied down to anyone all these years.

Maybe all he needed was his son and heir, but not her, the unwanted, unloved wife.

He had a mistress, after all. Didn't he?

Maybe it was all a mistake and she should have stayed dead.

She forced a stiff smile. "Why did you never marry again?"

He opened and closed his mouth several times, his face a mask of conflicting emotions. It was strange to watch, almost as if he were struggling for air.

After what seemed to her an eternity, he replied curtly, "I simply preferred not to." Then he turned and stalked back to his room, leaving Lena in the corridor, staring at the closed door in confusion.

Chapter Twenty-Eight

Julius paced his room, wishing himself to Jericho.

What had that been all about, and why the deuce had he said all those things he didn't mean? He was supposed to be wooing her, not fighting her.

Someone who was a burden and a millstone around your neck.

By Jove.

How could she just say something like that so carelessly?

He collapsed in his chair with a groan, burying his head in his trembling hands.

When she had died, he had been so grief-stricken he'd been unresponsive for days.

He'd mourned her for eight blasted years.

That was why he hadn't remarried.

That was the plain truth.

He heard female voices outside in the courtyard, and he got up to look out of the window. There she was, her light blonde head and Mona's dark one, together, bent over a basket on the ground.

Lena's sweet, clear laughter drifted up to him through the window.

A memory struck him, of that same laughter, her in a simple blue dress, her eyes covered with a kerchief, her arms outstretched as she turned in circles in the middle of the meadow while a group of children danced around her, honey-gold hair blowing in the wind...

The sudden stab of longing piercing his chest made him gasp for breath. It was a very old, very familiar feeling.

He rubbed the spot on his chest.

Exactly when had he begun to love her?

When had he started to see her as more than the pale, characterless waif he'd always perceived her to be?

When had he become so entranced by her sweet charm?

He couldn't identify a specific moment. It had crept up on him like ivy tendrils crawling up the trunk of a tree, taking firm root and binding him with an iron grip he could never shake.

His mind wandered back to the spring after they'd been married. They'd been married in November, and he'd immediately travelled to London to be present at the opening of Parliament, leaving Catherine behind at Aldingbourne Hall. At the time, he was convinced that this arrangement suited them both. She was free to do as she pleased in the house, while he pursued his own interests in politics. He would not subject his young wife to boring political dinners and parties. No, she would be well off at Aldingbourne Hall, and he would not question her interests.

In retrospect, of course, he realised that he'd badly neglected his young bride.

Though not unusual, people in arranged marriages often led separate lives, in separate houses, and if they did share a house, it was in separate bedrooms.

He hadn't questioned it. He'd naturally assumed that they, too, would have this arrangement, and that Catherine would be amenable to it. It was the way of their class, after all.

It wasn't until much later that he'd realised how wrong he'd been.

He furrowed his brows, deep in thought.

That early spring, after Parliament had adjourned, he'd returned to Aldingbourne Hall suddenly without notifying Catherine of his impending return. It had been a difficult term. He was tired of all the debating and arguing, he was tired of London, of the crowded city, the dirt and the smog. He craved clean, fresh air, walks in the woods, and rusticating in his library without doing anything at all.

His carriage pulled up the sweeping drive of the house, and he'd climbed the steps to the porticoed entrance two at a time, until he reached the top where the butler greeted him.

"Her Grace is in the front garden," he informed him. "With some visitors."

He was annoyed. The last thing he wanted was to have to dance attendance on guests.

So he took his time, changed out of his travelling

clothes, had a cup of tea, and then strolled out into the garden, hoping the guests had left by now.

Laughter greeted him.

It had taken him by surprise. Laughter in Aldingbourne Hall? Were the walls still standing?

There were children in the meadow, and judging from the way they were dressed, barefoot and in simple clothes, they were his tenants from the surrounding farms. The smallest one toddled about, and the eldest was a youth about Catherine's height…

…Who was blindfolded, turning around in circles, laughing helplessly.

She was like a butterfly fluttering in the meadow, and the children were like bees buzzing around her.

What a child she was, he thought. It wasn't the first time he'd thought that. To be honest, he'd thought it every time he saw her, especially after a long absence, when he was reminded again of her youthfulness, that she was really no more than a child bride. However this time, the thought wasn't dismissive.

It was one of amusement.

And for the first time, he saw that there was something charming about her.

He'd stepped out into the garden and the children had fallen away. Catherine had turned and turned, laughing, confused by the sudden silence, her arms outstretched, stumbling forwards until her fingers brushed his arm. Then she'd stopped instantly, and her fingers had crawled upwards, to his shoulders, his neck, his cheeks, his ears, and he'd held his breath as they

The Forgotten Duke

moved over his face, brushing his lips, nose, his eyes as softly as butterflies' kisses.

She pulled her hands away and tore off the handkerchief.

She had smiled such a breathtakingly beautiful smile, brightening from the deepest depths of her being until it reached the surface, her lips arching up in a gentle curve.

"You are here," she had breathed.

For the first time in his life, he'd been at a complete loss. That's when those vines had begun to take root, and grow, ever so slowly, firmly, stealthily.

Of course, he'd been a complete dolt, incapable of admitting to himself that he was slowly falling in love with his wife.

Until it was too late.

It wasn't until after the funeral, when he'd found the diary, that he'd understood how deeply she had loved him.

He walked over to the dressing table, pulled open the bottom drawer, and took out a leather-bound diary.

The writing in it was round and childish.

She'd also written her version of that day in her diary. It had been the happiest day since she'd married him, she'd written.

Each day's entry was a love letter. First from a child, then from a young lady, finally from a wife. It was an outpouring of honest feelings that he had never again encountered from anyone. It had shaken him to the core, the realisation that he had discovered her love for him far too late. It was also about sadness and loneliness, borne with fortitude. That had cut him to the core.

He had carried the diary with him for years; it had given him some comfort at times when he'd felt particularly lonely. Later, he'd kept it on his bedside table. When he went to Vienna, he couldn't bear to leave it behind, so he'd taken it with him.

He knew the right thing to do was to give it to her.

It was hers, after all. It would help her remember.

His fingers flipped through the pages, wondering what he should do. After a while, he stood up and put the diary back in its place in the bureau.

Not just yet.

Chapter Twenty-Nine

"I believe," the Duke said the next morning at breakfast, carefully setting down his coffee cup, "that it is my turn to cook today."

Five astonished faces turned towards him.

The Duke raised an eyebrow. "Why do I detect a distinct expression of incredulity on your faces?"

"Well, I, uh...you know, it's just that..." Theo hemmed and hawed before finally saying, "It's because none of us believe you can cook, Your Grace."

"You may be right about that, but I don't see why that should stop me from trying."

The look on their faces changed from incredulity to scepticism.

"I thought the agreement was that we would all contribute equally to the welfare of the family, no discrimination?"

"Yes, that's what we said," Les piped up.

"Well then." He nodded. "The kitchen is mine today."

"Fabulous," Hector said with a grin. "I'll be your kitchen helper."

The Duke's gaze softened. "It will be an honour."

They were finally bonding, Lena realised with a soft glow in her heart. Hector was no longer as hostile to him as he had been at first. The Duke, it appeared, seemed to regard him with increasing affection. She was glad.

"Do you know what he did the other day?" Hector chattered. "When we flew the kite?"

"I thought that was supposed to be our secret?" he murmured.

Hector blithely ignored him. "We went to the meadow by the river to fly the kite. Only it got tangled in a tree, and we couldn't get it down. So he—" Hector pointed to the Duke "—took off his hat and coat and rolled up his shirt sleeves and climbed up the tree and untangled it, and do you know what happened then?" He laughed.

"What?" Theo and Mona asked in unison.

Hector could hardly speak he was laughing so hard. Les joined in.

"He got stuck in the tree! He climbed up so high that he couldn't get down again."

The Duke ignored the conversation as if they were not making fun of him and continued to drink his coffee.

"Oh dear." Lena held back her laughter. "What did he do to come down again?"

"He was stuck in the tree for a good half an hour, and there was no one to call for help. I would have run to the neighbour for a ladder, but I had a better idea." He grinned.

"What did you do to get down?"

"Hector and I found a pile of hay, and we carried it under the tree. With all that hay, it was safe to jump without breaking your legs," Les explained.

Lena's eyes grew round. "He jumped into the haypile?"

"I jumped," the Duke said with a deadpan face. "As you can see, my limbs are intact, thanks to the quick thinking of Hector and Achilles. Otherwise, I would still be up in that tree as we speak."

"He had hay all over him." Hector giggled. "In his hair, in his collar..."

Mona snorted a laugh, and even Lena couldn't resist a chuckle. She watched in amazement as a small smile flitted over his face.

Was that really the Duke of Aldingbourne? The stiff, starchy Duke without a sense of humour, who flew kites, climbed and jumped from trees, bought stockings, probably hung laundry on a rope, and now even cooked?

A warm smile tugged at the corner of Lena's mouth. "It will be a pleasure to have you cook today. I am looking forwards to this culinary adventure. Mind you, no cheating! No secretly ordering food from a tavern or asking one of your servants to do the deed."

"I will certainly not do so," the Duke promised. There was a hint of subtle teasing in his voice. She may have imagined the brief twinkle in his eye, but it was gone before she could register it.

THE DUKE WAS true to his promise.

He served a ragout made of hearty chunks of beef, carrots, potatoes and onions, and a hearty dose of paprika. He'd boiled it in the pot on the stove, ladled it out into bowls, and garnished the plates elegantly.

The boys sniffed at it suspiciously. Lena tasted it cautiously.

To her great shock, it was actually quite good. It wasn't charred to cinders, it wasn't over- or under-flavoured, and the soup had the right consistency. Mind you, the pieces of beef were huge chunks, and the potatoes were half cooked, but the overall flavour was excellent.

She put down her spoon and looked at them with astonishment. "How on earth did you know the recipe?"

Hector and the Duke exchanged glances. "That will be our secret," the Duke said. Hector nodded emphatically.

"I saw Hecki ask Frau Bauer!" Les declared. "She told him how to do it, of course."

"Traitor," Hector hissed.

Les grinned and proceeded to spoon the soup into his mouth. "If it is Frau Bauer's recipe, then of course it is good."

"It appears I missed my vocation," he said after tasting the soup. "This is not bad at all. What do you say, Hector, should I give up my duties as a Duke and become a cook?" There it was again, a twinkle in his eye. Was he now getting into the habit of joking?

Lena looked away in confusion and concentrated on her soup.

The Forgotten Duke

Theo said, "It is good! His Grace cooks better than Mama."

After supper, the Duke approached Lena in the kitchen as she dried the last bowl and put it away. "I would like to have a private word with you."

She dried her fingers on her apron. "Now?"

"If you please."

"Let us step outside for a walk, then," she said as she removed her apron. "The evenings have been mild, and it is not yet dark." She fetched her shawl and her bonnet and joined the Duke, who was waiting for her at the gate.

He offered her his arm, and after some hesitation, she took it.

THEY WALKED in silence along the riverbank.

"This is where the kite got entangled in the branches," the Duke said, pointing to a tree by the river.

"That's a huge tree! It's a wonder you didn't break any bones."

"Thanks to the boys' quick and creative thinking, I did not."

They walked on in silence, and Lena became acutely aware of him—the smell of his cologne, the heat he radiated.

She turned her head. "Was there anything in particular you wanted to talk about?"

"Yes." He paused as if gathering his thoughts. "A dispatch has arrived from England, along with some private items I requested." He must have been referring to the packet delivered earlier. He pulled an object from his waistcoat and handed it to her.

It was a small miniature that fit in the palm of her hand. It was a picture of a boy with dark hair, a serious expression, and sombre eyes.

"That's Hector!" She pulled the miniature closer to her eyes. "No, it's not. Hector would never have that serious expression on his face." She gasped. "It's you!"

"Yes. If you turn the miniature, you can see the date is 1787. I was nine years old."

"The resemblance is uncanny." She held it up to his face. He had been a pretty boy—softer, sweeter, and with a trace of loneliness in his eyes. Now his face was all angles and planes, high cheekbones and a strong chin. The thought that one day Hector might look exactly like the Duke of Aldingbourne gave her goosebumps. She dropped her hand.

"This is the proof, I suppose," she murmured more to herself than to him. "Have you shown it to Hector?"

"Not yet."

Her eyes flew up to his face. "What do you intend to do now?"

He turned away and walked slowly along the gravel path. "Isn't the question what are *we* going to do now?"

"Yes," Lena stammered. "I suppose so."

"I'd like to make it official," he said curtly. "With your permission, and that of your family."

She licked her dry lips and her heart began to pound. "Make it official. Like, an announcement in the *Wiener Abendblatt*: Dead English Duchess Returns to Life." Her hands framed the imaginary headline in the air.

His lips quirked upwards. "Not quite that dramatic. Now that you mention it, I suppose we must expect it. It will draw much curiosity, and there will be talk. It would have to be an official introduction to society here. You would appear at my side, as my duchess."

Lena swallowed. That sounded daunting.

"Your parents would also have to be informed."

"My parents...Are they well?"

He hesitated. "As well as one would expect them to be after the death of their only child."

She looked at him, stricken. "Poor Father. Poor Mother. I must write to them at once."

He nodded. "Then there is something else." He hesitated again. "We need to talk...about our marriage."

She braced herself. "Yes." Her eyes focused on the riverbank where some laundry women were washing clothes.

"It is difficult for me to find words, because I am, in general, not a man who is used to talking about these things. Feelings. Marriage." His Adam's apple bobbed up and down as he swallowed. "But you have a right to know the truth. Maybe it will help you remember."

"The truth. What is the truth?" she whispered.

"The truth, Catherine," he said with emphasis, as if he had deliberately chosen that name instead of Lena, "the truth is that our marriage was...not as good as it could have been." He did not meet her eyes.

A murder of crows rose up from the fields beyond, squawking.

"Why wasn't it good?" she asked after a pause, eager to hear his side of the story.

"It was...all my fault."

"How?"

"I failed to be a good husband. I take full responsibility for what happened."

A steep wrinkle formed between Lena's eyebrows. "A marriage, by definition, involves two people. It seems absurd for you to take full responsibility. Half of it might be yours. The other half is mine. As for what happened... what, specifically, do you mean?"

He looked to the horizon, where the sun was slipping behind the hills, his eyebrows forming dark, steep slashes against his pale face.

"The truth is that you could no longer bear it." There was a beat of silence. "And so, you packed your trunks and left me."

Lena's heart skipped a beat. "I did?"

He ran a hand through his thick hair. "We had an argument. Truthfully, I can't recall what it was about now. At the time, it must have seemed trivial to me, but to you, it must have been significant enough to leave. We didn't know where you had gone for three days. By the time we found a trace of you in Scotland, it was too late."

Lena rubbed the side of her nose, feeling a knot tighten in her stomach. There was so much more to the story. Why was he holding back? "Are you certain? It doesn't seem like me to run off over a minor argument."

There was a tightness around his eyes and mouth and a weariness seemed to settle over him. "Believe me, I have searched every recess of my mind, gone over it a thousand times, wondering what I could have said or done differently. I've thought about it every day for eight long years."

She did believe that to be true. His regret was genuine. She wanted to touch the line of suffering that had etched itself in the corner of his mouth but forced herself to hold back.

"Are you certain that I left you?" she asked softly. "Maybe I was visiting a friend or a relative. Didn't I leave a letter?"

"No." His expression tightened with some unspoken emotion. "But you did leave this." Once more, his hand reached into his waistcoat, pulling out the slim leather volume she had seen in his room. "I believe it is right that I return it to you."

Lena took the diary, her fingers brushing the worn cover. She'd seen it before, knew it was hers. Inside, the pages were filled with what she recognized as her own handwriting. "My diary." She turned it in her hand. "Papa gave it to me on my fourteenth birthday."

His lips twisted to a faint smile. "I see it is working, and your memory is returning. The answer to your questions might be in that journal, but the entries stop shortly before your departure for Scotland. You never wrote about why you decided to leave. I didn't give this to you earlier because—" He paused, searching her face.

"Because?" she pressed.

"Because I was afraid," he admitted. "Afraid of what you'd remember. Afraid it might drive you away."

She observed him closely. A breeze blew a strand of hair over his forehead, and suddenly he looked younger, more vulnerable.

"Why tell me all this now? You could have easily said

everything was perfect, that our marriage was a success and that we couldn't have been happier."

"Truth be told, I wanted to do just that." He sighed. "To paint the past as a picture of bliss, to convince you that it was all roses, milk and honey, and that it couldn't have been better. But that would have been a lie, and I realised…I want a new beginning—with you. Now. Based on the present, not haunted by the past."

Her breath caught. "Are you sincere?" she whispered.

He brushed a loose strand of hair from her face and his knuckles gently grazed her cheek. He traced her lips lightly with his thumb.

She shivered at his touch.

"Yes," he said huskily.

Her heart quickened, an ache forming deep within her chest as she swayed towards him.

His pupils were dark and deep, endless wells in a sea of molten silver.

There was nothing she wanted more than to lean against him, lift her mouth and—

A bang tore them apart, and the sky exploded in fireworks.

Lena licked her lips and pressed her hand against her racing heart.

"The festivities are ongoing," the Duke said, his voice slightly breathless. "I believe Count Razumovsky is hosting a party."

"Shouldn't you be there?" Lena asked after collecting herself.

"I prefer to stay here." He lifted his face to watch the

The Forgotten Duke

fireworks in the sky, but Lena watched him instead—the line of his jaw, the delicate curve of his mouth, remembering how close they'd come to kissing.

She cleared her throat.

"I suppose we should go back. The children..."

"Yes. The children." After a moment's hesitation, he held out the diary. "Don't you want it?"

Lena glanced at the journal, its brown leather faded and cracked. She knew what it contained. Minute descriptions of her daily life at Aldingbourne Hall. Embarrassing, childish confessions for the man who had been first her betrothed, then her husband. Love poems, filled with naive hope. And later, entries that spoke of growing loneliness and longing.

All that pain, that sadness. She needn't relive all that.

She shook her head. "I don't want it."

An incredulous look passed over his face. "Don't you want to know what you wrote? Don't you want to remember?"

Once more, she shook her head. "Perhaps I will, one day. I trust you'll keep it safe for me. As you have done so far."

His expression softened. "It's my greatest treasure. I'll guard it with my life."

They walked back home in companionable silence, but Lena felt as if they had reached a new level in their relationship; something there that hadn't been there before. Was it friendship? Was it trust? Or something deeper? Whatever it was, she was certain, for the first time, that it was not the hollow memory of a bygone love.

That was why she had refused the diary—her past

emotions confused her. She wanted what was here now. Something real, solid and present. Something new, and something to build on.

And it was all within her grasp.

Chapter Thirty

After supper, the Duke gathered the whole family in the drawing room. He placed his miniature in the centre of the table, and everyone stared at it.

"This shouldn't surprise any of us," Theo eventually spoke up, rubbing his forehead. "But it's still shocking to see such an incredible likeness."

Hector's reaction was interesting. He threw a quick glance at it and shrugged. "I will look exactly like you when I am old," he remarked. It was the closest he had come to acknowledging the Duke as his father.

"It is time to bring this experiment to a close. Starting tomorrow, I will turn the tables. You will join me in the city for an entirely different kind of life. You may perform if you wish, but only for private functions held in my house, and not for pay. You may continue your interests and medical studies." He nodded at Theo. "But you will have additional responsibilities."

"Such as?" Theo asked.

"You and Mona will be introduced to society and

expected to attend social functions. Achilles and Hector will have a new tutor to teach them the basics: Classics, arithmetic, science, history, and geography."

Both boys started to protest, but the Duke raised his hand. "You will also have lessons in dancing and fencing."

"Fencing?" the boys exclaimed in unison. They looked at each other, then at the Duke.

"Of course. Every gentleman of breeding must know how to fence properly. I will hire the best fencing master in all of Vienna to teach you."

"*Famos!*" the boys said together.

"You will have to earn your fencing lessons by proving that you learn diligently in all your other subjects. I will receive daily reports from your tutors, and if you have studied well, you will earn your fencing lesson."

"That is a very wise decision." Lena nodded. "How wonderful for you, boys. And me, what will I do?"

"You will remain by my side at all social functions as my duchess."

Lena bit her lip. After a while, she gave an almost imperceptible nod.

That evening, after the children had gone to bed, Lena went to the Duke's bedroom and knocked gently on the door. She heard his footsteps, followed by the creaking of the hinges as the door opened. He stood before her in stockings, his shirtsleeves rolled up to reveal powerful forearms. For a moment, she was distracted by the sight.

"Lena. It is late. Is something the matter?" he asked, his voice soft but firm.

She blushed and blinked quickly. "I need to talk to you. Could we talk outside in the garden, please?"

He arched an eyebrow. "It just started raining. May I suggest the parlour downstairs instead?"

She nodded. "Very well."

In the parlour, she added several logs to the fire, which crackled warmly in the fireplace. The Duke joined her, now wearing his coat, and Lena couldn't help but feel he was less approachable with it on.

"What is it you want to talk about, Lena?"

She took a deep breath. "I've thought about what you said earlier. I'll accompany you to all the social functions you need and do my best to be a hostess you won't be embarrassed by. I can't promise perfection. I tend to trip over my own feet and drop things at the worst possible times, oh, and have you noticed that I have a tendency to spill things on my clothes? If I was ever good at this—" she made a vague gesture with her hands "—this thing that duchesses are supposed to do, which I doubt I ever was, I've forgotten all about it by now."

A hint of a smile flickered across his face. Lena treasured those moments when he smiled; it was like sunlight breaking over a desolate landscape, turning it into honeyed gold.

"We never entertained on a large scale at Aldingbourne Hall," he said, "but I remember you liked to host tea parties in the gardens to which you invited our tenants' children."

Her eyes were wide. "I did? Truly? Did I spill the tea over them when I poured it?"

A laugh escaped him.

"My point being, I'll try my best to be a proper duchess." She folded her hands meekly.

"But?" he asked. "I sense there is a 'but'."

Lena heaved a deep sigh. "But I can't give up performing. It's the only thing I do well, and it brings in money."

The smile vanished. "There's no need for you to earn money," he said in a level voice. "My funds are sufficient for everyone."

She shook her head. "No."

"No?" he repeated softly.

"I can't give it up. Music is who I am. It defines me."

"I am the Duke of Aldingbourne. I cannot and will not allow the Duchess of Aldingbourne to perform in public. It's grossly inappropriate and simply not done. You may perform privately, organise musical soirees, invite everyone you wish, but you will not earn a penny. Once you are my duchess, you will no longer be a working musician."

"How can you be so certain of everything?" Lena burst out, unable to contain her frustration.

"What do you mean?"

"Certain that I am your wife, that Hector is your son, that I'll be a worthy duchess, that it will all work out and we'll be happy together?"

He stared into the fire. "If there's one thing I know for certain, it's that nothing in life is ever certain."

The Forgotten Duke

"You see? That's why I need some independence. I don't want to give up my income, meagre as it is."

"Independence," he mused. "Security. Is that what this is about?"

How could she explain the terror she felt at the thought of losing her independence and sole source of income? What if things went badly? What if he changed his mind about her and her future?

"Tell me what is troubling you, Lena."

"I'm frightened," she confessed. "In case this—" she gestured between them again "—fails. What if you decide it was a mistake? What if you change your mind? What if you find us a burden and no longer want us? What if I am a dreadful duchess? I'm no longer accustomed to social functions." She took a deep breath. "I'm afraid I'll embarrass you."

His gaze softened and he took her hand. "It concerns me, too."

She stared at him. "You're afraid?"

"You disappeared once. What if you disappear again?" His voice was rough with emotion. "Who's to say you won't change your mind? That you won't disappear like you did eight years ago?"

"Oh. I...see." Tenderness flooded through her.

"As for your music," he continued, "let's make a compromise. Perform as much as you like, but without payment. Continue your correspondence with Metternich and let him pay you. In fact, tell him to increase the payment. Now that you will be back in society, you have even closer access to the kind of intelligence he wants. You can charge double what he pays now."

Her eyes widened. "You don't mind if I keep on spying?"

He smiled thinly. "Feed him carefully controlled information, some true, some not. Let him figure out what is what."

Her eyes sparkled with understanding. "Mislead him. It would serve him right!"

"It would serve him right, indeed."

Chapter Thirty-One

The children stood in a line; their heads tilted upwards as they gaped up the magnificent baroque mansion that was to be their new home.

"This is a palace." Theo was the first to find his voice.

"Are you sure the coachman didn't make a mistake?" Mona asked sceptically.

Since several footmen rushed out of the front door to help unload the luggage from the second carriage that arrived behind them, Lena assumed that this must be the right place.

They were ushered into a splendid marble hall with a sweeping staircase leading to the upper rooms, from which Mr Mortimer hurriedly descended to greet them.

"His Grace is not here at present, having been called to an urgent meeting. It has therefore been left to me to welcome you here." He opened his arms as if to embrace them all. "Welcome to the current residence of the Duke of Aldingbourne. I hope you will feel at home here. If you would please follow me."

There were enough rooms in the palace for every child to have their own.

Lena did not have a room; she had a whole suite. The room covered in blue and gold velvet left her speechless. Even the stucco on the ceiling was gilded. It was almost too much.

"The canopy bed is so big, we could all sleep in it," she said to the maid, who was busily unpacking her trunks.

She smiled politely. "Yes, Your Grace."

"Do let me help." Lena took the nightshirt out of her hands. The maid's eyes widened in horror.

"Oh no, Your Grace. You mustn't. This is my work, if you please."

Your Grace!

The words were strange, and Lena's first reaction was to correct her. Then the echoes of the past came back. It was not the first time people had called her 'Your Grace'.

"His Grace has cancelled all events for tonight, saying you and the children need time to get accustomed to being here. Tomorrow will be a busy day, with the dressmaker coming here to measure you for a new wardrobe."

Lena ran her hand down her faded dress. "I suppose I do need something a little more appropriate to wear." She could hardly continue wearing Emma's dresses from the attic that she usually used for performances. She had to be more fashionable now. She supposed having one or two additional dresses wouldn't hurt.

She ended up having two walking dresses, four morning dresses, four afternoon dresses, two carriage dresses, three ballroom gowns, a riding outfit—even though she protested that she did not know how to ride; or did she? A vague memory of her nervously riding on a vast green estate in England resurfaced, but the image slipped from her mind before she could grasp it. Then two new nightdresses, spencers and redingotes, shawls and shoes and fans and gloves and petticoats, and oh! More stockings! The most beautiful things of the finest silk. Lena stroked them but found the first pair the Duke had given her was her favourite. She was wearing them now.

"That is only the beginning," the dressmaker had said, satisfied when everything fit her to perfection. "More is to come."

Mona and the boys also received new outfits, much to the chagrin of Les and Hecki, who insisted that their new satin suits were stiff and uncomfortable, and "one could hardly go fishing in them."

Lena adjusted the plainly tied neckcloth around Hector's neck after he'd tugged at it. "You look like a young gentleman now, Hector. Behave like one."

"I'll make sure he does. Come on, Hecki, let's slide down the banister in the great hall. I wonder if we can go all the way from the fourth floor to the ground floor in one ride?" Before Lena could say another word, the two boys had scampered off.

Mona was in seventh heaven. Not only was her room pretty in pale lemon, but she had an extra room of her own, her very own drawing room, where she could play her viola to her heart's content, without being disturbed.

"I like it here, Mama. I can read, play my viola, draw,

because there's plenty of light, and if I get bored, go shopping, because the best shopping street in Vienna is right outside!" Her eyes sparkled with excitement.

Only Theo was subdued. Lena assumed it was because he was still struggling with his broken heart, because moving into the city meant being away from his Rosalie, even though she had made it clear that they could never be together. She had become engaged to someone else. Somehow this move made things even more final. Also, the hospital and the Josephinum where he had his anatomy and physiology classes were further away.

"On the other hand, it is exciting to live in the heart of Vienna, isn't it? You won't have to perform anymore, and you will be able to focus entirely on your studies. That is an advantage, isn't it?" Lena stroked his hair.

"Yes." Theo moped. "I suppose so."

Lena's suite of rooms contained a pianoforte in her drawing room. It was a Walter piano, an elegant pianoforte of walnut wood, the kind that the great masters like Beethoven, Mozart and Haydn owned.

Lena ran her fingers reverently over the black ebony keys and pressed them down.

The instrument was finely tuned with full sound.

She sat down, closed her eyes, and played.

"This Congress doesn't move forwards, it dances!" the Prince of Ligne complained to Julius after a particularly harrowing diplomatic meeting. They'd conversed in French, and Julius had been contemplating the wit of the remark and how difficult it was to translate the double entendre of '*ne marche pas*' into English. On the one hand it referred to a lack of forwards movement, but on the other, in simpler language, it meant that the thing was simply broken and didn't work.

Julius could not but affirm the truth of these words. Not only did they all prefer dancing the waltz to sitting down and working in the literal sense, but the few who were actually working—often in smaller, private groups gathered informally amid social functions like balls, soirees, ridottos, and dinners—found themselves treading in place as if stomping grapes in a vat, or, at best, moving round and round in circles, making no progress at all. At least if they'd been treading real grapes they'd end up with some good wine. In this case, there would be no such reward.

It was enough to make even the most patient man lose his temper.

Julius rubbed at his eyes tiredly.

They'd just had another pointless four-hour meeting, and it had ended, as it so often did, with the Tsar storming out of the room and slamming the door like an overindulged infant.

Come to think of it, even infants were better behaved than that.

Then Metternich had sidled up to him with a smug smile and poked him in the waistcoat with his lorgnette. "I know who paid you a visit the other day."

"Do you now?" Julius had replied wearily. "How extraordinarily shocking."

"I have known about your friendship with Lindenstein for a long time, of course. You and Lindenstein and Hartenberg are exceptionally close friends, almost like brothers. The three of you met on a Grand Tour when you were but young, green boys. Where did you meet, again? Ah yes, I recall. I have an excellent memory, you see. I remember every detail, no matter how insignificant. It was at an inn in the Tyrolean Alps, before the revolution and all the other madness broke out." He grinned suavely. "Impressed by what I know, aren't you?"

Julius shrugged. "It is no secret that the three of us have known each other since our youth."

They'd all been stranded in a seedy inn due to inclement weather, the road blocked by a mudslide, making it impossible to continue their journey. Julius had noticed two youths sitting at a table by the window, a good-looking blond and an older, edgier, darker-haired one with sharp eyes, recklessly gambling as if the sky was falling, with real money, too. The older one had a cigar dangling from the corner of his mouth and they were drinking huge jugs of what looked like beer. He couldn't help being impressed by them and sneaking glances at their game, for his tutor had strictly forbidden him to touch cards, cigars, and heaven forbid, beer. His tutor was now sick in bed, and Julius was bored.

The two boys must have noticed his interest, because they put their heads together, whispered, and looked at him slyly.

Without much ado, Julius had got up and walked over to them.

"Julius Stafford-Hill, the Marquess of Drayton." He bowed stiffly.

The blond boy grinned, raised his mug and drank deeply, not wiping the foam from his mouth, never taking his eyes off him. "English?"

"Yes."

"That would explain it."

"Explain what?"

"Why you're sitting there all stiff and straight as if you'd swallowed a steel pole."

The older boy looked him up and down with narrowed eyes, a cigar still dangling from his mouth. "Georg von Hartenberg." He lifted his chin to the blond boy. "My cousin Lindenstein."

"Just Lindenstein?" Julius enquired.

"Just Lindenstein," he confirmed, his teeth still clenching the cigar.

"How do you do." Julius nodded at them both.

"Do you play Faro, Drayton?" Lindenstein smiled beatifically at him.

"I do," he lied.

They'd fleeced him quite spectacularly. In the end, Hartenberg had clapped a hand on his back and declared him a good loser. The next morning, Julius had left his tutor at the inn and gone to Innsbruck with them. He'd been delighted by Lindenstein's wit and daring, and Hartenberg's dry humour and courage. By the end of the week, the three had sworn eternal friendship and blood brotherhood, and to top it all, Julius had promised Hartenberg his sister Evie's hand in marriage.

"How old is she?" Hartenberg enquired.

"Almost five."

Hartenberg seemed to think for a moment. "Very well, then. We'll tie the knot in twenty years, brother."

"Don't you want to know whether she's beautiful?" Julius couldn't help asking.

"No. She's your sister. That means she's not a doormat. That's all that matters to me."

That was all that was said on the subject.

Julius sighed. How long ago that was. The years had passed, they weren't boys anymore, but their friendship had withstood time and distance and they were as close to each other as ever. Like brothers, they guarded each other's secrets with their lives.

Metternich still watched him closely. "I am, of course, particularly interested in Lindenstein, as you call him. We all know who he really is, do we not?"

Julius stiffened. He would only reveal that secret over his dead body. "What about Lindenstein?"

"There's been considerable upheaval, I hear, involving the father. Quite shocking, really. The father-son relationship is not the best, I find. There was much shouting, swearing, and slamming of doors." He leaned forwards curiously. "Surely you have heard of it?"

"I don't listen to gossip," Julius said stiffly.

"It involves, as usual, a woman."

Julius shrugged. "What's new? Who isn't involved with a woman these days? What about your own amorous relations with the Duchess—or is it Princess? Or both? You should have heeded my wife's advice."

Metternich grimaced. "Don't remind me. I have had many sleepless nights because of that." He sighed deeply. "But let us not change the subject. You do not happen to know the identity of the woman in question? I have my suspicions, but I must confess, it has been maddeningly difficult to discover the identity of the lady who has captured Lindenstein's heart. She must be someone quite impressive."

"I do not know."

"Somehow, I do not believe you. I suspect an Englishwoman…" His words trailed off.

But Julius' face remained blank.

"As for your own domestic affairs, I see that you have them in good order." The Prince patted Julius on the shoulder, and it took all his effort not to flinch at the touch.

Now, having finally arrived at his residence, with all the windows alight, he found it strange that for the first time the sprawling mansion was full of people.

His family.

His wife.

The tinkling sound of a piano reached him.

He took two steps at a time and reached for the door.

That melody.

A lonely, but sweet tune, simple and charming.

He could play it on the piano with one finger. It had haunted him for eight long years.

He opened the door and entered.

She was sitting behind the piano, dressed in a new gown, her hair coiffed upwards in a new style.

His eyes drank in the image.

Catherine. His duchess.

She looked up and smiled as he entered but continued to play the melody to the end.

"I just remembered that melody," she said with a smile.

"Yes," he whispered.

"I composed it for you."

"Yes." His voice was hoarse.

He'd heard it for the first time in a similar way he'd heard it now. She was playing it, a much younger version of herself, and he'd walked in unexpectedly.

She'd jumped to her feet and joy had lit up her face. "Your Grace!" She'd blushed fiercely. "I composed something for you."

"You composed this yourself?" He was surprised. He knew she played the piano, but not that she also composed.

"Yes." She had blushed scarlet. She handed him the sheets with trembling hands.

"Play it for me again."

She did.

That was the first time he had consciously listened to her play. Certainly, she'd played before, but it had always been calmer, more conventional pieces in the background. He discovered her favourite pieces were by Beethoven; heavy, passionate pieces hardly suitable for a young woman like her. She'd played them perfectly and with verve and zest.

The piece she'd composed for him began with a slow tempo, with long legato notes, thoughtful and slightly heavy, building into an intense, rich, and more complex melody, followed by an unexpected turn that expressed softer, warmer harmonies. It was a beautiful piece that expressed longing and yearning.

When she finished, she waited for the notes to fade. "This melody is you."

He grasped for words. "That was extraordinary."

Her smile lit her up from within and for the first time, he realised how beautiful she was.

That had been in the past. Now, it was the same. Hearing her play the tune that she'd composed for him brought back feelings he'd thought he'd long forgotten.

"This melody is you." She used the same words now as she did then.

"It is beautiful," he heard himself say.

As the last note lingered in the air, so did the memory, refusing to let go.

Chapter Thirty-Two

It wasn't easy being a duchess.

Certainly, there were advantages. Her spectacularly beautiful new wardrobe and the jewellery the Duke had given her: an emerald necklace that matched her sage green dress perfectly. Her hair was expertly pinned up and a green ribbon woven through it, with several longer curls allowed to fall over her shoulder.

As she descended the stairs, the Duke had given her a long, lingering look that had made her blush.

Unfortunately, Mona was feeling unwell with a head cold and had to stay in that night. It was a pity, for there was a grand ball at the Imperial Palace to which they had been invited.

"It's a shame," she said, with a stuffy nose. "But if I go, I will sneeze all over the Emperor and that would not be good, would it?"

Lena had tucked her in tightly. "It would have been nice if you could have joined us, but your health is more important now."

She had been immediately awed by the glitter and glamour that greeted them. She tightened her grip on Julius's arm.

"Never fear," he murmured, noticing her nervousness.

"I won't know a single soul here," she muttered as the footmen opened the wide doors for them.

"You know me," Julius replied.

Metternich descended the stairs, saw them, and headed straight towards them.

"And him," Julius groaned.

"What a pleasure to see you here," the Prince said, kissing her hand effusively. "Your Grace. Your presence brightens the place." He said that with such sincerity and charm that she smiled. Suddenly Lena understood why he was so popular with the ladies.

"Thank you, Your Highness," she replied, "but I dare say the hundreds of chandeliers do a better job of it than I do."

He threw back his head back and laughed. "Not only beautiful but witty. You are to be envied, Aldingbourne."

The Duke smiled a cool smile that did not reach his eyes. "Your purpose has been accomplished, Highness. You have her attention, and she seems jealous."

Metternich's smile did not falter. "Is she, indeed? A little longer, if you don't mind."

Lena's head swerved from one to the other, slightly tilted, trying to understand what they were talking about.

"But I do mind." Julius clasped his hand over Metternich's and removed it from Lena's. "I believe your own wife is waiting for you at the door."

Metternich laughed softly. "Always the jealous husband, I see."

He bowed and strolled to the door, where his wife, a tall, thin woman with a kind but anxious face, awaited him.

Julius took Lena's hand firmly and led her up the stairs. Halfway up the staircase stood a gorgeous creature in white and silver. She had a round, expressive face framed by tiny, dark curls, and looked at them with open curiosity.

Julius nodded curtly at her. "Duchess." He swept past her, not pausing to introduce Lena.

"That was the famous Duchess of Sagan," he murmured in her ear. "The one who broke Metternich's heart."

"Oh!" Lena turned to look at her again, but she had slowly descended the stairs and uttered a sound of delight as she hurried towards a uniformed man who had just entered.

"Her new lover. Or old lover." Julius explained. "Depending on how one sees it." His forehead puckered to a frown. "Metternich was just trying to use you to make her jealous. With his wife standing at the door, watching."

"Dear me. His poor wife! How complicated everything is." She shook her head.

"These are the games Metternich plays, and I have no sense for them."

"It is all rather childish, is it not?"

"You don't know the half of it," Julius said heavily.

That elicited a chuckle from Lena.

"I vow, if the Duchess of Sagan would just elope with her new-old lover and remove herself from Vienna, I am certain Metternich would stop being distracted and finally focus on what really matters, and that is to move this deuced Congress forwards. As for now, as things stand, he is allowing himself to be drawn further and further into her snares. That woman over there, by the by, is her rival." He nodded to another glamorous creature in a revealing dress that clung to her curves so voluptuously that it made Lena blush. She stood against the wall, slowly fanning herself.

"That is Princess Katharina Bagration, another of Metternich's former lovers."

The Princess stared daggers at the Sagan, then moved her narrowed gaze to Metternich, who was offering his arm to his wife.

The orchestra began to play the stately strains of a polonaise that always opened the ball. Only the highest and most noble dignitaries, princes, and monarchs entered the ballroom with their ladies, starting with Emperor Francis. There was Metternich, of course, and Tsar Alexander. He was a tall, blond man with a charming face and full lips. He nodded to all right and left, especially to the ladies. The line of couples in the polonaise was almost endless.

Lena grabbed Julius' arm. "I may be imagining it, but isn't that—Lindenstein?"

She hardly recognised him. There was not a trace of the cheerful boyish charm that she'd come to associate with him. He was in a white uniform, looking proud and bored, leading a haughty-looking lady who wore one of

The Forgotten Duke

the most extravagant tiaras Lena had ever seen. He raised their joined hands, forming a bridge so that other couples could pass underneath. She had never seen anyone dance with less enthusiasm.

"Correctly observed." That was all Julius said.

Lena turned to him, blinking. "But that means that he—"

"Yes."

"Shouldn't we go and greet him?"

"No."

"But...why?"

"Because he asked us not to."

Lena digested this.

"He threatened fire and brimstone to hail down upon us if we do," a deep voice spoke up next to her, seemingly out of nowhere. "I have yet to test the matter."

She jumped and whirled around. A man in a field marshal's uniform stood beside her. He had short greyish brown hair, and his sharp grey eyes sparkled merrily at her.

"Blast you to hell and back," Julius exclaimed. "You just appeared out of nowhere. What the devil are you doing here?"

"Likewise, brother, likewise." He thumped him on the shoulder. "I see you are healthy and well. Since you are as rude as ever and not introducing me to your wife, I must do so myself." He made a military salute. "*Gestatten*, Field Marshall Georg von Hartenberg at your service. It is a delight to finally make your acquaintance, Your Grace."

"Oh! I have heard of you. You are one of Julius's, I

mean, Aldingbourne's friends." She had met Lindenstein before, but never Hartenberg.

He took her hand and kissed it. "I hope only good things. As for the things I have heard about you, I had to come and hear the story with my own ears. Before we do so, where is she?"

"Who?"

"My lovely betrothed." He raised a jagged eyebrow that looked like a comma. "Your sister, Lady Evie, of course. The woman I am to marry. I presume? Though she may be in the frame of mind to call it off at the moment."

"Evie?" Julius's brows puckered to a frown. "She said she was visiting a friend—the devil."

"She was indeed visiting a friend." Hartenberg's face was deadpan.

"And now?" Julius barked. "You've met? She is back? Since when? Is she here?"

"So I assumed. But it appears I lost her. Again," he muttered.

Before Julius could ask what the deuce he meant, he patted him on the shoulder. "Do not worry, my friend. Dance with your lovely wife. We shall talk another time."

He disappeared as quickly and unexpectedly as he had appeared.

"He is rather...fast," Lena said.

"He is good at that. Military training in stealth and whatnot." Julius tried to get a last glimpse of his friend, but he'd already gone. "Strategising and sneaking up on enemies and friends are his forte. Apparently, it helps him survive in the field."

"You certainly have interesting friends." Lena turned to watch Lindenstein again, who was staunchly ignoring them. "He is a good dancer."

"It's one of those new-fangled dances," the Duke observed. "I believe they call it a waltz. Would you like to give it a try?"

Lena knew how to waltz. Every peasant child in Vienna did. They danced the waltz at every village fête, in every restaurant, café, and wine tavern. When the violins began to play, it was usually to the lilting 3/4 time of the waltz. The common folk had been doing it for centuries. The upper aristocracy had taken notice of it only recently. Tired of their stiff minuets and formal polonaises, they found the waltz's lively and intimate nature intriguingly different. The close embrace of the dancers, considered scandalous by some, only heightened its appeal at aristocratic balls.

The Duke danced it well.

Lena danced on a cloud. Her feet were light, and he led her in twirls and turns about the dance floor, expertly manoeuvring them to avoid collisions with other couples.

By the end of the dance, she was rather breathless, but exhilarated and happy.

The Duke led her to the side of the ballroom, next to a huge marble urn. "Wait here, I'll procure some refreshments."

Lena leaned slightly against the urn and fanned herself with the fan attached to her wrist. A dreamy smile played on her lips.

The dance was beautiful. She hadn't wanted it to stop, ever.

"Did you see that?" a female voice said from the other side of the urn. "That English Duke's wife. I saw Metternich fuss over her, no doubt to make the Duchess of Sagan jealous. Her stare had the force of a hundred daggers. How he flirted with her, and right next to his wife, too." The voice sniffed scornfully. "I vow I have seen her somewhere. But where?"

Lena's movements froze.

"You are right. I saw her dancing with the Duke. It is a familiar face. Oh! I know! Wasn't she at Metternich's soiree? Wasn't she one of the—performers?"

A queasy feeling settled in her stomach.

"You're right!" the other voice said gleefully. "But surely not? Can the English Duke's wife truly be a mere performer?" She gasped. "I can hardly say it, it is such a preposterous notion, but can she be—a commoner?"

"Does Metternich know? Oh. Surely not! Can you imagine the scandal if it were true?"

"It is not true," a cold, cutting voice interrupted.

Lena jumped, as did the other two ladies.

"Oh. Your Gr-Grace. I didn't see you there," the first voice said weakly, followed by a nervous giggle.

"If you must spread rumours, do so with a hint of truth, if you please. My wife Catherine is the daughter of His Grace the Duke of Maplethurst, and the granddaughter of a cousin to the current King of England. To call her a "commoner" is to insult the King of England directly."

The ladies spluttered. "We were merely conjecturing—"

"Do not conjecture. Nothing good ever comes out of

it. Now, if you will excuse me, I must deliver this to my duchess."

There was dead silence.

Lena's hand had gone to her mouth.

Julius appeared, scowling, holding a glass of champagne to her. "I got held up for a minute."

"Thank you." She took the glass and sipped from it.

He nodded.

"I mean, thank you for defending me from those two harpies."

"I cannot bear it when people spread untruths. Especially about you." He touched her cheek gently.

"Thank you," she whispered a third time, fighting the sudden urge to weep. He had defended her publicly. As far as she could remember, no one, not even Simon, had ever done that before.

He nodded again, and there was something in his eyes that made her heart leap.

Chapter Thirty-Three

Lady Evie had indeed returned from her travels.

She stood bright-eyed at the top of the marble staircase, still in a rumpled travelling dress, greeting them effusively as they arrived back from the ball.

"Catherine, I mean, Lena! And Julius. I'm back!"

"So I see," Julius replied. "And somewhat earlier than anticipated. How was your journey?"

"Awful. However, I am back now, and all is well." She descended the stairs quickly and clasped Lena's hands. "I'm so glad you're here. You must tell me everything."

Julius cleared his throat. "Your friend, I take it she is well?"

"Hm? What fr—oh. You mean Pippa? Yes, of course. Yes, she is fine. That is, she was ill, but she's better now." Evie's gaze flickered away to avoid meeting Julius's eyes.

His brows furrowed. "I ran into Hartenberg at the ball."

Her head whipped around. "You did? He's here?"

"Yes." He watched her closely.

Evie looked away again, fiddling with the fringe of her scarf. "Oh."

"It is high time you two met formally."

Evie shrugged nonchalantly.

He lifted an eyebrow. "Is there something you need to tell me?"

She shook her head. "No. I can't imagine what that could be. If Hartenberg is in Vienna, I suppose I can't get around meeting him. Finally."

"Granted, the war made it difficult, if not impossible, for the two of you to meet sooner. But when he finally managed to come to England against all odds eight years ago, you ran off."

Evie lifted her chin defiantly. "That's not true. How was I supposed to know he'd choose to visit the one time I was taking the waters in Bath? Besides, Aunt Agatha needed me."

"Conveniently so," Julius commented dryly. "After all, Aunt Agatha could never manage without you. The distance to Bath is insurmountable, far more difficult than his journey from Vienna, of course."

"Precisely." Evie sniffed dismissively. "The man is used to travelling through battlefields. Surely, a trip to Bath would have been easy enough for him. But no, he couldn't be bothered. Come, Lena, let us leave my insufferable brother before I lose my temper. I've just returned and I've no patience left for him."

Lena, who'd been looking from one to the other in

bemusement, patted her arm. "Come and tell me everything."

The two women ascended the stairs together, leaving Julius to watch after them thoughtfully.

He had just finished a meeting with Castlereagh at the Minoritenplatz. The day was clear and brisk, so he decided to walk back to his residence. It wasn't far, and the walk would help him gather his thoughts.

The weather had turned cold, and a crisp edginess was in the air, heralding that winter was coming soon. The chill cleared his mind, which had been clouded all day with a restless fog. He found his thoughts drifted constantly, making it difficult to concentrate.

During the meeting, Castlereagh had to ask him three times if he agreed to the proposal. He'd blushed like a schoolboy who'd been caught stealing sugar plums from the pantry.

Fact was that his thoughts had been miles away with Catherine and how lovely she'd looked at the breakfast table this morning. They'd made it a habit to eat breakfast together, both rising before the children, savouring that quiet hour alone. He cherished these mornings, his only time with her before the demands of the day took over.

Today, she had tilted her head, her rosy lips curved in a smile. The entire day Julius had been unable to shake the thought of how much he'd wanted to kiss her.

Why the devil hadn't he?

She was his wife, after all.

Would they taste as sweet as he remembered?

What was he waiting for?

"Your Grace," Castlereagh repeated for the third time, his voice laced with amusement. "The proposal?"

He blinked, startled. "Ah yes." He cleared his throat, heat washing up his neck. "The proposal. Of course."

As wholesome as the walk was, the crisp air did little to cool the feverish heat that seemed to have taken over his entire being. He felt as if his blood had turned to honey mead, oozing hot and slow through his veins. As he reached the bustling Graben, where carriages and pedestrians crowded the wide street, he paused. Perhaps he ought to visit that hosiery shop again to pick up another pair of stockings. No, this time he ought to buy her something less ordinary.

A piece of jewellery perhaps. It occurred to him that other than the family heirlooms, he'd never given her any trinket. Something personally made for her. Something that reflected the colour of her eyes. They lit up when she smiled, like sparkles in a diamond.

He walked happily down the road ruminating on her eyes, when he was interrupted by a familiar voice calling from across the street.

Julius looked up and there she was, as if he had conjured her from his very thoughts.

She stood at the other side, waving. But not at him, no.

In front of him were the children gathered near the house.

An unexpected feeling of elation washed over him.

He had a family now.

Not only Catherine, but a son, and the other children, too. A surprising warmth bloomed in his chest. He had to confess he'd miss them if they were ever to part now.

Lena called again, waving at the children as she began to cross the street.

Julius saw the coaches coming.

Two of them, barrelling down the street at a reckless speed. Lena, her focus entirely on the children, had not noticed them.

"Mama!" the children screamed.

"No!" It broke from him.

The scene unfolded in a blur of chaos. Shouts, screams, the shrill whinny of panicked horses. The deafening crunch of splintering wood as the two carriages collided, and there—caught between them—was Lena.

Julius was running before he even realised it, his heart pounding in his chest. He reached her in what felt like an eternity.

Her pale arm lay on the ground and her hair spread across the cobblestones—streaked with blood.

Chapter Thirty-Four

It was happening all over again.

A horrific accident.

His wife.

Limp and broken in his arms.

Dead.

Once more, he had arrived too late.

Violent sobs tore out of the depths of his soul. "Catherine, my God. Catherine, Catherine."

"Your Grace. Your Grace. We must move her," an urgent voice said, but he did not register what was being said. "Your Grace, begging your pardon, but you must move aside." Someone grabbed his arm to pull him away from her, but it had taken a hold of him, the black despair of old, tearing through him with a pain stronger than a dozen swords piercing through his heart.

"Catherine," he gasped.

"We have to move her," the voice said urgently. "We can save her, but you must allow us to move her."

They separated him from her, and she was carried

into the house. He stumbled after her, feeling as if he was trapped in an eternal nightmare.

The children huddled in a corner, weeping quietly.

Evie, red-eyed and shaken, attempted to comfort them.

Julius had refused to be separated this time. "I will not leave her," he'd bitten out, not allowing any contradiction. He was there when the doctor and the nurse had undressed her, examined her, and washed away the blood and bandaged her head. He'd held her hand, cold and limp, the whole time.

"A head injury," the doctor explained. "She is unconscious."

Unconscious. It took a while for the word to sink in.

"You mean, she is not—not dead?" It fell from his lips.

"No, Your Grace. Her pulse is beating, though faintly."

Relief spread through him and left him weak in the legs and he'd toppled into a seat.

"And now?"

"Now you must wait. God willing, she will regain consciousness soon. We must wait."

He nodded. "I will stay here and wait."

He remained by her side all night and all day, watching her white, immobile face, the soft curve of her lips, and the shadow of her long lashes as they lay against her creamy cheeks.

His hand shook violently as he rubbed his forehead.

Once again, he'd been too late to prevent disaster.

Too late to tell her the one and only thing that ever mattered, that he loved her.

Why hadn't he done it before? Why was he so consistently unable to protect her? Why was he always too late?

Why did she always die?

She, the only love of his life.

He'd barely survived the last time. He knew he would not survive this time. If she died, he would die right there with her. He would be done, and they could bury him right next to her. The mere thought of the yawning emptiness of a life without Catherine was so agonising that he gasped with pain.

"Oh God, let her live," tore from his soul.

Something hot rushed into his eyes and he blinked. It filled his eyes and trickled out, down his cheeks and onto the hands he clasped tightly.

At first, he did not know what it was.

His fingers touched his cheeks and came away wet.

Tears.

He hadn't wept in eight long years, not since he had broken down at Catherine's grave so long ago.

As he had then, he wept now.

It burst from him like a broken dam, shaking his whole body. He lowered his head and leaned it against hers and wept.

Maybe it was hours, maybe it was minutes, but he was sure that there was not a drop of water left in his entire body, and a despairing lethargy heavier than lead took over his body and dragged him down into a merciful blackness.

He slept.

In dreams, miracles happened.

In dreams, the dead came back to life.

In dreams, you could hear them laugh again, hear their sweet voices, feel their touch. Soft, gentle fingers ran through your hair in a rhythmic, soothing motion.

In dreams, ah, so much was possible in dreams.

He did not want to wake up, if only to continue feeling her fingers on his head. Caressing, stroking, playing with his hair...

His eyes popped open.

He stopped breathing.

And he felt it, still, fingers caressing the top of his head...

He turned his head, slowly, carefully.

And met her gaze.

Tired, sweet, and full of love.

"I'm afraid I bumped my head again," she whispered wryly, as if she'd merely banged it against a kitchen cabinet.

"Catherine," he whispered, incredulous.

"My head is quite hard, you see, and not easily broken. I might forget a thing or two, at worst it might take me eight years to remember that I am married. Aside from that, I think I am perfectly fine." She winced as she moved her head.

"My God. Catherine."

The Forgotten Duke

And he burst into tears again.

LATER, much later, after the doctor had been called and the bandage had been changed, she had been examined once more and told to remain in bed for observation. Though she declared that she was otherwise as fit as a fiddle, he climbed into bed and cradled her in his arms.

"I thought you'd died," he said, his voice cracking.

"I am sorry. It was a stupid thing to do, to run across the road without looking." She sighed. "I keep warning my children not to do that, and there I was, doing just that."

She licked her dry lips. "Pray, a favour?"

"Anything."

"Would you tell the children that I am well, and I shall be very cross if they stopped their studies and music practice because of me?"

He stared at her for one moment, blinked, then he said with a hoarse voice, "I will tell them, in these very words."

HE WENT to Hector's room.

The boy was in bed, his bedclothes on the floor, thumping a ball against the wall. It was a small, irregularly shaped ball made of a pig's bladder wrapped in leather and tied with string.

He did not stop when he entered the room but staunchly ignored Julius and continued to bang the ball against the expensive silk wallpaper.

Julius sat down on the bed beside him. "She is awake and fine."

The ball dropped to the floor. "Mama?"

Julius nodded. "She will recover. She says you must continue your studies, or else she will be very cross."

The boy's face contorted. His eyes filled with tears, and he buried his face in his elbow, sniffling.

Julius stared at him helplessly for a moment, then reached out awkwardly and pulled him into a tight embrace.

Hector wrapped his arms around him and wept loudly into his chest. "I thought she was going to die and go away. Like Papa Simon."

"I know. I know," Julius said thickly. "I thought so too."

He allowed the boy to finish crying, then tucked him into bed and brushed a strand of dark hair out of his face. The emotion he felt for the boy was unlike anything he'd ever felt before. Catherine was one thing, but this boy, this child, was his. He felt a fierce protectiveness, pride, and love for the boy.

"Sleep now," he said. "Everything will be well."

He went to the door.

Shortly before he reached it, Hector called out, "Your Grace."

"Yes?"

There was a pause, then so quietly that he thought he'd misheard, "May I call you Papa?"

Chapter Thirty-Five

A MIRACLE HAD OCCURRED.

The Duchess of Aldingbourne had been involved in a horrific accident but had miraculously escaped with nothing more than a bump on the head.

Now she sat in the morning room, wrapped in a blanket, the sun streaming through the windows. Her children had just left her. She'd been cosseted, reprimanded, hugged and kissed, and made to swear that she would never cross the street alone again.

After they had gone, Lena leaned her head against the sofa, savouring the warmth of the sun on her face.

"I'd like to have a moment with you, if you please." Julius's voice penetrated her thoughts.

She opened her eyes to find him standing in front of her, looking down at her with a soft expression in his eyes.

She smiled faintly. "I thought you'd already left."

"I postponed the meeting." He pulled up a chair and sat across from her.

"You've had to postpone a lot of meetings lately because of me," Lena said.

He waved a hand dismissively. "It is of no consequence. You are more important to me than any of that." His voice was rough.

Her eyes flew up to meet his, searching. "Am I?"

His face was a study in emotions. What had happened to the cold, emotionless, stiff Duke she'd always thought he was?

He leaned forwards and took her hands, opening and closing his mouth as he visibly searched for words. "Yes, you are. More than words can say." He took a deep, shaky breath. "I have been meaning to talk to you about us, about the truth of our past long before this latest accident."

She kept looking at him steadily and he continued.

"The truth is what happened back then was my fault. You were very young and lonely, and I was too absorbed in my own world to notice. I was oblivious to your feelings. I was a fool," he said bitterly. "You were unhappy, and I did not see it, and I did not try hard enough to understand what might have made you run away that day. The diary later helped me understand. There was nothing in it, no record about what had gone through your mind to make you decide on such a course of action. I questioned the servants, and eventually something came to light."

He looked tired and sad.

"They confirmed the loneliness, just as you'd written. They also told me that the day before your sudden departure, you'd received a visitor." He paused, as if he found it difficult for him to continue. "Violetta Allan." He swallowed. "She was an opera dancer…and my former mistress."

The silence in the room was so absolute that only the ticking of the clock on the mantelpiece could be heard. Lena did not move a muscle in her face but continued to look at him.

"She and I had been involved before our marriage," Julius continued, his voice heavy with remorse. "I ended the relationship before we wed. I set her up with a house and enough jewellery to live comfortably on the condition that our relationship was over. She didn't take it well. I must have been a cork-headed fool, as somehow she'd got it into her head that she would become the next Duchess of Aldingbourne. I learned too late that she'd done the unseemly thing and sought you out in public, and then again in Aldingbourne Hall. I can only imagine what she must have said. She admitted it when I confronted her much later, and she'd bragged about what she'd done.

"The servants confirmed that you were distraught. Understandably so. The next day you packed your things and left. We didn't immediately discover where you'd gone. You'd taken the public stagecoach to the North. By the time we caught up with it, we'd heard of the accident. Many bodies were not found, washed away by the river. Yours included. We had search troops—" His voice failed. He cleared his throat and started over again. "We had search troops scour the entire area. A week later we found a body that we mistook to be yours."

"Martha," Lena said mournfully. "Poor, loyal Martha.

She hadn't wanted to come along. She'd tried so hard to talk me out of it. I bribed her by giving her one of my dresses, allowing her to wear it on the trip."

The Duke closed his eyes, as if seeing the horrific images of those days flash in front of him once again. "Martha was the same height and had the same hair colour as you. Since she wore your clothes, we mistook her for you."

Lena wept quietly. "It is my fault she is dead."

"No, Lena. The accident was not your fault. None of it was."

There was silence as she chewed on her lower lip, deep in thought.

"That is the whole truth," he said quietly. "I kept it from you, thinking it would spare you pain. I have decided that secrets only fester. I want us to have no more secrets."

Lena's voice was steady when she finally spoke. "Did you love her?" It was a question she hadn't intended to ask, but she knew it would haunt her if she didn't.

Julius rubbed his forehead, a stricken expression on his face. "I was young and foolish. There was a time when I thought I loved her. That was before I understood what love really was."

"Were you ever unfaithful to me while we were married?"

He shook his head firmly. "No, never. The thought of having a mistress while being married, as so many in our class do, is abhorrent to me. She lied to you that day. Our relationship had long been over by then."

There was silence once more. Lena regarded him for a long moment.

"I believe you," she said softly.

He closed his eyes in anguish. "I should have done more for you. I should have been there. I should never have let you feel so alone. I have failed you in so many ways, Lena. I don't expect your forgiveness, but I wanted you to know the truth. I know this is eight years too late. I have loved you all along, even when I was too blind to see it myself. Every day I regretted the moments I let slip away without showing you how much you meant to me. I should have been shouting it from the rooftops and from every hill in England. Instead, I allowed fear to get the better of me and I retreated into my shell and abandoned you. I will never forgive myself for that."

Lena considered his words. Her voice trembling slightly when she finally spoke. "About that woman, Violetta Allan," she began carefully. "What happened before our marriage isn't something I can hold against you. We were both young then. Yes, I felt insecure and unworthy, especially after she came to me." She glanced down at her hands. "She told me you were still involved with her, that you loved her. And I believed her lies." She sighed softly. "But you ended things with her before we were married, and you were never unfaithful to me."

He nodded solemnly. "I swear on my life, that is the truth."

"What matters to me now is our marriage, not the relationships you had before. I could have done more too. Instead of reaching out to you, I withdrew into my own sadness. I could have accompanied you to London, or insisted we spend more time together. But I didn't. I buried myself in Aldingbourne Hall and wallowed. So when your former mistress crossed my path and couldn't resist bragging, all the insecurities of my youth came rushing back. I didn't know how to handle it. Instead of asking you the truth or fighting for us, I ran away."

He stared at her and his eyes widened as the truth dawned on him. "You remember?"

She nodded. "Yes. I've known for a while."

"Since when?"

"Since the day you spent in town on a meeting. I entered the room to sniff your cologne. It all came back to me then."

He shaded his eyes. "All this time you've known, and you've never said a word? Why?"

"Because I needed to hear it all from you. I was afraid of remembering, but I was even more afraid of losing what we have now." She reached for him. "But that is all in the past, Julius. I want us to move forwards. I want us to start again." She laid her hand on his wet cheek.

He grasped her hand tightly. "I don't deserve you. These last few weeks have been the happiest of my life. The thought of you remembering, of the past catching up, terrified me. I did not know what to do. Remind you of the past? Or let you forget it? I was torn. But never, not once, did I cease loving you."

"Hush," she whispered, drawing him closer. "No more regrets. No more torment. We have now. The present to focus on. A family to care for. A love to rediscover." She smiled warmly, her gaze locking with his as she pulled his face down to hers and kissed him, deeply, passionately.

Julius's voice softly echoed against her skin. "A love to rediscover."

Epilogue

TEA AT THE PALAIS ON THE GRABEN IN VIENNA, where the Duke of Aldingbourne resided, was always a grand affair. Musical entertainment filled the gatherings, creating a charming and lively spectacle, with the Duchess herself performing alongside all the children. The music was exquisite—a true feast for the ears—but the food presented a curious challenge for the Viennese palate. Afternoon Tea was served in the traditional British style, complete with delicacies bearing strange names: scones with clotted cream, crumpets, scotch eggs, and—could one even believe it—jellied eels, among other peculiar dishes that some guests found positively barbaric.

"Why do they call it clotted cream when it is just plain cream? And what is this?" the Duchess of Sagan asked, plucking a cucumber from a dainty triangular sandwich and holding it between her fingers with a perplexed frown. "My eyes do not deceive me. These are cucumbers—sandwiched between slices of buttered bread," she muttered in disbelief. "Cucumbers. No meat. No cheese. Of all vegetables, cucumbers. I don't understand. Are these meant for children? Are they supposed to be nutritious? Or is this some kind of aesthetic choice? How quaint." She shook her head, genuinely baffled.

"It's a staple of British afternoon tea," Lena interjected, trying to keep her tone light. She found the Duchess to be beautiful and intelligent—a star of society—but also demanding and difficult company. Convincing this elegant creature that cucumber sandwiches were not some barbaric concoctions but rather a cherished delicacy was proving to be a challenge.

Meanwhile, guests couldn't help but notice a change in the Duke of Aldingbourne. The usually reserved and stiff Englishman appeared softer of late, and shockingly had even been caught smiling once or twice. He hovered near his wife, the recently rediscovered duchess, who had been the subject of so much gossip. The couple's obvious affection had set tongues wagging. They were clearly deeply in love. The Duke held his wife's hands on all occasions. Once or twice, he was caught trailing his fingers over her cheeks, her arm, and once—gasp!—her neck. He was making love to her in plain daylight. In public.

How utterly scandalous.

"Have you heard about the latest scandal?" Lady Castlereagh interjected, her feathers bobbing brightly as she leaned in, her voice a conspiratorial whisper. "There's quite an uproar at court. It's truly shocking." She took a noisy slurp from her teacup before continuing. "The

Emperor's youngest son—well, one of his many children; he's had so many wives, he's on his fourth one now, or is it his third? Honestly, who can keep track of all these wives and their impossible German names! Anyway, the youngest son of the oldest wife—or is it the oldest son of the youngest wife?—oh, who knows. You must hear this: one of his sons, a prince of the house of Habsburg, an archduke, no less"—she paused for dramatic effect, leaning forwards—"has declared that he insists on marrying a commoner!"

Gasps circled the room as Lady Castlereagh sat back, clearly pleased with herself for delivering such tantalising news. "The Emperor threw a fit that rattled the palace walls. The archduke may never inherit the throne, but he remains in line of succession. Where would we be if we all married commoners?"

Lady Castlereagh paused, savouring the anticipation in the room. "And do you know the most delicious part of it all? They say this mystery woman is a foreigner. No one knows who she is—not a clue. It's whispered she's already at court, incognito! She could be anyone. Here's the best bit—she's one of us. British! Now, what do you make of that? Isn't it just the most thrilling piece of gossip?"

Lena stood by the windows, lost in thought, when the Duke stepped up behind her, so close she could feel his heat.

"Who on earth could she be talking about?" she murmured. The Duke leaned in so closely his lips brushed her ears. Quite accidentally, of course. Lena's eyes widened suddenly with a spark of realisation. "I know who she's talking about. It must be Lindenstein, of course!"

"I wouldn't know," he said. "And frankly, I wouldn't care." He paused, his smile curving in a way that was meant only for her. "Send them all home?"

She searched his eyes, finding everything she needed there. "Yes." Her heart caught at the warmth between them. "Let's."

A Note from the Author

It seems a tad redundant to say this, but here goes: This is a historical *romance* novel, not a factual treatise on the Congress of Vienna. Many events and characters depicted are works of fiction, and I've taken great (and joyful) liberties with history to create this story. In other words, I've stirred a mix of historical figures, imagined personalities, and invented happenings into one big, delicious pot—because that's what makes storytelling fun!

For example, there was never a Duke of Aldingbourne in Lord Castlereagh's delegation (shocking, I know!), and some of the shenanigans and dramatic love affairs are entirely my own creations. However, several characters and events are rooted in historical truth, and I couldn't resist sprinkling in some real, juicy tidbits along the way. For a guide on which characters are real, please check the beginning of this book.

Here are just a few of the true morsels I've woven into the tale:

A Note from the Author

- The bed-hopping, love triangles, and rivalries between Metternich, Tsar Alexander, the Duchess of Sagan, and Princess Bagration? Oh, yes—their affairs were notorious and very much real. They were the talk of the town. Metternich's lovelorn demeanour, complete with dark circles under his eyes from sleepless nights, did not go unnoticed by the Congress attendees.
- Those same ladies, bitter rivals, lived in the Palais Palm, where Metternich made his infamous rounds: to the right for Sagan and then left for Bagration. And yes, the Tsar swooping in after Metternich's visits? That's all documented in the spicy *gossip* sheets of the time. (Note the emphasis on 'gossip').
- Metternich's spy network really was the stuff of legend. It was the most sophisticated at the time, snooping on everyone and everything, right down to the contents of wastebaskets and unopened letters. The saying "My daughter cannot sneeze without Metternich hearing about it" captures just how pervasive his espionage was.
- Poor Lady Emily Castlereagh was indeed known for her dowdy appearances and odd habits, including visiting shops only to leave without buying anything. The shopkeepers were not pleased and considered her 'stingy'. Her infamous appearance at a ridotto dressed as a vestal virgin, with her husband's order

A Note from the Author

pinned on? Happened! How could I *not* include that?

While I've endeavoured to capture the spirit of the era, artistic licence abounds, and any historical inaccuracies (intentional or not) are entirely my own doing.

I hope you enjoyed this mix of fact, fiction, and a little bit of whimsy!

Also by Sofi Laporte

Merry Spinsters, Charming Rogues Series

Escape into the world of Sofi Laporte's cheeky Regency romcoms, where spinsters are merry, rakes are charming, and no one is who they seem:

Lady Emily's Matchmaking Mishap

A scheming spinster's matchmaking plans for her sister take an unexpected twist when she finds herself entangled in a charade of love.

Miss Louisa's Final Waltz

When a proud beauty weds a humble costermonger, their worlds collide with challenges and secrets that only love can conquer.

Lady Ludmilla's Accidental Letter

A resolute spinster. An irresistible rake. One accidental letter... Can love triumph over this hopeless muddle in the middle of the London Season?

Miss Ava's Scandalous Secret

She is a shy spinster by day and a celebrated opera singer by night. He is an earl in dire need of a wife - and desperately in love with this Season's opera star.

Lady Avery and the False Butler

When a hopeless spinster enlists her butler's help to turn her life around, it leads to great trouble and a chance at love in this rollicking Regency romance.

(*more to come*)

The Viennese Waltz Series

Set against the backdrop of Vienna's 1814 elegance, diplomacy, and intrigue, this series twirls through the entwined destinies of friends, enemies, and lost lovers in charming tales of love, desire and courtship.

My Lady, Will You Dance? (Prequel)

A Lost Love. A Cold Marquess. A Fateful Christmas Country House Party...

The Forgotten Duke

When a penniless Viennese musician is told she may be an English duke's wife, a quest for lost love begins.

The Wishing Well Series

If you enjoy sweet Regency novels with witty banter and a sprinkle of mischief wrapped up in a heart-tugging happily ever after, this series is for you!

Lucy and the Duke of Secrets

A spirited young lady with a dream. A duke in disguise. A compromising situation.

Arabella and the Reluctant Duke

A runaway Duke's daughter. A dashingly handsome blacksmith. A festering secret.

Birdie and the Beastly Duke

A battle-scarred duke. A substitute bride. A dangerous secret that brings them together.

Penelope and the Wicked Duke

A princess in disguise. A charming lord. A quest for true love.

A Mistletoe Promise

When an errant earl and a feisty schoolteacher are snowed in together over Christmas, mistletoe promises happen.

Wishing Well Seminary Series

Discover a world of charm and wit in the Wishing Well Seminary Series, as the schoolmistresses of Bath's most exclusive school navigate the complexities of Regency-era romance:

Miss Hilversham and the Pesky Duke

Will our cool, collected Headmistress find love with a most vexatious duke?

Miss Robinson and the Unsuitable Baron

When Miss Ellen Robinson seeks out Baron Edmund Tewkbury in London to deliver his ward, he wheedles her into staying—as his wife.

NEVER MISS A RELEASE:

To receive a FREE GIFT, exclusive giveaways, review copies, and updates on Sofi's books sign up for her newsletter:

https://www.sofilaporte.com/newsletter-1

About the Author

Sofi was born in Vienna, grew up in Seoul, studied Comparative Literature in Maryland, U.S.A., and lived in Quito with her Ecuadorian husband. When not writing, she likes to scramble about the countryside exploring medieval castle ruins. She currently lives with her husband, 3 trilingual children, a sassy cat and a cheeky dog in Europe.

Get in touch and visit Sofi at her Website, on Facebook or Instagram!

- amazon.com/Sofi-Laporte/e/B07N1K8H6C
- facebook.com/sofilaporteauthor
- instagram.com/sofilaporteauthor
- bookbub.com/profile/sofi-laporte

Printed in Dunstable, United Kingdom